"Turn this boat aro **and take me ashor**

Samantha demanded. "You have no right to take off like this. This is kidnapping."

"Kidnapping...? Kidnapping!" Marc's jaw went slack. The audacity of the woman, he thought as he stared at her crouched in the doorway to the cabin. Long, blond hair, tangled from the wind, and angry, green eyes were all he could see.

"Lady, you're crazy. This is my damn boat and you're a stowaway. Trespassing, that's what you're doing."

"I just wanted to help. Could you please just turn this thing around and take me back?"

Marc shook his head. "I can't do that, and I can't explain why. Believe me, it's for your own safety...."

ABOUT THE AUTHOR

Anne Logan lives in Luling, Louisiana, (not far from New Orleans) with her husband of twenty-four years. The couple has three grown children.

Gulf Breezes is Anne's first Superromance novel, and was inspired by the somewhat colorful politics of her home state and by her love of sailing. The family owns a sixteen-foot catamaran, which they sail along the Mississippi coastline in the Gulf of Mexico.

Gulf Breezes

ANNE LOGAN

Harlequin Books

TORONTO • NEW YORK • LONDON
AMSTERDAM • PARIS • SYDNEY • HAMBURG
STOCKHOLM • ATHENS • TOKYO • MILAN
MADRID • WARSAW • BUDAPEST • AUCKLAND

Published July 1992

ISBN 0-373-70507-7

GULF BREEZES

Printed in U.S.A

To David (my beloved) and my children,
April, Charles & Cristi
With thanks to Jessica, Karen, Emma,
Jean, Erica, Metsy, and Linda
for their help and encouragement.

that I wanted to in the first place."

CHAPTER ONE

THE HAIR ON THE BACK of Samantha Bradford's neck stood on end when she heard the noise again. She scrambled back across the yacht's deck to the bow.

"Tommy, there's someone on board," she hissed as she leaned over the rail.

The young college kid looked up at her from his small catamaran. "Aw, come on, Sam," he said. "Stop kidding around, and let's get out of here." Tommy shifted his eyes to stare longingly across the stretch of water to the narrow strip of Mississippi beach beyond. He still couldn't believe he'd let her con him into sailing her out to the yacht.

"There's someone down below," she insisted. "I heard a groan."

Tommy glanced back at Sam. "So what? Hey, Sam, wait. Come back here. Don't go down there by yourself." He stood up just in time to see her disappear. "Oh, no," he whispered as he grabbed the yacht's tow rail and pulled himself up and over, onto the deck. For a normally conservative and safety-conscious twenty-seven-year-old woman, she sure could be stubborn and persistent at times. "Should never have let her talk me into this," he grumbled. "Should've called the Coast Guard like I wanted to in the first place."

Samantha stepped down the companionway. She paused for a few moments until her eyes adjusted to the dim light.

Nice, she thought as she surveyed the rich beauty of the room. Whoever had designed the boat was a genius, and whoever owned it had spared no expense. The large L-shaped galley was equipped with a stainless-steel double sink, gimballed stove and oven, two iceboxes, and teak crafted cabinetry.

Hesitantly, she stepped farther into the room. So far, so good, she told herself. She took a deep breath and let it out slowly; her eyes darted back and forth as she searched for the source of the groan she'd heard earlier. At first, she barely heard the sound, but as she inched forward, the heavy breathing grew more audible.

Through an open doorway, she could see the large, huddled form of a man lying on his back across a bunk. He was as still as death except for the erratic movement of his chest. Again, fear battled with curiosity. Two days ago she'd noticed the yacht as she'd walked along the beach, and there'd been nothing—no movement, no activity. For two days she'd wondered and worried about it. With good reason, she thought.

Cautiously, she entered the cabin and slowly approached the bed. Even in the dimly lit room, she could see the man's dark hair was damp and disheveled. A heavy beard shadowed his face. His broad chest rose and fell with each labored breath, the sound alarmingly raspy. His shirt and shorts were rumpled and stained with dark circles. His long, bare legs were tanned and muscular.

Samantha drew closer and leaned over the man. She felt heat radiating from him as if he were the sun itself. Tentatively, she reached out to feel his forehead. The moment her hand touched his hot skin, he jerked in response.

Startled, Samantha snatched her hand away. Still leaning over him, she hesitated for a split second, undecided whether to stay or hightail it topside to safety.

Suddenly, he grabbed her around the neck and yanked. His unexpected movement caught her off guard. She fell forward, and his iron grip tightened.

With her face shoved against his chest, her scream was muffled and ineffectual. Terror raced through her blood. She couldn't breathe. Samantha reached up and clawed at his arm as she fought for air.

Useless thoughts raced through her head as she struggled to get free. She should have listened to Tommy. They should have called the Coast Guard. For all she knew, this man could be a criminal—a murderer or a drug runner.

Seconds seemed like an eternity. Then, as suddenly as he'd grabbed her, she felt his stranglehold loosen. His groan vibrated through her before the sound ever reached her ears. His arm fell back limply onto the bed and she was free.

For a moment she lay still, stunned, gasping for breath. It was the realization that his hot body was pressed intimately against her own that jarred her to her senses. Dressed in a bikini with only a tailored shirt as a cover-up, she felt almost naked and extremely vulnerable. She scrambled off him, each second wondering if he would attack her again.

"Sam . . . Sam! Where are you?"

Samantha took several steps backward toward the door, her hand raised protectively against her neck. "Here." Her voice sounded weak and tremulous even to her own ears. She cleared her throat. "Back here, Tommy."

Just knowing Tommy was nearby, she breathed a sigh of relief. The odor of the man's sweaty clothes clung to her skin and filled her nostrils. She hadn't noticed how rank the air smelled, but now, suddenly, she was conscious of the mustiness of the room.

Fear, she thought. Fear always intensified one's senses. Part of her could hear Tommy rushing toward her, but part of her was still recalling the terrifying moments of struggling to breathe. The only other time she'd felt that way was in the midst of one of her phobia attacks ... no, she wouldn't, couldn't think about it.

Tommy grabbed her shoulder from behind and Samantha jumped.

"Sorry. Didn't mean to startle you, but I thought I heard a noise. What's wrong?" Tommy pushed past Samantha and stepped into the room. "Phew." He wrinkled his nose. "What's that smell ... ?" Tommy's voice trailed off.

Samantha motioned toward the bed.

"Oh lord! Is he ... is he ... dead?"

Samantha shuddered, remembering just how alive the man was. "No. He's not dead. But I almost was, or at least, it felt like it."

Tommy's head snapped around. "What do you mean? What happened in here?"

Samantha shook her head. Telling him what had happened would be pointless. He'd just say I told you so. "Nothing," she said. "Nothing at all. I'm just jumpy, I guess."

"Are you sure? You look pale."

Samantha summoned a shaky smile. "I'm fine. It's just stuffy in here."

Tommy didn't look convinced, but to Samantha's relief, he turned away and slowly approached the bed.

"What's wrong with him?"

"I'm not sure." Still feeling uncomfortable, Samantha stared at the man. His breathing seemed even more labored than before. With Tommy close by, her fear began to dissipate and common sense and compassion surfaced in its place. Looking at the stranger lying still as death, it was hard to believe he was capable of trying to strangle her. Besides, she thought, she couldn't be sure he'd actually tried to strangle her. He was probably delirious.

"He has a fever," she said softly. "And from the looks of him, I suspect he's dehydrated." Samantha moved closer to stand beside Tommy.

"Wonder who he is."

"Maybe we should go through his pockets," Samantha offered.

"I don't know about that. What if he came to or something. He might accuse us of...of...well, anything."

Amazed, Samantha watched Tommy back away. Who'd ever have thought the Greek god of the catamarans would have turned out to be such a chicken? "Don't you even want to examine him? After all, you are studying to become a doctor."

He shook his head. "Sam, I'm not qualified to examine anyone, yet. I'm just a third-year pre-med student, and don't look at me like that. If he's got a fever, the only thing you can do at this point is try to cool him down. We ought to sponge him off with water and try to get some *qualified* medical help."

"What about aspirin?"

Tommy shook his head again. "Too risky. He might be allergic to it."

"Okay, okay. You're right. I just wasn't thinking. Why don't you go look for a radio, and I'll see what I can do about his fever?"

Tommy vigorously nodded in agreement. "Just be careful. He doesn't look as if he's in any shape to do any harm, but whatever's wrong with him could be contagious."

Samantha didn't comment. She was well aware of the man's shape, intimately aware. As far as being contagious, she figured it was a little late to worry about that.

Samantha left the room and searched the galley until she found a glass and large bowl. She filled both with water, grabbed a dish towel and headed back toward the cabin. She could hear Tommy's voice in the background.

"Mayday, Mayday, Mayday, this is the yacht *Jenny II* located five miles west of Gulfport. Over. Mayday, Mayday, Mayday..."

Samantha looked down at the man and wondered whether she had the courage to get close enough to sponge him down.

He'd turned on his right side and his face was half-hidden between his crossed upper arms. She set the glass and the bowl on the cabinet beside the bunk. Placing her hands on her hips, she stood, still hesitant to touch him.

"Don't be ridiculous," she scolded herself softly. She took a deep breath and reached out. "He needs help," she whispered as she pushed against him. His shoulder was firm and muscular, and he was heavy. Samantha shoved until he rolled onto his back.

Pity welled within her and she unconsciously moved her hand to smooth his dark hair away from his hot forehead. He looked so helpless, so vulnerable.

She shook her head at her foolish thoughts and reached for the glass of water. Lifting his head with one hand, she put the glass to his lips.

"Hey, can you hear me?" she asked softly. "Mister, you need to drink this." Praying he wouldn't choke, she tilted the glass slightly. Water dribbled uselessly down his chin.

"Come on," she encouraged. "Drink a little."

He grimaced as if irritated and turned his head just as she tried to give him another swallow.

"Wonderful!" she muttered. "What do I do now?" For a moment she simply stared at him. Somehow she had to get him to swallow. "One more time," she breathed, determined to get him to drink at least some of the water.

"Water. Drink," she commanded sternly as she tilted the glass against his lips.

As if he'd heard her, he swallowed once, twice, and then reached for the glass for more.

"Whoa. Not too much—" Samantha's words froze in her throat when she saw his eyes twitch and blink open.

"Angel...no...who..." his raspy voice came in gasps, then his lids fluttered and closed, and his hand fell back against the bed, "...are you...?" His words died away.

Samantha couldn't speak, couldn't move.

"Hey, Sam!" Tommy's voice grew louder the closer he came.

Samantha quickly lowered the man's head back onto the bed and turned just in time to see Tommy standing in the doorway.

"Something's wrong with the radio. I can hear everyone in the state of Mississippi talking," he exaggerated. "But nobody's hearing me or responding. It looks like one of the dials is broken."

Still shaken and with a thousand questions racing through her head, Samantha just stared at Tommy.

"Sam? Did you hear what I said? The radio is—"

"I heard. That's all we need—a broken radio."

Tommy looked down at the sleeping man, then back to Samantha. "What do you think we should do?"

Samantha reached up and rubbed the back of her neck and tried to think. What could they do? "He's too heavy for us to move by ourselves and it would be too awkward getting him on the cat, but still . . . I hate to leave him by himself."

"Oh, no, you don't." Tommy shook his head decisively.

"You know it's the only way," Samantha said, realizing their minds were on the same wavelength.

"I'm not leaving you here alone."

"I won't be alone."

"Sam, that's not what I meant and you know it. Look, he's already been by himself for a couple of days. He'll keep for another hour or so until we can get help."

What Tommy was saying made perfect sense, but for some inexplicable reason, she couldn't just leave. She knew that if their circumstances were reversed, and she was the one lying sick and unconscious, she wouldn't want to be left unattended.

"I'm staying here," she insisted. "The sooner you get going, the sooner you'll be back with help."

Tommy stood for a moment and stared at her. "Women!" he muttered, then turned and walked away. "I knew it. I just knew it. Should never have let her talk . . ."

Tommy's voice faded. Samantha glanced down at her watch. It was a little past three, and she'd have laid odds Tommy would be back before four. He'd probably break every speed limit in the book trying.

She turned to her patient. Something tightened in her stomach at the sight of him. He was a complete stranger and had only mumbled a handful of words when she'd given him water, yet she couldn't deny the affinity she felt . . . or the fear. Despite her brave words to Tommy, unease gnawed at her.

Samantha reached for the dish towel, immersed it in the bowl, and wrung it out. Tommy would return soon with help, she kept telling herself. For now, the important thing was to get the stranger's fever down. She began gently wiping his face. In sleep, he looked harmless. Even with several days' growth of dark beard, he was a handsome man in a rugged sort of way. Samantha guessed he was about thirty-five or thirty-six. By the faint lines radiating from his eyes, she figured he was an outdoorsman. Probably sailed a lot. His nose was nice and straight, his lips, smooth and full. She wondered about him. What had made him so sick? Did he have a family? A wife? Kids? Maybe she should go through his pockets, after all.

Samantha glanced down at his snug-fitting shorts. If he had a billfold, it would be in his back pocket. That meant turning him over since he was sprawled on his back.

"Hmm." Samantha straightened, folded the towel, and laid it on his forehead. There would be time enough later to find out who he was. For now, his fever was still alarmingly high. He needed more than just water and a wet towel on his forehead. Ideally, he needed to lie in a whole tub of cool water, but she knew that was impossible. She figured the next best thing was to strip him and soak him as best she could.

Samantha remembered how her grandmother used to give her cool rubdowns when she had fever, and a pang of grief shot through her; her eyes misted and blurred. Two weeks had passed since the funeral, and she still couldn't believe Gram was gone, gone forever.

She drew a deep, shuddering breath and glanced down at the stranger. The rubdown could wait a little while longer, she decided. Maybe help would arrive, and it wouldn't be necessary.

THE SAIL on the catamaran caught the wind, and the little boat flew across the water. Tommy hated leaving Sam on the *Jenny II*. He'd had an uneasy feeling about the yacht since he'd first sighted her. It wasn't that he thought the man would harm Sam. The stranger wasn't in any condition to harm anyone, but there was something odd and disturbing about the whole setup, and he didn't trust any of it.

He skillfully maneuvered the cat within a few feet of shore, jumped off, and with the momentum of the waves, pushed the boat onto the sand. Without stopping, he ran across the beach toward his Jeep.

There was a pay phone a few blocks over. With a little luck, he could be back on the *Jenny II* in less than an hour. The sooner he got back, the better he would feel.

His mind was racing with thoughts of the *Jenny II*, the sick man, and Sam, when he slowed for a left turn off the highway. As he sat waiting for an opening in the oncoming traffic, he glanced in his mirror and saw a delivery truck bearing down from behind. Certain the truck would take the other lane, Tommy concentrated on the traffic in front of him; he didn't give the truck a second thought.

Tommy heard the screeching of brakes and tires and looked up in the mirror just in time to see the truck sliding sideways toward the rear of his Jeep. His eyes widened and his heart pounded. Belatedly, he remembered he hadn't fastened his seat belt; he tried to brace himself. His last thoughts were of Sam before he heard and felt the impact of crumpling metal against metal. There was pain, the sensation of being airborne, and then, oblivion.

SAMANTHA'S EYES squinted against the glare off the water as she stood in the cockpit of the *Jenny II* and searched the distant shoreline. Nothing. Not another boat was in sight.

Two hours had passed since Tommy had left. Two hours in which she'd had her hands full. The man below was extremely ill, his fever dangerously high. One minute he'd thrashed about and talked out of his head, and the next, he had begun to moan and shiver. She'd been right not to leave him alone.

She quickly scanned the water one more time, and she prayed for the sight of brightly colored sails. She was suffused with dread as she turned away and entered the companionway.

"Stop it," she admonished herself. "Tommy's okay. He'll be back soon." But Samantha didn't believe it. She knew something had gone wrong. Tommy should have returned long before now.

She didn't have time to worry further. As she entered the cabin, she saw the stranger had rolled to the edge of the bunk and was trying to get up. There was an urgency about him, and even though his eyes were glazed with fever, they burned with determination.

Immediately, she was in front of him, pushing against him. She knew if he ever got off the bed, she'd never have enough strength to get him back on it.

"Whad're you doing?" His words were broken and slurred. "Got...to...get up. Can't stop."

For long seconds, Samantha wasn't sure if she would be able to handle him. Even ill, his strength was incredible. But it was short-lived. She gave one final push, tumbling both of them onto the bed.

Once again, she found herself in the precarious position of being sprawled on top of him, but when she started to crawl off, his arm snaked around her waist like a vise.

"Nice...feel good," he groaned. "So...cool."

For an instant, Samantha ceased struggling. She was trapped with her face buried in his neck, and her breasts flattened against his chest. Each time she took a ragged breath, her lips brushed against his warm, salty flesh. The heat from his feverish body penetrated her thin shirt. His fever was worse, not better. She feared he would go into convulsions, and she had no idea what to do if he did.

Just as before, his strength was short-lived. Suddenly, she was freed as his arm went slack and fell away. Quickly, Samantha slid to the edge of the bunk. She pushed herself off the bed and hurried straight to the head. The stranger remained quiet for the moment, his breathing even. Samantha soaked as many towels as she could find.

Returning to his side, she hesitated for only a second before she leaned over and tugged his knit shirt off. He offered no resistance as she pulled it over his head. She stood for a while, allowing her eyes to rove over his broad, tanned shoulders. A thick mat of dark hair covered his chest and tapered to a vee, then disappeared beneath the waistband of his snug shorts. She noticed the flatness and firmness of his stomach, the narrowness of his waist.

Suddenly aware of what she was doing, Samantha felt her cheeks grow warm and quickly she reached for a wet towel. For the next hour, she thought of little except cooling him down.

It was almost dark; the afternoon had been long and wrought with tension. Samantha had forced herself to continue her ministrations, and he was quiet for the moment.

Her intuition told her something terrible must have happened to Tommy. In between soaking towels, she'd tried the radio to no avail and had finally given up. She'd searched the yacht thoroughly, but other than a three-day-old newspaper, an old magazine, and a few personal items, she'd found nothing that could give her a clue to the identity of the man lying so ill in the forward stateroom.

Earlier, she'd thought of using the dinghy attached to the stern to row ashore, but then the stranger had once again become restless, and it had taken all her strength to quiet him down. By the time she could have safely left him, the dark shadows of night had made the trip impossible.

Samantha went through the cabinets in the galley until she found the canned goods. At least the yacht was well stocked, she thought as she heated tomato soup on the small stove. Her patient needed nourishment, and she had steadily grown hungrier herself. This in itself seemed strange considering she hadn't felt truly hungry since Gram's funeral.

Samantha poured two cups of soup. While waiting for one of the cups to cool enough to feed her patient, she took the other one and climbed the steps of the companionway onto the deck. A gentle breeze played in her hair. All was quiet and peaceful. Samantha sat, leaning against the backrest, the cup cradled in her hands. It was a clear night with the stars and moon suspended against the blue-black ceiling of the sky. Twinkling lights lined the shore in the distance. The phrase "so near and yet so far away" flitted through her mind.

Outwardly, she tried to remain calm, but her insides knotted with worry. And she was beginning to panic. She wondered again if she should try to row ashore. Samantha closed her eyes. She couldn't do it, couldn't chance it. Distance was misleading on the open water, and she knew she'd never hold up to the physical demands of a long row.

Her hand began to shake. The soup sloshed precariously close to the rim of the cup. The twilight had faded and as the darkness had increased, she'd felt the tension building. As always, nighttime on the open water reminded her too vividly of the black fury of the storm that had taken her parents' lives twelve years ago and left her with an uncontrollable fear. Samantha shivered and gripped the cup tighter. Over the years, she'd learned to contain her phobia to a certain degree. Seeing the lights in the distance gave her comfort and helped to keep her anxiety somewhat at bay. As long as she could return to the deck periodically for reassurance, she could convince herself the shore was close by.

Samantha raised the cup to her lips. The soup was still hot, so she blew on it, then sipped. If she was to survive the long, dark night ahead, she needed strength ... and courage.

She'd just finished the last of her soup when a loud curse sounded from below. Startled, she almost dropped the empty cup. "Damn," she mumbled. "What now?"

When she rushed into the stateroom, she found the stranger sitting on the floor moaning and holding his head. "Great! Just wonderful," she said sarcastically. Worry and exhaustion had robbed her of what little patience she had left. "Now what am I going to do?"

The stranger didn't answer but continued to sway and mumble.

Samantha took a deep breath and calculated the distance from the floor to the bed. She approached him warily from behind. She bent down, gingerly wrapped her arms around him and pulled. Heat seeped from his body to hers as she tightened her grip and attempted to ignore the feel of his hot, bare skin. The sensation was unnerving at first but quickly forgotten with the frustration of being unable to budge his deadweight. God, he's heavy, she thought.

Samantha grunted. "Come on, mister. Up you go. You've got to get back to bed." She braced her legs and pulled again. Nothing. He didn't move. He just sat there, holding his head and mumbling as if she didn't exist.

Samantha released him and straightened. Hands on her hips, she stood over him and glared down at his dark head. Without his cooperation, she'd never get him back on the bed. Samantha stepped around in front of him and squatted. Maybe if she could get his attention, she told herself, make him understand . . .

She reached for his hands. They were large hands, callused and strong. As she pulled them away, he lifted his head, opened his eyes and stared at her. Dark blue, almost navy, they were bloodshot and glazed with pain. Was it true, she wondered? Were the eyes truly the window to a person's soul? If so, his soul was in torment. A tug of compassion and pity warred with determination; determination won.

"Can you hear me?" she asked.

He didn't blink but continued to stare at her as if he were looking right through her.

Samantha squeezed his hands and gave them a little shake. "Listen to me. You're sick and I want to help you, but you've got to help me first." He didn't respond.

"Hey!" she shouted. He winced as if the sound was painful. Good, she thought. At least he'd reacted to something. "You've got to get up." Samantha tugged on his hands. "You can't stay on the floor. You need to be in the bed."

The stranger blinked several times, and Samantha knew he'd heard her. Irritation replaced his glazed look, and he frowned in confusion.

"Who're you?" His eyes lowered to their joined hands.

"Never mind who I am." Samantha shook his hands to regain his wavering attention. "It doesn't matter. What matters is you've been very sick, and you need to be in the bed."

The stranger began shaking his head. "No...can't stop...got to keep going." His confused expression hardened into a scowl. "They might find me!" He groaned; his hands squeezed Samantha's, causing her to wince in pain. "They're dead...all of them...murdered them." His voice lowered to a growl. "Bastards deserve to die."

Samantha heard his words, but she was too aware of the bone-breaking grip he had on her hands to be too concerned with his ravings. She'd already dealt with his sudden surges of strength and knew if he really got riled, she'd be helpless against him. She had to calm him down. The compassion she'd felt fled in the face of the anger emanating from him. The same hands that were crushing hers could just as easily be around her neck squeezing the life out of her.

Samantha shivered and fought down her fear. Now was not the time to panic. "It's okay," she soothed. "I only want to help you...it's okay."

"Help me?" He looked confused again, then relieved. "Good...need help...got to keep going."

Samantha relaxed somewhat as he loosened his grip. "Yes, I'll help you. Up you go...on the bed," she coaxed. "You need to rest for now...just rest. Don't worry. I'll take care of everything."

Her words seemed to reassure him. He nodded, and together they struggled until he was sitting on the edge of the bed. Samantha trembled from the exertion. Her breath came in gasps. She felt light-headed and dizzy but didn't have time to dwell on her weaknesses. She was too worried about the stranger. His face had turned pale and beads of sweat popped out on his forehead. "You okay?"

He nodded. "Thirsty... hot in here."

Samantha remembered the soup. "Promise me you'll stay right here, and I'll get you something to drink."

He agreed with another nod.

"Don't try to get up again." She stepped back toward the door. "Just sit there. I'll be back in a second." She continued talking, as she quickly grabbed the soup and a glass of water. He needed nourishment. That he'd asked for something to drink was surely a good sign, she thought. "Don't move—I'm coming," she called out.

He allowed Samantha to feed him the soup and gulped down the water she held to his lips. Water dribbled down his chin, and without thinking, she reached out and wiped it away with her finger. When she touched his lips, he automatically opened his mouth and then closed it around her fingers. Hot fire shot up her arm, and her lower stomach contracted at the completely innocent but intimate gesture. Samantha jerked her hand away. "Time to sleep again." Her voice had come out sharper than she'd intended. Since she'd first seen the man, she'd felt drawn to him. But this was not the time to think about her disturbing reaction to him.

His eyes clouded; his forehead wrinkled in confusion. "Who are you?"

Samantha pushed against his shoulder. "Nobody. Just lie down and rest for now. I'm nobody."

Several hours later, Samantha jerked her head straight up after almost nodding off to sleep. The newspaper she'd found earlier slid to the floor. She bent to pick it up.

Between the stranger's fits of delirium, Samantha had searched for something to keep her mind occupied and the three-day-old newspaper had served this purpose. Since her grandmother's death, Samantha's grief had taken precedence over everything. It had been days since she'd looked at a paper, and since Gram had never believed in owning a television set, Samantha hadn't even known the governor of Louisiana had been assassinated.

Samantha stared at the front page. The bold headline jumped out at her again: Eyewitness Narrowly Escapes Death. There was a picture of the governor, and beside it was a picture of his leading opponent, Congressman Bobby Landry. Samantha had read the articles under the pictures, which seemed to suggest that the congressman might have hired the assassins. The whole thing seemed unreal.

Samantha shivered. It was hard to believe the governor had been killed, and it was even harder to believe a murder attempt had been made on the journalist who'd been an eyewitness.

As she folded the newspaper and laid it on the table, she wondered about the journalist. Where was he? The article had said he'd disappeared. Was he on the run—traveling across the country or maybe abroad? Just thinking about him conjured up images of foreign places, excitement and danger. How would it feel to lead such a life? About the only danger she came into contact with as a high school English teacher was a brawl in the school yard.

She rubbed her eyes, then stretched. She could do without the danger, but the exotic places and excitement were appealing, and possible. Her relationship with Clark was over. She'd made the mistake of falling in love with a married man. And she'd believed him when he'd said he was going to divorce his wife. Instead, his wife had become pregnant, Clark had returned to her and Samantha had been humiliated and almost destroyed.

Suppressing these painful memories, she turned her thoughts to her grandmother. The previous day, she'd had an appointment with her grandmother's attorney to settle the estate. She'd sat stunned as Mr. Potter had read the will. As the only living relative, she'd inherited her grandmother's Mississippi beach house in Pass Christian and money she hadn't realized her grandmother had, half a million according to Mr. Potter. When she'd questioned him about the money, he'd gone on and on about insurance, stocks and investments, but what she'd been thinking of were all the penny-pinching years she'd lived with Gram. Not that she'd minded for her own sake. She'd loved living with her grandmother. But all those years of scrimping and making do as if it were some grand game they were playing still confused Samantha, and she wasn't sure if she'd ever be able to enjoy her inheritance without remembering those lean years.

Enough, she decided, as she yawned and stood. She didn't want to dwell on the ramifications of her inheritance; at least, not yet. It was time to see about her patient.

Samantha peeked around the corner of the door. He was still resting peacefully. She glanced at her watch and yawned again. Two o'clock in the morning. She was exhausted. For now, all she wanted was to sleep. Just for an hour or so, she thought.

She glanced longingly toward the companionway. Beyond was a second stateroom, containing an empty double bed. What could it hurt? she silently argued. If he became restless again, she'd be close enough to hear him. To reassure herself, she checked him for fever; then, like a sleepwalker, she made her way toward the other stateroom. The bed was covered with a fluffy, royal blue com-

forter. It looked so cool and peaceful, so inviting—
Samantha couldn't resist.

"Ahh." She moaned in pleasure as she stretched out on
the bed, then curled up on her side. It felt so good to lie
down. Just for a few minutes, she told herself.

Something in the back of her brain nagged at her, worried her, something the stranger had said, but her eyes
were too heavy. She needed a nap, just a short one. Later,
she'd remember . . . after she'd rested.

CHAPTER TWO

MARC DUREAUX awakened with a start. Where was he? His eyes searched the small room. Instantly, he recognized the tiny cabin with its teak paneling, its narrow slit of a window, but he was confused. Why was he on the *Jenny?* He lay still, trying to remember just when and how he'd gotten on board.

He stared at the ceiling and concentrated. Flashes of memory wove in and out of his mind, sketches of blurred scenes played behind his unseeing eyes. And there were voices; he recalled there had been voices. Just dreams, delirious dreams, he decided.

When the memories finally returned, they did so with such force, Marc groaned from their sheer magnitude. And with the memories, the scenes came into focus. But the voices . . . the voices still remained a mystery.

A sense of urgency gripped him. He had to get up, had to keep going. But when he attempted to raise his head, a sudden wave of dizziness hit him, and dark spots danced before his eyes. He eased his head back onto the pillow and blinked rapidly. Easy, he told himself. Take it nice and easy. Wait a few moments, then try again. He wondered how much time had passed since he'd anchored. Hours? Days? There was no way to tell. The last thing he remembered was how miserable he'd felt as he'd sailed through the night. He'd kept falling asleep over the wheel. He'd been tired, so tired, and ill.

Inch by inch, Marc raised himself until he was half sitting on the bed. He used his elbow as a prop to steady himself. Carefully, he slid his legs until they hung over the edge. His whole body felt sore; each movement was an aching reminder of how weak he was. Still, he pushed himself. Even now, someone might have spotted the *Jenny*. If they found him, his life wouldn't be worth a plugged nickel.

He rested on the side of the bed for several minutes. One step at a time, he reminded himself. Urgency again tightened his gut. The fight for survival had a strength all its own.

If he could just get topside, just get under sail, the *Jenny II* would do the rest. Distance was what he needed—distance and open water between herself and them.

One hour later, Marc sat in the cockpit. Leaning on the steering wheel, he concentrated on guiding the *Jenny* on course. Several things were still unclear, still confusing. He didn't remember cooling himself off with the wet towels strewn about his cabin. He'd fed himself; that was evident from the dirty cup beside his bed still half-full of congealed tomato soup. But he didn't remember doing so, and it didn't matter. Those riddles had quickly taken second place to the more pressing problem of getting topside. Still weak, he gripped the wheel tighter to steady himself.

Sailing southeast, Marc had a spectacular view of the rising sun. He watched it as it climbed from its watery bed, its rays glittering over the open sea like scattered diamonds. He was grateful for the stiff, salty breeze that filled the *Jenny*'s sail. It felt refreshingly cool against his bare chest.

With the slow return of his strength came a surge of memory, and he recalled the circumstances responsible for his predicament.

The phone call had come at six-thirty two mornings before, or was it three or four? Marc grimaced. Hell, he still didn't know what day it was. For weeks before the call he'd heard rumors. Governor John Henry Jackson's only real competition in his bid for reelection was a young congressman from Lafayette, Louisiana. Marc's informant, a sleazy little man he'd used for other stories, suggested that the congressman's people had made a deal with the governor. There was to be a meeting between the two for a payoff.

Marc remembered he'd had a devil of a time locating the small, secluded park where the meeting was to take place. Hidden behind a sprawling oak, he'd watched and waited. The governor had arrived first, then two other men had shown up. They'd argued. The governor had shouted something about a double cross, and one of the two men had pulled a gun, pointed it and squeezed the trigger twice. Marc closed his eyes against the memory of Jackson clutching his head while his blood formed a pool beneath him. God, there'd been so much blood.

A crash from below jarred Marc from his memories, and he tensed. Something or someone was down there.

SAMANTHA AWAKENED with a half-conscious sensation she was moving. Sunlight streamed through the tiny window above her bunk. Disoriented, it took her several moments to remember where she was. Then sheer terror raced through her.

The yacht *was* moving. Impossible, she told herself. But the rocking sensation was too familiar, and the sounds of water slapping against the sides of the boat confirmed her suspicions.

Suddenly, she felt her throat tighten, she couldn't breathe. She was trapped. The walls were closing in. "Got to get out," she whispered.

Wildly, she scrambled off the bed. The minute her feet touched the floor, her legs gave way with the movement of the boat. She reached out to steady herself but smashed sideways into the cabin wall and sprawled on the floor. Unwilling to fight the swaying floor, she crawled toward the companionway. She had to get topside. Please let this be a nightmare, she prayed silently as she pulled herself up and through the narrow opening to the fresh air above.

"Who the hell are you?"

Samantha's head snapped forward to confront the angry stranger.

"I asked you a question." Marc stared at the wild-eyed woman. Who the devil was she and how had she got on his boat?

Samantha tightened her grip on the doorway and ignored his question. Frantically, she surveyed the surrounding water. No land, no land anywhere. Nothing but water—water and blue sky.

God, what am I going to do? she thought. Her body was besieged by a series of tremors. Stop it, she told herself. Stop thinking about it. Concentrate on something else, anything. Samantha gulped in deep breaths of air and focused her attention on relaxing.

For several moments, she didn't speak. Warily, Marc continued to watch her. She was clinging to the doorway as if her life depended on it. She gazed straight ahead as if he didn't exist. He'd never realized before how many different emotions were reflected through a person's eyes. One moment hers were wild and fearful, the next, distant

and focused. He knew the exact moment she acknowledged his presence. Her eyes narrowed and she glared at
him.

"Turn this boat around and take me to shore," she demanded. "You have no right to take off like this...to
leave. Why...why, this is kidnapping," she accused.

Marc's jaw went slack. His eyes widened. "Kidnapping? Kidnapping! Lady, you're crazy. This—" he gestured widely with one hand "—is my damn boat, and
you...you're a...a stowaway. Trespassing, that's what
you're doing, trespassing." The audacity of the woman,
he thought as he stared at her crouched in the doorway.
Long blond hair tangled from the wind and angry green
eyes were all he could see.

Samantha opened her mouth to deny his accusations,
but the words wouldn't come. Angry demands weren't
going to work. She should have known. Anyone that had
been as sick as he'd been, yet had found the strength to
pull himself out of it, wasn't going to be intimidated so
easily. Still, she had to make him take her back to land.
She couldn't pretend forever that the shore was close by,
that she wasn't in the middle of the Gulf...on a sail-
boat...no, she wouldn't think about it. Maybe he'd be
more responsive to humility and contrition. "Okay, okay.
So I exaggerated. I'm sorry." Her eyes pleaded with him.
"Could you please turn this thing around and take me
back?"

Marc ran his fingers through his hair, his eyes rolled
upward. "Why me? Why me?" he muttered. Crazy, he
thought. The whole world has gone crazy. He'd seen a
man murdered, he'd been shot at and chased, and now he
was stuck in the middle of nowhere with some crazy
woman.

"Well?"

Marc closed his eyes and didn't answer right away. When he opened them again, he gazed at her thoughtfully. "I might consider it," he finally answered. "But first, I want to know who you are, and how you got on my boat."

Better, much better, thought Samantha, as she eased out of the doorway and slid onto the contoured seat that wrapped around the cockpit. Seated opposite the stranger, she eyed him cautiously. Should she trust him? "And you'll take me back to shore if I answer your questions?"

"I said I'd consider it."

Samantha hesitated and tried to sort out her options. Unless she wanted to swim for it, she didn't have any, she decided. "Okay. My name is Samantha Bradford."

"And," he prompted.

"I saw your boat anchored for a couple of days and got worried." Samantha could tell he didn't believe her. "Boats this size don't usually anchor in unprotected waters for that long," she emphasized, "so I figured either it was abandoned, or someone was in trouble."

"That still doesn't explain how you got on board."

"I'm coming to that." Samantha glared at him. "A friend of mine owns a fleet of catamarans. I persuaded him to take me out."

"So where is this friend of yours?" At least now he knew he hadn't been hallucinating. The mysterious voices he'd remembered had belonged to her and her friend.

"I . . . I don't know. He left—"

"My God, you mean he just dumped you and took off?"

"No," she denied hotly. "He wouldn't do that. For your information, he went to get help. We'd found you delirious with fever, and the radio was broken, and . . . oh, never mind. I've told you what you wanted to know. Now, will you take me back?"

Marc shook his head. He felt rotten now that he knew she'd only been trying to help him. No wonder she'd acted crazy. But still, he couldn't chance going back to shore. It was too risky. By now someone might have figured out that he'd hightailed it to the *Jenny*. They could be searching. "I can't. Sorry."

"What do you mean you can't?" Samantha doubled her fists; her fingernails bit into her flesh. "You said you would!"

"Well, I can't."

His jaw tightened, but just as he looked away, Samantha thought a hint of regret clouded his eyes. "Why not?" she demanded, but even as she asked the question, a vague uneasiness flitted through her. Something, some distant recollection nagged her, something he'd said the night before, when she'd been too tired to pay much attention.

For the first time in his life, Marc didn't have a pat answer. Up to now, words, like his life, had been easy. Too easy, too glib, he thought. In view of the present circumstances, his whole existence had been a fairy tale. But this was reality. The only other time he'd even come close to the fear that gripped him now had been during his short stint in the navy. But even then, his assigned ship had never seen any action. He'd never been shot at or seen men killed. He still couldn't believe the two policemen who had been assigned to him were dead. And the other two, the two who were supposed to be driving the van. He didn't even know their names. That they'd died protecting him gave him a sense of guilt he didn't know how to deal with, and now here was yet another victim. He couldn't chance jeopardizing the safety of another innocent life. He didn't want more blood on his hands. The less she knew, the better.

Marc turned back to Samantha. She was staring at him as if he'd suddenly sprouted two heads. Her green eyes were wide with fear. But this was different than when she'd first appeared through the companionway. Then, he'd known instinctively her fear hadn't been of him. He was sure of it. In fact, she'd completely ignored him. No, this was different. He could almost smell it the way a predator senses the terror of his prey. Well, so be it, he thought. Better she's afraid of me than dead.

"I won't take you back and I can't explain why, not now. Believe me, it's for your own safety."

Samantha didn't believe a word he was saying. She was sure her safety was the least of his concerns. She began to remember bits and pieces of what he'd said the night before—something about them all being dead and something about murder. Suppressing a small shiver and the urge to scream, Samantha glanced away. Could he see how frightened she was of him? She'd have to make sure he didn't. She couldn't risk it.

What was it he'd said? She tried to think of his exact words. Her eyes darted back to him, then away again. He didn't look like a murderer, but then how many murderers had she come across in her twenty-seven years? And to think, she'd actually felt sorry for him. Samantha shied away from the other thoughts she'd had about him when she'd undressed him and bathed away his fever. Instead, she concentrated on trying to recall what he'd said. Snatches of his words surfaced. Something about the bastards deserving to die. Think, Samantha. Now is not the time to panic, she told herself. You'd better come up with something fast.

If she pretended she didn't suspect anything, didn't know anything, he might decide she wasn't a risk. Eventually, the supplies would run out, she reasoned silently. At some point, he'd have to anchor. If she was convincing, maybe, just maybe he'd let her go. And then there was her phobia. If she told him about it, it might add a little more weight to her argument, especially if he thought it could cause him problems.

Samantha schooled her features and swallowed the lump lodged in her throat. "Look, I'm really sorry about everything. You don't owe me any explanations. It's just that I panicked for a few minutes. It's something I can't help. I have this phobia. It's okay as long as I don't think about it. I can half control it." She gazed at the stranger. Did he believe her? After all, she was telling him the truth.

Suddenly, it didn't matter. The stranger turned a ghastly white and slumped forward. The boat lurched crazily, and without thinking, Samantha quickly scrambled around to him and grabbed the wheel. He seemed to sense she had control. He loosened his grip and slid backward onto the seat.

"Sorry," he muttered. "Still weak . . . be okay in a minute . . . just dizzy."

Samantha's fingers tightened on the wheel as she brought the boat back around until the sail once again filled with the steady breeze. Not since she was fifteen had she been at the helm of a boat, but it was just like riding a bicycle, she thought. Once a person mastered it, they never forget how it was done. If only she knew what course he'd set, maybe . . . Samantha ventured a quick glance . . . no, color was already returning to his face. She'd never get away with it. Even when he'd been delirious with fever, he'd possessed an uncanny strength. There was no hope she could overcome that strength.

"I'll take it now."

Samantha hesitated. "Are you sure?"

"I'm sure."

His voice brooked no argument. Silently, Samantha relinquished her position and moved away. His color had returned. With his dark, windblown hair, shadowy beard and hard, determined eyes, he reminded her of a fierce pirate. All he needed was a black patch over one eye. And like a pirate, any moment now, he could toss her overboard, and no one would ever know, ever suspect...except Tommy. But Tommy hadn't returned. Samantha fought against the tears building behind her eyes and blinked rapidly. She didn't want to think about why he hadn't.

"You were saying something about a phobia. What kind of phobia?"

Samantha felt uneasy talking about what she considered her weakness, but reminded herself it might just save her life. "When I was fifteen, both my parents died in a boating accident. We'd been out for several days when an unexpected storm hit—"

"You were with them?" he interrupted.

"Yes. I was below, strapped in a bunk. It was horrible, the darkness, the sounds...." Her voice trailed away to a whisper. "When I awakened, I was in a hospital. Ever since then, I-I've had this fear of being on a boat in open water. I do okay as long as I can see land and don't think about it. It's just that this morning, finding myself out here was so unexpected...I panicked."

"But you're all right now?"

Samantha eyed him warily. He'd really sounded concerned. Just wishful thinking, she decided. He was probably worried she'd go bonkers on him. "Yes," she answered curtly.

"If it helps, we'll only be in open water for three or four days if the wind holds."

Samantha chanced a fearful look at the endless expanse of water, but quickly averted her gaze and concentrated on her hands when her throat began to tighten. Three or four days. She wasn't sure she could control her phobia that long. And if she did, then what? Would he let her go?

"I really am sorry about all of this," he said. "Especially since you were just trying to help me. But for now, all I can guarantee is that, eventually, you'll get back home safely. I promise. I just can't turn around and take you back now, and it's best you don't know why. I realize it's asking a lot." Marc hesitated. Was he even making sense? "But you'll just have to trust me."

He sounded sincere, Samantha reasoned. Because her choices were decidedly limited, she decided she'd have to humor him, pretend to agree. But trust him? No way on God's green earth would she trust him.

"You do understand what I'm telling you?"

Samantha nodded. "Yes, I understand." More than you think, she added silently.

"And you'll go along with me on this?"

Samantha glared at him. "I don't have a hell of a lot of choice in the matter, do I?"

Marc ran his fingers through his hair and briefly closed his eyes. "No...no, I don't guess you do," he replied wearily. "But could we at least call a truce for now?"

"Yeah, might as well," Samantha said grumpily and started toward the companionway. His voice halted her at the doorway.

"Where do you think you're going?"

Samantha turned to face him. "I thought we'd called a truce," she answered sarcastically.

"Well yes, but—"

Throwing all caution to the wind, Samantha decided whatever he intended to do, she wouldn't cower. She wouldn't give him the satisfaction of knowing he could intimidate her. She glared at him, and her chin jutted forward. "I don't know about you, but I'm hungry. If it meets with your approval, I'd like permission to go below." She wasn't really hungry. She'd rather do anything than go below, but she was too confused at the moment to worry about it. She needed to think . . . away from . . . God, she didn't even know his name—didn't want to. The less she knew about him, the better the chance he would let her go.

Several tense moments passed before he answered. "Okay. I could use something myself if you don't mind."

A small sigh of relief whispered past her lips, and Samantha shrugged. "Sure. What do you want?"

"A steak, medium rare with baked potatoes and sour cream, would be nice."

"Sure," she answered, her tone tinged with irony. "I'll just whip one up out of thin air." She couldn't believe it. He was actually teasing her . . . and grinning.

Marc watched her disappear below, and his smile faded. He didn't like her being out of sight. Something about her sudden acquiescence didn't ring true, but he just couldn't put his finger on it. It wasn't that he didn't believe the bit about her phobia. No one could have made up a story like that, and she had definitely been scared. No. There was something else. And the food. He couldn't believe he'd actually asked her to prepare him food. For all he knew she could poison him. Were there any poisons or medications on board? He couldn't remember. He'd have to be careful.

Below, Samantha gripped the edge of the cabinet. Already, the familiar tightening in her throat was making breathing difficult. "Dammit, relax!" she whispered harshly. Think of something else. Breathe deeply and concentrate. The face of the stranger came to mind, and Samantha cursed again. Stupidity, sheer stupidity. Why hadn't she listened to Tommy? If they'd called the Coast Guard as he'd suggested in the first place, she wouldn't be here. She'd be back at Gram's house, nice and safe. Hindsight was a wonderful thing, she thought scornfully, as she slowly loosened her death grip and made her way to the two iceboxes.

Was he a murderer? Instinct denied it while logic insisted it was possible. Samantha reached into the first icebox and pulled out a package of sliced ham. Maybe she was mistaken. Maybe his feverish ramblings had been just that, the mutterings of a delirious man. But no, if that was true, then why wouldn't he take her back to shore?

Samantha shook her head and slammed the icebox door. Crazy. Trying to figure him out was making her crazy. She searched the cabinets for bread and found a still-sealed loaf behind some tins of soup. There had to be something she could do to get out of this mess, but what? He was too big and strong to overpower unless she could catch him off guard and knock him out with something. A shudder ran through her. She'd never hit anyone in her life. What if she hit him too hard and killed him? No, she couldn't do it. Besides, the possibility of his leaving the wheel was unlikely. Samantha slapped a piece of ham on top of a slice of bread and covered it with another slice.

If she had some sleeping pills, she could slip him a few   and then what? she asked herself. She had no idea what course he'd set or their location, and her knowledge of navigation was nil She could sail for days and days and never reach land. Samantha felt her head begin to throb and the familiar tightening in her throat warned her to breathe deeply and evenly. There was nothing she could do for now, nothing but be patient and wait.

A few minutes later, carrying a plate with two sandwiches on it, she started back toward the companionway. Halfway there, she stopped as it suddenly dawned on her that with all the worrying about her circumstances and speculations about the stranger, the usual symptoms of her phobia didn't seem as strong as they had when she'd first awakened. Best not to dwell on it, she thought, as she quickly climbed the steps to the deck above. What she needed to do was concentrate on finding some way out of the predicament she was in.

Once on deck, Samantha pasted a too-bright smile on her face. "Sorry. We're all out of steaks. You'll have to settle for ham sandwiches, instead."

"Thanks." Marc eyed her warily but took the plate of sandwiches she offered. "You were down there a long time...I mean...well, your phobia. Are you okay?"

Samantha curtly nodded. "Better than before."

"Good." Keeping one hand on the steering wheel, Marc put the plate down behind him on the contoured seat, and when she turned her back, he hurriedly lifted the top slice of bread and peered at the ham. She'd been just a little too bright and cheerful for his peace of mind, but everything looked normal enough, nothing unusual. Satisfied, he took a bite, and chewed slowly. Nothing funny about the taste. In fact, it tasted pretty damn good, he thought. He hadn't realized how hungry he was, and within minutes, he'd devoured the first sandwich and started on the second.

"I thought about using poison, you know."

Marc stared at her and forced himself to swallow. The look on her face told him she was serious. And that look also reminded him he'd best continue to be on his toes.

CHAPTER THREE

SAMANTHA BRADFORD. She didn't look like a Samantha. Marc's gaze strayed to the slender woman sprawled on the cabin top soaking up the last rays of the sun. Her hair was blond, cut in a casual, carefree style. Her bikini-clad body looked firm and capable. He hadn't touched her, didn't have to; he could see the subtle muscle definition each time she moved. He'd have bet his next exclusive she pumped iron on a regular basis. Marc's eyes slid down to her legs—honey-colored, slim and long. Legs like hers could wrap around a man.... Marc quickly glanced away.

How long had it been? If just looking at a pair of legs put those kinds of thoughts in his head, it had been too long. Marc reached up and smoothed the beginnings of a mustache, then rubbed his jaw and thought of Angelique. Already his stiff whiskers had grown enough to begin softening. Angelique had always insisted he shave before they made love. It had turned into a damned ritual, Marc remembered. Everything had to be just so, and even then, there was no satisfaction. It had been like making love to a robot.

Marc looked up to the cabin top again. No, she didn't look like a Samantha, and physically, she was the complete opposite of Angelique. Sam, he decided. She looked like a Sam. She'd told him about her parents and her phobia, but other than that and her name, she was a complete mystery. Did she have any other family, people who would miss her, search for her? And what about her friend with the catamaran? What had happened to him?

Was she single, married, or divorced as he was? Marc glanced upward to check the sail and automatically adjusted the wheel accordingly. Technically his divorce wouldn't be final for another month, but it might as well have been; his marriage had been over for a long time. His only regret was that he hadn't been the one to initiate the legalities. When they'd first separated, he'd felt guilty— that somehow it was his fault the marriage hadn't worked. Then, in a fit of temper, she'd told him there was someone else. She'd made a fool of him and that was still a bitter pill to swallow. Thank God, in just one more month, he wouldn't have to deal with her—someone else could have that privilege, he thought sarcastically.

But Samantha Bradford *was* someone he had to deal with; he had no choice. He needed to know more about her for both their sakes if they were to stay alive, and it was doubtful she would volunteer any information if he allowed things to continue as they were. After the sandwich incident, she hadn't spoken a word to him.

Over his right shoulder, the sun, now a fiery orange ball, was slowly easing its way to the edge of the horizon. The afternoon had been a long one, fraught with tension, and the night promised to be longer. Even if he'd been in top physical condition, sailing single-handedly day and night without relief was exhausting. Because he was still weak, Marc knew he'd never manage. Before long he'd have to make a decision.

He glanced at Samantha. He smiled bemusedly as he watched her ease up from the deck. She made a face, and gingerly touched her shoulder.

"Too much sun?"

Her chin jutted forward, but she gave him only a cursory glance.

"You really have to be careful in open water." He watched her as she silently headed for the companionway door. That she continued to ignore him both irritated and amused him, but he couldn't allow it to go on any longer.

"As long as you're going down, would you bring me a cup of coffee? I think there's some instant down there somewhere."

She paused, but only to glare at him.

"Oh yeah," he said as she turned away. "Another thing. Could you fix something to eat besides poison sandwiches? You can cook, can't you?" When her back stiffened, Marc fought the urge to grin. She didn't like being ordered around, but even her anger was preferable to the silent treatment he'd been receiving.

Again Samantha faced him, her eyes widening in mockery. Placing one hand on her hip and motioning toward the door with the other one, she asked, "Any other orders, Captain?"

Marc hesitated for a moment. "Not now, but I may ask you to relieve me at the wheel for a while, later."

Samantha stared at him. "You'd trust me?" she blurted out.

"It's not exactly a matter of trust, but one of necessity. Wouldn't you agree?"

"I'm not so sure."

"Sure that it's necessary?"

Samantha shook her head vigorously. "No...not that. I'm not sure I can do it."

Understanding suddenly dawned. "Of course, you can. There's nothing to it. Besides, you did okay earlier." She'd done better than okay, and as sick as he'd been, he'd noticed. He'd figured it was the only solution to his problem, but he hadn't been sure she'd go for it, especially after he'd refused to take her ashore.

"You're not afraid I might head for shore?"

Marc laughed. "Even if you tried, by my calculations, we're at least three or four hours from land. I don't plan on leaving you at the wheel that long. And just in case you get any other ideas, I warn you, I'm a light sleeper."

Samantha felt deflated. She should have known he'd figure it all out and leave nothing to chance. The only thing she could do was bide her time. She turned and focused on the setting sun. She didn't trust him, but so far, he hadn't threatened or harmed her. He'd pretty much left her alone. Several silent moments passed. She knew he was watching her, waiting for her to say something. "You don't have anything to worry about," she finally mumbled.

"What was that?"

Samantha swallowed hard and turned to face him. "I said, you don't have anything to worry about."

"Good. That's what I thought you said. Now that we've got that out of the way, will you answer my earlier question?"

"What question?"

"Can you cook?" Again, Marc felt a grin tug at his lips when he saw her stiffen. He'd known before he asked what her reaction would be, and she didn't disappoint him. Her green eyes narrowed and glittered, and her lips thinned with irritation, and he wondered why he took such pleasure in aggravating her.

Samantha didn't answer him. Instead, she stomped below as best she could in her barefooted state and fumed. Slamming cabinet doors as she searched for coffee gave her some satisfaction. While waiting for the water to boil, her stomach growled. As she opened a can of beef stew and searched for spices to make the food more palatable, she told herself she was doing the cooking only because *she* was hungry. It had nothing to do with him. By the time she'd finished eating, she'd calmed somewhat, and after she thought about it, she realized that not once had her throat even threatened to tighten on her. She rinsed her dirty dishes, and leaving the food on the stove and a cup of steaming coffee on the counter, she returned to the deck.

She was startled at the change in him. He was half sitting, half leaning against the wheel. Even the twilight didn't hide the pallor of his skin. Was he ill again? Had his fever returned? The thought made a knot of fear grab her stomach as she approached him.

"I left you some stew on the stove. Why don't you go below and eat?" Her instinct was to reach out and feel his forehead, but common sense told her he wouldn't appreciate the gesture. Instead, she took the wheel.

Marc gladly relinquished control. "The wind is still steady, so you shouldn't have any problems. Just keep an eye on the compass and yell if anything changes."

Samantha glanced at the compass, noted the readings, and nodded. Any fears she wouldn't be able to handle the boat took a second seat as she watched him move away. His progress was slow and erratic, and she held her breath until he disappeared below.

By the time he reached the settee in the dining area, Marc was breathing heavily from the exertion. He collapsed on the cushions and leaned forward. With his elbows propped on his knees, he closed his eyes and held his head as he waited for the wave of dizziness to pass. The enticing aroma of coffee and stew filled the cabin. Maybe if he could eat, he would feel better. But first, he had to find the strength to make a trip to the head to relieve himself. He'd been ready to burst for the past hour.

WHEN TWO HOURS had passed, Samantha began to worry, but she hesitated to call out to him. If he was sleeping, she didn't want to disturb him, at least not yet. But what if he'd passed out, maybe even hit his head in the process? He could be lying there, bleeding to death. Just as she'd made up her mind to call him, he appeared in the doorway, and she breathed a sigh of relief. He looked better, much better. His color had returned, and his movements were strong and certain.

He seemed in no hurry to take over the wheel. Instead, he seated himself across from her and looked up to check the sail.

"Still on course?"

"Yes." She followed his gaze. The wind was brisk, the white sail rigid. "She handles like a dream."

"Who taught you how to sail?"

"My father." Her face seemed to soften when she mentioned her father.

"You still miss him."

"Sometimes, but that was a long time ago."

"Your father," Marc repeated. "And you haven't handled a boat since?"

"No."

"You said you were fifteen when your parents died. Who took care of you?"

Her hands tightened on the wheel. Was he just making conversation, or did he have an ulterior motive for his subtle interrogation? If he found out there was no one who would miss her, then it wouldn't matter what happened to her. While he was still weak, he needed her help, but later... Samantha figured the best way to handle the situation was to simply sidestep the personal questions.

"My grandmother, my father's mother, took care of me." She stood. "If you don't mind, I need to go below. I got a little too much sun this afternoon, and my legs are beginning to burn. I'd like to put something on them."

Marc frowned but took the wheel. "Sure. There should be something in the first-aid kit." He'd been too obvious, he decided. She'd caught on to what he was doing. Still, there was plenty of time. He'd learned, with some people, it was better to be patient and wait.

"You might as well try to sleep. I'll need you to spell me for a while around midnight—that is, if you think you can."

"As you said before, it's necessary. I'm prepared to do what's necessary."

Her double meaning was clear, and the long, lonely evening provided him ample opportunity to think about her parting words.

A LITTLE PAST NOON the following day, the heat in the cabin was becoming unbearable. Samantha pulled at her shirt which insisted on sticking to her sweat-soaked back, and wished for a cool shower and a change of clothes. To keep conversation to a minimum, she'd made it a point to stay below, using her sunburn as an excuse. Still, she shivered, remembering the torturous two hours she'd spent at the wheel the night before. He'd awakened her around twelve-thirty to take over. There had been no stars, no moon. Only the soft glow from the cabin and the masthead light had afforded any relief from the eerie blackness of the night. But she'd done it. She'd fought her demons and won; not once had she panicked.

Samantha glanced at her watch and fanned herself vigorously with a magazine she'd found and read from cover to cover. She figured now might be a good time to go above and take the wheel for a while.

When she peeked out the doorway, the first thing she noticed was his concentrated frown. With his furrowed brows and dark beard, he looked fierce and angry, and seemed unaware of her presence as he continued to stare past her.

Curious, Samantha turned her head in the direction of his gaze. All sane thoughts fled her mind. Her knees turned to jelly, and her heart skipped a beat only to begin pounding twice as fiercely a moment later. He shouted something at her, but she couldn't respond. She felt frozen as she continued to stare with fascinated horror at the approaching blackness as it swallowed the sun.

The storm had appeared out of nowhere. Deadly lightning cut a jagged path in its midst and thunder rolled from the heavens in protest. It all seemed so unreal until the palpability of it hit her—a fine mist of salty spray stung her cheeks and burned her eyes. The sound of Marc's voice reached her but his words were lost, whipped away by the wind.

"Sam! I need your help, now!" Marc shouted. She still didn't move. He tried again. "I need you to take the wheel." But she didn't heed his command. And then he remembered. With the sudden appearance of the squall, he'd only thought of getting safely through it. He'd forgotten about her phobia.

Marc quickly lashed the wheel. He cursed and fought against the stiff wind. They didn't have much time before the storm hit, and he feared it might already be too late. When he was finally within reach, he grabbed her upper arms and turned her to face him. The glazed green of her eyes stood out against the paleness of her face. Marc's fingers tightened. "Samantha . . . Sam, it's okay. We can ride it out." She didn't respond, but continued to stare through him. "Sam…listen to me." He rubbed her arms up and down, as if soothing an injured child. "It's only a small storm, but I need your help."

"We're going to die, just like . . . we're going to—"

"No, we're not going to die." Marc reached up and smoothed her hair away from her face. But she wasn't listening. Her entire body began to quiver and she continued to mumble incoherently.

The boat suddenly pitched and she grabbed at him. Marc's hands slipped around her and hugged her close as he tried to balance them both against the rolling deck.

Pressed against his body, she gave way to spasmodic sobbing. With each breath she drew, the pressure of her firm breasts pushed against his chest. Not sure of what she might do next, his arms tightened. "Sam, please listen," he murmured close to her ear. "We don't have much time." Already the edge of blackness had reached them. The roar of the wind was growing louder.

Her arms fell to her sides like limp dishrags. "We'll both die," she said.

"No, Sam," he soothed. "We won't, but—"

"Now you won't have to kill me," she continued as if he hadn't spoken, her voice eerie and low. "But the joke's on you. You'll die, too."

What on earth was she babbling about? Marc wondered. Did she actually think he was going to murder her? But she was already sobbing again, and time had run out. The blackness was all around them. Since there was no way he could hold her and fight the storm, he decided she'd be better off below, out of harm's way.

"Sam," he pulled her toward the companionway. "I want you to go below."

Samantha stumbled and the inky darkness of the cabin yawned out menacingly; something within her snapped. "No," she pleaded. "I can't go down there. Please, I'd rather die up here."

There was no time to reason with her. Keeping one hand firmly on her arm, Marc had to shout above the increasing cry of the wind as he guided her over to the corner of the cockpit. "Sit here and don't move." He grabbed a nearby life jacket, and quickly pulled it on her and fastened it. "Please, just stay here," he said as he backed away, but he wasn't sure she'd heard him.

Memories of that other storm kept reverberating in Samantha's mind as the sea tossed and pitched around the yacht. Mingled with those memories were Marc's soothing words. Was he a murderer or had it been his fever and delirium talking? Samantha huddled in the corner where he'd left her and watched as he struggled to single-handedly turn the boat into the center of the storm. Murderers weren't kind or compassionate. He'd had ample opportunity to do anything he wanted to her, including kill her. Yet he hadn't touched her except to try to reassure her.

She thought of her parents. Her mother hadn't huddled like a coward in a corner feeling sorry for herself. Without an ounce of trepidation, she'd followed her husband and bravely fought at his side. Samantha began to feel ashamed, and in the aftermath of that shame, a curious calmness washed over her. All around her, the sea churned and spat into the wind, the thunder rumbled, but Samantha no longer felt afraid. Her shaking body stilled, and her sobs subsided into an occasional hiccup.

Her common sense reasserted itself, and she began to remember other things she'd forgotten in the wake of her crippling fear. Being unable to transmit messages over the broken radio hadn't kept them from monitoring weather bulletins. There'd been no reports of tropical depressions, no hurricanes. That meant the storm had to be an isolated summer squall. He'd said it was small, that they could ride it out. The *Jenny* was a strong, sturdy boat. If they dropped the mainsail, but ... he couldn't do it all by himself. He needed help. Without further thought, Samantha struggled up and made her way toward the wheel.

Marc saw her move and watched her slip on a safety harness. Calmly, she snapped it to the lifeline, then turned and reached for the wheel. He hesitated briefly, but the clear, determined look on her face eased his uncertainty. He moved away without a word passing between them.

During the following thirty minutes, they crewed the ship as a team with Marc working the control lines and barking out orders, and Samantha obeying his commands unquestioningly. Through the blinding rain, Marc lowered the mainsail and replaced it with the storm jib. To slow the impetus of the *Jenny,* he dropped the anchor and allowed it to trail the stern.

Just as he'd thought, the small thunderstorm passed quickly, and the *Jenny* sailed through it with ease.

When the sea was once again calm, Marc began the task of hoisting the mainsail. It was only then that he allowed himself to remember Samantha's accusations. As the full impact of her words registered, the implications left him shocked, confused and angry. In the beginning, he'd thought it best for both their sakes if she remained ignorant of the facts, even if it meant she feared him. Being afraid of him was one thing, but thinking he was a murderer who intended to kill her was something entirely different.

Marc paused to stare at her, wishing he could read her mind. Even after the storm had passed, she'd remained at the wheel. Her hair was slicked back and hung in dripping tendrils down her back, but her face still had that same stubborn set to it. He turned away and began the task of hauling in the anchor. Just as he finished, the sun reappeared from behind the clouds, and he squinted against the glare bouncing off the waves.

His head began to ache. The benefits of the two-hour nap he'd had the night before had long worn off. He closed his eyes and reached up to pinch the bridge of his nose. "God, what a mess," he muttered as he stumbled toward the cockpit. He had no choice now. Her accusations left him none. He couldn't allow her to believe he was a murderer, but he dreaded telling her what her Good Samaritan deed had sucked her into. And even after he told her the whole bizarre story, would she believe him? There was only his word for it; he had no concrete proof to offer her.

Samantha watched him make his way toward her. She felt a knot form in her stomach. From the set of his jaw and the determined gleam in his eyes, she knew all her unvoiced questions were about to be answered.

"We have to talk."

He was standing opposite her with only the wheel separating them. The knot in her stomach tightened as she looked up at him. "Yes, I agree." For a second he continued to stare at her, then he motioned toward the wheel.

"Do you want me to take over?"

Samantha slowly shook her head. "No, I'm fine." He appeared relieved by her answer. The hard luster of his eyes faded momentarily with uncertainty and something else. Pain?

"I'm going below for some aspirin. Do you want anything while I'm down there? Something to drink?"

Samantha nodded. "Something cold, please."

A few minutes later, he returned carrying two cans of beer. He popped the top on one and offered it to her. Samantha grimaced, but took it anyway. She hated beer; still, it was cold, and she was thirsty.

Marc popped the top of the remaining can and seated himself along the side of the cockpit. He took a long drink and wiped his mouth with the back of his hand, then leaned forward and braced his forearms against his spread thighs. One hand held the suspended beer can while the fingers of his other hand made circles in the beaded condensation. When he finally spoke, his voice was low and resigned.

"Not once have you asked my name. Why?"

Samantha shrugged. "I figured the less I knew, the better off I would be."

"Why?"

His eyes had darkened to navy, and Samantha squirmed uncomfortably. "You know why."

"Because you think I'm a murderer, that I'm going to kill you."

Samantha took a sip of her beer. The cool wetness of the bitter liquid slid down her throat. She couldn't deny she'd thought those things, but after what they'd just been through, and now face-to-face with him, her suspicions seemed ludicrous. When she didn't answer right away, he let loose a string of profanities.

"Where did you get such a screwball idea?"

Samantha swallowed and opened her mouth to answer, but he continued speaking.

"Have I threatened you?" He didn't wait for her answer. "Dammit, not once have I laid a hand on you." A mounting rage rose in his gut. "Not once have I said or done anything to warrant an accusation—"

"You have," she shouted defensively.

Angrily, Marc crushed the beer can.

"It was when you were sick."

Marc's head snapped up.

"You said you murdered them . . . an-and the bastards deserved to die." She glared at him.

"Good Lord!" Disgusted, Marc threw the can down the companionway and reached up to massage his throbbing temples.

"Well, what was I supposed to think?"

"I'm no damned murderer. I'm a reporter, a newspaper reporter. My name is Marc Dureaux."

Samantha's eyes grew wide. Marc Dureaux. Where had she heard that name? The newspaper! He was the one she'd read about. "Oh, God," she said, staring at him, her heart pounding.

"Indeed."

She leaned forward until her forehead was resting against the wheel. She closed her eyes. No wonder he wouldn't turn back. Then the enormity of her situation began to sink in. "Be careful what you wish for, you may get it." Her grandmother's words popped into her mind and she groaned, remembering her silly notions about travel and excitement the night she'd read the article about him.

"I'm sorry, Sam."

His voice was husky and filled with remorse. She began to shake her head and was startled when he squeezed her shoulder. A tiny shock of awareness radiated from his touch. She looked up at him. "No . . . I'm the one who's sorry." Her eyes held his. "When I think of what you saw...what you've been through...and I...then I called you a—"

His lips thinned. "It doesn't matter. I'm just relieved you believe me."

"I read about it in the paper I found the night you were so ill." His hand fell away, but she could still feel the warmth and strength of it pressed into her flesh.

"I didn't think about that, but I should have known you'd have read or heard it somewhere," Marc said, standing up and stepping away. With his back to her, he braced both hands on the ledge of the cockpit and stared out over the empty expanse of water.

Samantha couldn't help but notice how the muscles in his broad shoulders strained against his shirt, and she couldn't help but remember how he'd looked without the shirt when she'd bathed away his fever.

"Do you want to talk about it?"

"No," he said quickly and shook his head. "I mean, not now," he amended. "Maybe later." Marc turned sideways to face her. "Right now I'd like to get some sleep without worrying about being bashed in the head."

Samantha felt her color rise and started to deny that she could do such a thing. As if he'd been waiting for her reaction, his blue eyes sparkled mischievously, then he grinned.

"You would have worked up enough nerve sooner or later."

"I may do it yet if you keep on," she retorted, and smiled sweetly.

Marc chuckled. "Just remember I'm still a light sleeper."

CHAPTER FOUR

SAMANTHA GLANCED toward the setting sun and squirmed again. Nature called and she was going to have to answer soon. But she hated to wake him. Even his attempt at humor hadn't hidden the exhaustion emanating from his body. The seas were calm, the breeze had died to an occasional gust. A few minutes below wouldn't matter, she decided.

Samantha noted the readings on the compass, lashed the wheel and switched on the automatic pilot. When she tiptoed past him, Marc was sleeping soundly, his breathing deep and even.

On her way back up, she stopped by the icebox to grab a soft drink. The cabin was beginning to lose the heat of the day and felt cooler than the deck. Samantha took a long drink of her cola, then rubbed the wet can against her forehead.

"Nooo...don't!"

Marc's moaning words sent chills chasing down her spine.

"Son of a bitch...stop...nooo."

Samantha slammed the canned drink on the counter and rushed to the stateroom. Marc was thrashing about as if he were fighting the demons of hell. She grabbed his shoulder and shook him.

"Marc...wake up. It's just a dream." She shook him again, using both hands. "Marc—" His lids flickered as his body jerked beneath her fingers. When his bloodshot eyes snapped open, they still reflected the horrors of the nightmare.

"What!" Like a steel trap, he jackknifed to the edge of the bed.

Samantha quickly backed away. For a moment he sat as if suspended in time, then slowly, he took a ragged breath and ran shaky fingers through his hair.

"Okay now?"

Samantha's soft voice was a balm to his jagged nerves. Marc looked up and tried to reassure her with a smile, but he knew from her worried expression, the attempt fell short. He shrugged, and without thinking, held out his hand to her.

Samantha understood and clasped his hand in both of hers and knelt in front of him. He needed human contact, tangible proof that the nightmare was just that—a nightmare. And for some strange reason, she needed to feel his touch again.

"Have you ever had a dream so real, yet you knew it wasn't, and no matter how hard you tried, you couldn't wake up? Each time you think you're awake, you find yourself back in the damned dream?" Marc's hand trembled. "I kept trying to wake up, but every time I thought I was awake, I was back in the police car staring down the barrel of a gun. And each time..." He closed his eyes and shook his head.

"Each time what?" she gently encouraged.

"I guess it's time to tell you the whole story," Marc said softly.

Even though he opened his eyes and began to talk, Samantha knew he was with her in body only. His mind and soul were elsewhere, reliving the horror he'd witnessed.

"After the governor was shot that morning, I hightailed it to a telephone to call in the story to my editor before I turned myself in as a witness. The authorities questioned me throughout that day and most of the night. It was early the next morning before they decided to place me in protective custody. For safety precautions, I was to be driven around for a while by two policemen, then handed over to two other cops who would meet us at a designated place and take me to a safe house. Taylor and Wilson, the two detectives assigned to drive me around, were in the front of the police car, and I was in the back."

Marc knew as long as he lived, he would remember the two men. Taylor was a black-haired, slim, almost effeminate man with nervous brown eyes, and his partner, Wilson, was the complete opposite. Tall and broad-shouldered, he'd reminded Marc of a red-haired wrestler he'd once interviewed. "I remember thinking that Wilson's size alone was enough to intimidate anyone," Marc said. "I was tired, and I had a headache. The least bit of light or noise hurt and every second was a pounding eternity. One of the officers at the police station had gone home ill with some kind of flu virus, but not soon enough. I guess I caught whatever he had.

"Anyway, we'd been driving around for what seemed like hours. My headache was so bad, I'd shut my eyes...." Marc stared past Samantha, his eyes wide and unseeing as he continued talking.

Eventually the police car had slowed and turned and he'd opened his eyes and sat forward. He'd spotted the brown van immediately and had chuckled to himself as they pulled alongside it. Of all the unlikely places to make the exchange, they'd chosen a restaurant's parking lot. Marc had been tempted to suggest they all take a break from cops and robbers and go in for eggs and bacon.

Wilson might have gone for it, but Marc figured Taylor wouldn't think much of the idea.

Marc watched as the passenger side of the van opened. Neither Taylor nor Wilson made a move. They just sat watching. From the back seat, Marc could see the man who got out only from his chest down—white shirt, navy tie, light blue suit coat with matching slacks.

"Don't remember seeing him before," Taylor said, his voice low and suspicious.

Marc rolled his eyes upward and almost groaned out loud. Taylor was unbelievable—ever-determined to play detective to the hilt.

"Could be a new man," offered Wilson.

Good old Wilson, thought Marc. At least one of them was in the real world.

"Maybe," Taylor replied.

As the man approached the car, Marc shifted uneasily in the back seat. Maybe Taylor's doubts were contagious. Maybe, but there was something familiar about the way the man moved.

The man leaned against the car with one arm draped along the top, but Marc still couldn't see his face.

"Got the transfer papers?" Taylor asked.

Out of the corner of his eye, Marc saw Wilson slowly reach toward the shoulder holster concealed by his suit coat.

"Sure. Right here," the man answered.

Warning bells went off in Marc's head even as his body tensed. He'd heard that voice before. It came to him at the exact moment the man reached into his coat pocket. He was one of the men in the park, the one who'd cold-bloodedly murdered the governor. But his recognition came too late.

Instead of the transfer papers, the man pulled out a gun, complete with silencer. He squeezed the trigger twice, swiftly and accurately, with an economy of movement. Wilson's hand never had time to reach his gun. It all happened too fast. Neither Wilson nor Taylor knew what hit them as Taylor slumped forward, and Wilson fell sideways.

Suddenly, everything seemed to move in slow motion as Marc watched the gun slowly turn and point toward him.

Marc heard the thugging zing and felt a small puff of air near his forehead as he ducked. Instinctive need for survival lent him uncanny agility as he dived into the seat and reached for the door handle in the same swift movement. With his head pressed hard against the vinyl seat, he felt his heartbeat pulsing in his temple. He tensed in readiness for action as adrenaline pumped through his veins.

Without a moment's hesitation, he yanked the handle and shoved the door with every ounce of strength he possessed, successfully slamming it into the killer. The corresponding groan of surprise was a welcome sound to Marc's ears. He hadn't been sure the man was positioned in its path but he had taken the chance anyway. All he needed was time, just a second of precious time to buy him his life.

The killer was doubled over in pain. Before he could recover, Marc rolled out of the car, landing on his feet. He kicked out and his foot connected with the man's hand; the gun skidded across the concrete. With one hand, Marc grabbed the killer's tie. He drew back his other hand, doubled in a fist, and slammed it into his assailant's face. Blood spurted. The man went limp and fell to the ground. Marc scooped up the gun, and without a second glance, took off. Keeping low, he dodged around the parked vehicles. If he could just reach the building, he knew he'd have a chance.

There'd been no movement from inside the van yet, but Marc knew the killer hadn't come alone. Any minute, the driver of the van could come out shooting. Marc wasn't about to wait around to be on the receiving end of the fireworks. The picture of Taylor's and Wilson's lifeless bodies was still vividly imprinted on his mind.

When he reached the side entrance to the restaurant, he glanced back in time to see a man running from the van. Without hesitation, Marc plunged through a group of people inside the doorway. Trays flew, food spilled and people yelled. He ignored the indignant shouts as he continued to push and shove his way through to the opposite side of the building, where he was sure there'd be another exit.

Once outside again, he tossed the gun in a nearby trash can and quickly scanned the area. Out of breath, he sucked in huge gulps of air and swiped at the blinding sweat stinging his eyes. Across the rear parking lot, he spotted a low, stone fence covered with ivy. Bushes and trees blocked his view beyond that point.

Within seconds, Marc vaulted over the fence and ran down the narrow alley beyond. The end of the shaded alley brought him to another barrier. He didn't stop when he reached the six-foot-high chain-link fence. He grabbed the bar on the top and pulled himself up and over, landing with a thud on the other side. As soon as he hit the ground, sharp pain shot up his right leg from his ankle, but he continued, half limping, half jogging across the well-manicured lawn.

"Son of a bitch!" Marc cursed and halted dead in his tracks, gasping for breath. Only a few yards in front of him was his gate to freedom. Beyond the gate he could see a bus stop. Farther down the street, as if on cue, a city bus rounded the corner and headed his way. If he could just get through the gate and get on that bus...

"Son of a bitch!" he repeated. Between him and the gate to freedom stood the biggest, ugliest Doberman pinscher he'd ever seen.

A low growl rumbled in the black dog's chest as his pointed ears flattened against his head; his lips quivered and curled back in a snarl, revealing vicious fangs.

"Easy boy... nice dog," Marc whispered, careful not to stare directly into the animal's eyes. He'd read somewhere that dogs considered a direct stare from a human as a challenge. Slowly, Marc took a tentative step backward. The bus roared in the distance. Marc's eyes darted from side to side. He was careful to keep his movements to a minimum as he searched for another route of escape.

As far as he could ascertain, the most logical choice was to go over the fence again. The most logical, maybe, but certainly not the easiest. The nearest part of the fence was still several yards away. Easing away a step at a time would take forever. By then, the bus would be gone and he'd probably be feeling the bite of a bullet with his name on it.

The dog raised off its haunches and growled louder. Marc took one look at the animal's sharp teeth, remembered how he felt having a gun pointed at him and made his decision. Later, when he thought about it, he wasn't even sure if his feet touched the ground. All he remembered was lunging for the fence and feeling the snarling dog nipping at his feet.

The bus was pulling away when Marc reached it. He chased along beside it, shouting and pounding on the door with his fist.

When the driver finally stopped, Marc pulled himself up the steps inside. He felt the stares of every person on board. He paid his fare and stumbled down the aisle toward the back, where he collapsed on an empty seat.

When he looked up, he caught a glimpse of his reflection in the window. No wonder everyone had stared, he thought. His hair was sticking up in spikes worse than a punk rocker's. His face was shadowed with an overnight beard and streaked with dirt, and his wrinkled shirt was soaked clear through with sweat. He looked like a bum. Marc wrinkled his nose. He probably smelled like one, too. Suddenly, none of it mattered. Beyond his reflection in the mirror, Marc caught a movement outside the bus.

Marc jerked his head around to the back window. Sure enough, two men—one of them holding a handkerchief to his nose—ran out into the street just as the bus turned a corner. For a brief moment, they both stood and stared. One signaled to the other and then they disappeared. Marc felt reasonably sure they'd noted the bus number and were probably hotfooting it back to the van.

Grim faced, he turned away. It had been too much to hope for. Safety was still a long way off.

Marc changed buses two more times before allowing himself to relax. He glanced at his watch. It had been exactly two hours since Taylor and Wilson were killed. The early-morning clouds had darkened and rain beat down, keeping a steady rhythm with the windshield wipers of the bus. Marc shivered and stared at the back of the driver's head two seats in front of him. The last time he'd changed buses, he'd got soaked in the process. His headache was back with a vengeance and his ankle was throbbing like an abscessed tooth. Marc closed his eyes. He couldn't think, didn't know what to do next.

"HEY, BUDDY. This ain't no motel on wheels."

"What!" Marc opened his eyes and jerked himself up-right. His jumbled mind tried to make sense of what was happening. Standing over him was the bus driver.

"I said this ain't no motel. Go somewhere else to sleep it off."

Still groggy, Marc asked, "Where am I?" His mouth felt like it was stuffed with cotton, but his head was fi-nally clearing; it was all coming back—the governor, Thompson, Taylor and Wilson, the killers chasing him.

"Look, buddy, we're a few blocks from the corner of Airline and Florida. You've been asleep for about a half hour. Either get off the bus or I'll have to call the cops."

"Okay, okay. You've made your point." Marc pulled himself out of the seat and made his way to the door. The last thing he wanted right now was a visit from the cops. He'd already seen the kind of protection they gave.

Outside the bus, the humid air hit him in the face like the steam from a pressure cooker. The rain had slacked off to a slow drizzle, and a sickly sun was trying to burn its way through the lingering dark clouds.

A block away, Marc spotted a flashing sign advertising an Always Fresh Donut Shop. He checked his pockets for change but only came up with a few pennies, some nick-els and a couple of quarters. He reached in his back pocket and pulled out his wallet. A ten, a five and a cou-ple of ones were all he had left besides his charge cards.

"Thank God for plastic money," he whispered. He hadn't figured out what he was going to do yet, but whatever he decided, he was going to need money.

When Marc entered the donut shop, he found it empty except for a waitress and a couple of teenagers sitting at one end. The waitress ignored him and continued wiping the counter. Both teenagers had headsets on. Their bodies jerked and convulsed to the silent beat of the music on their radios; they were oblivious to anything outside their self-contained world.

Marc stopped at the counter long enough to order coffee and a couple of glazed donuts, then headed to the men's room. A quick glance told him it was empty. He went straight to the sink. Without looking in the mirror, he turned the hot water on full force. Bent over the sink, he splashed his face with the warm water and groaned. He was beginning to feel human again. He dried himself off with paper towels, and using the small black comb he always carried in his back pocket, he smoothed his hair. His shirt was beyond redemption; nevertheless, he tucked it into his pants as neatly as possible.

When he returned to the counter, the waitress had poured his coffee; the rich aroma filled his nostrils as he took a tentative sip. The donuts were a poor substitute for a steak but starving men couldn't be choosy, he decided as he wolfed down the first one and started on the second.

The food helped, but his head still ached. He rubbed his temples. He had to be able to think, and think clearly. His life depended on it. He decided the best course of action would be to contact his father. By now he would know what had happened and Marc didn't want him worrying. Marc placed a credit card call from the pay phone at the end of the counter. After several rings, he hung up. Odd, he thought, that no one was home.

A few moments passed before he reached for the phone again and punched the operator button. "Operator, I need to get in touch with Police Chief Investigator Harry Thompson.

"No," Marc told the operator. "I don't want to dial the number myself. Yes, it's an emergency."

The memory of his all-night interrogation conducted by Thompson still rubbed him the wrong way. Thompson had asked him the same tired questions over and over. He'd made Marc feel as if he were the criminal instead of a volunteer eyewitness. But even so, Thompson might be able to fill him in on what was happening. Before he did anything else, he needed more information.

It seemed to take forever to locate Thompson. Marc looked up to see the waitress eyeing him suspiciously.

"Thompson here."

Marc turned his back to the counter and lowered his voice. "Thompson, this is Marc Dureaux—"

"Where in the hell are you?" Thompson shouted into the phone. "I've got every officer in Baton Rouge looking for you."

"Never mind that. Just listen."

"Listen! Fat chance," Thompson said, his voice lowering menacingly. "Four of my men are dead because of you and all bloody hell has broken loose around here. I've got the lieutenant governor breathing down my neck, not to mention your father ranting and raving. Now tell me where you are, and I'll send some men to pick you up."

"Fat chance," Marc mimicked Thompson's own words. "I've been shot at, chased, attacked by a dog, harassed, and you want me to let *your* men pick me up? No way, man. No way!"

"Okay, okay. Just calm down and let's talk this over."

"The only person I'm going to talk with is my editor," Marc answered. "How do you spell your name again? I want to make sure I get it right along with the spelling of other words such as inept, bungling, negligent—"

Thompson interrupted in a strained voice. "You've made your point, Dureaux. If you won't talk to me, will you talk to your father?"

"Is he there?"

"Yeah, just a minute."

While Marc waited, it occurred to him the police could be tracing his call. He glanced at his watch and tried to remember how long it took to trace a call.

"Marc?"

"Dad?" Marc breathed a sigh of relief.

"Are you all right, Son?"

"Yeah, Dad. I'm fine. How about you?"

"I've had better days, but never mind that. Thompson tells me you refuse to turn yourself in."

"Dad—"

"No," Edward Dureaux interrupted. "I understand. Just listen and listen well," he whispered, then louder he said, "We've all been worried about you—especially Jenny. She's already gone out and stocked up on all your favorite foods and is waiting for you to come home when it's safe." He paused, giving Marc time to absorb what he was saying.

At first Marc was confused. Why was his father rambling at a time like this? And who the hell was Jenny? He didn't know anyone named Jenny, except…Marc grinned. Of course. Jenny. Why hadn't he thought of it himself? Jenny was their family's yacht and was actually the *Jenny II*. *Jenny I* had been bought and named after Marc's maternal grandmother and later replaced with the *Jenny II*, a newer, more sophisticated boat.

Apparently, as he'd suspected, there was a leak somewhere in the police department, and this was his father's way of telling him his safest bet was to set sail for the open water until things could be worked out.

"Thanks, Dad. I needed to hear that. You tell Jenny, I'll be there as soon as I can."

"Just take care of yourself, Son."

Marc hung up the phone, a smile tugging at his lips. The *Jenny II* would be stocked and waiting for him. The only problem was getting to it without being picked up by the cops. His smile faded to a frown as he reached up and rubbed his aching temple. If what Thompson had said was true and every cop in the city was looking for him, it wouldn't be easy.

"Will that be all, sir?"

Marc glanced around to see the waitress glaring at him as she slapped his bill on the counter. She made "sir" sound like a dirty word. He figured she probably thought he was going to skip without paying his bill.

Marc pulled out his wallet and threw a couple of ones down on the counter, then winked at the scowling waitress.

"Thanks, sweetheart. You're a real doll," he called out as he walked toward the door.

As soon as he stepped outside, he searched the street to orient himself. The street was lined with a mixture of small boutiques, office buildings, and much farther down the block was a sign with the red, white and blue logo of the First National Bank. Noisy traffic crawled by, people rushed past him.

A yellow cab stopped ahead and a middle-aged couple stepped out. Marc wondered what a taxi would cost from Baton Rouge to Mandeville, where the *Jenny* was docked. "More than you've got, buster," he said under his breath and watched the cab pull away. Even if he didn't take a taxi, he was going to need more cash, and the fastest way to get it was with his credit card. Marc headed for the bank.

Just as he reached the end of the block, he looked up, swore, then quickly ducked into the nearby alley. After the police car cruised on by, he stayed flattened against the

building and silently counted to fifty. Cautiously, he
emerged from his hiding place and scanned the streets.
Breathing a sigh of relief, he continued walking toward the
bank.

Twenty minutes later, he was back on the street.

His next stop was a sporting-goods outlet where he
purchased a pair of navy shorts, a polo shirt, tennis shoes,
socks, sunglasses and a baseball cap. As soon as he walked
out of the store, he dug into the sack for the sunglasses
and baseball hat. It wasn't much of a disguise, but it
would have to do until he could change into the rest. Marc
removed the sales tags, slipped the glasses on and pulled
the cap low over his forehead.

He caught the public bus and rode it as far to the east
of the city as it would take him. After dismissing several
other modes of transportation as easily traceable, Marc
decided to hitchhike to Mandeville. Hitchhiking on the
highway was illegal and chancy, but it was the best he
could come up with.

Marc got off the bus and walked several blocks to a gas
station located near the Interstate 12. He slipped into the
men's rest room, quickly stripped and donned the shorts
and shirt. He stuffed his old clothes into the empty sack
and deposited them in the trash can on his way out. Pre-
tending he was a stranded motorist, he purchased a gas
can and then pumped a gallon of gas into it. Marc smiled
grimly, thinking if worse came to worse and a state
trooper stopped him, he would at least have an excuse for
hitching.

The highway stretched out before him as car after car
sped by. With each step, Marc became more exhausted.
He glanced at his watch. Even though it was almost eight
p.m., he was sweating profusely, his headache was now
really bad and his body ached. The gas can was unwieldy

and the gallon of gas felt as if it had expanded to ten. According to the mile markers, he'd walked five miles and not one person had stopped to offer him a lift.

Then the worst happened. Marc didn't see the navy-and-gold car approaching. It seemed to come out of nowhere. Suddenly it was there, big as life. For several moments, it cruised along beside him. Finally, it pulled ahead several yards and waited. There was nowhere to run. Marc stopped when he was alongside the car.

"Got problems, buddy?"

Marc's mind raced to fabricate a believable lie. "Yes, Officer. My wife ran all the gas out and didn't bother refilling the tank. I thought I could make it, but..." He forced a laugh and held out the gas can. "Women," he said. "You can't live with them and you can't live without them."

Marc had to tell himself to keep breathing, keep smiling. The less nervous he appeared, the better chance his ruse would work.

The state trooper's face was noncommittal, his eyes hidden behind dark, reflector sunglasses. He seemed to study Marc carefully for an interminable amount of time before he finally smiled.

"Yeah, I know what you mean. Get in and I'll give you a lift."

Marc breathed a sigh of relief and climbed in beside the officer. He offered up a silent prayer that somewhere down the road there would be an abandoned car. He'd already made up his mind to claim the first one they came to as his.

For several miles, the trooper was silent.

Marc kept his eyes on the road and tried to think ahead. It felt good to sit again. The coolness of the police car was a welcome relief after the oppressive heat.

"How far's your car?"

Marc shifted uneasily in his seat. "Not too far. Just down the road a ways."

"What's the make and model?"

Marc hesitated, caught in his lie. Now what was he supposed to say?

The police radio suddenly crackled to life with a garbled mixture of words and code numbers, then was quiet. Marc grew more uneasy and prayed for divine guidance or intervention. He'd be grateful for either one. At this point he was past being choosy.

The silence seemed to last forever, but Marc couldn't think of an answer that wouldn't get him into more trouble than he already was.

Once again the radio broke in. "Marc Dureaux." The two words came through the mixture of code numbers and words loud and clear. . . .

"MARC... MARC!" Samantha squeezed his hand. "Don't stop now. What happened?"

Startled, Marc looked down at Sam. He hadn't realized he'd stopped talking. In the dim light of the cabin, her eyes glowed with curiosity. Her expression, the tenseness of her small hand in his, the eagerness in her voice, all reminded him of a small child waiting for the punch line to a scary bedtime story—the kind children tell to frighten each other. But Samantha wasn't a child, he thought as the last remnants of his nightmare faded. He allowed his gaze to lower to her body for a brief moment. Definitely not a child, he decided, but it was also definitely not a good idea to dwell on her womanly attributes, not in the present situation.

"Well?" she asked, fully aware of the way he was looking at her.

A smile tugged at his lips.

"The trooper shot me on the spot."

He'd said it in such a deadpan voice, it took several moments for the words to register. Samantha stared at him. She wanted to hit him and she wanted to laugh. "That's a rotten thing to do, Marc Dureaux."

"I know."

"You don't have to be so smug about it."

"Who's at the wheel?"

Samantha snatched her hand out of his and stood up. "You know good and well, nobody is. It's on auto."

"Guess I'd better check the readings then, huh?" Marc reached for the shirt he'd discarded on the floor earlier and tugged it over his head.

"You're not going to tell me, are you?"

When his head popped through the neck, he was laughing, and even though Samantha pretended to be miffed, it was all she could do to keep from laughing with him.

"Maybe...maybe not. Depends." Marc breezed past her.

"Depends!" Of all the nerve, she thought. "I didn't want to know anyway," she mumbled to his retreating back.

Marc stopped and turned, grinning from ear to ear. "Nothing really happened. When my name came over his radio, I thought I'd had it for sure. But believe it or not, static interference blocked out any description they were giving and the trooper switched the thing off."

"What about your fictitious car?"

Marc laughed. "The saint who looks out for fools and liars must have smiled on me. A few miles down the road, there was an abandoned car."

"And, of course, you claimed it," she finished for him.

Marc crossed his arms and leaned against the door-frame. "Damned straight. Beggars can't be choosers."

"So how did you get to the boat?"

Marc's expression grew pensive. "Actually, the car wasn't abandoned. It had overheated. The kid who owned it was napping in the back seat, waiting for the engine to cool. I gave him a twenty to drive me to the marina. By the time I got the *Jenny* to the point where I could anchor, I was so sick, I'd almost decided to radio for help. I remember stumbling to the radio and—" Marc shrugged "—anyway, when I came to, I managed to make it to the bed."

"Maybe that explains it."

Marc looked puzzled. "Explains what?"

"Tommy couldn't get the radio to work. Maybe you dropped it when you passed out."

"It's possible. I vaguely remember grabbing for it." He shrugged again. "Who knows?"

Samantha slowly shook her head. "Amazing," she said.

Marc looked at her questioningly.

"I still can't believe the part about the abandoned car," she explained. "Never in a million years would you be that lucky again."

Marc laughed but the sound oozed sarcasm. "Yeah, any luckier and I'd be dead."

A shiver of fear raced through Samantha as she watched him disappear up the companionway. His story had so intrigued her that for a moment she'd almost forgotten it was more than a story. It was real. Marc's nightmare was real, too, she thought. And the people chasing him wanted him dead.

CHAPTER FIVE

ANGELIQUE DUREAUX walked briskly through the crowd, her heels clicking against the concrete promenade surrounding one of New Orleans's favorite tourist attractions, Jackson Square. Thunder rolled in the distance as black clouds gathered to block out the late-afternoon sun. A stiff breeze whipped her silk skirt above her knees, revealing slim, shapely legs. Her dark complexion and black hair were an attractive contrast to the white dress that molded her petite body. She made a grab at her large-brimmed hat as the wind threatened to whisk it away and looked up just in time to see a sudden streak of lightning split the darkening sky over the Mississippi River.

She glanced at her gold watch and frowned. The heat and the brewing storm were the least of her worries. Nothing had gone as planned. Her breath caught and she fought against the familiar pressure building behind her eyes.

Determined not to cry, Angelique gritted her teeth as she continued to snake through the crowd. She'd shed enough tears to fill buckets the last two days. And just when she thought she had everything worked out, Marc had to go and ruin everything.

She sidestepped a group on the corner watching a juggling act. There was no turning back now, she thought. Everything had been set in motion and Marc had to be eliminated.

Too bad, she thought. Marc was a good man, an honorable man, but she didn't love him. He'd served her purposes for a while, and in the beginning, she'd been too desperate to care about anything but surviving in a world that had suddenly turned upside down. She still cringed each time she remembered the pain and humiliation she'd suffered after the sudden death of her parents. She'd lost everything, everything she'd ever cared about. The auction of the family estate had been the final blow. Like greedy vultures, her parents' so-called friends had shown up. She'd heard their whispers about her father and speculations about her financial situation. At times, she still heard them.

Angelique clenched and unclenched her fists; the need to cover her ears to shut out the voices was overwhelming. She was hearing the voices more and more these days. But this time she would control herself. She shuddered just thinking about the consequences if she didn't.

All she had to do was think positive and ignore everything else. Suddenly she smiled. All she had to do was go after what she wanted out of life. That was what the doctors had told her when she'd been released from the hospital, and she'd followed their advice with a vengeance. Think of yourself, they'd said, and she had. Instead of ending up a penniless pauper, she'd discovered Marc Dureaux.

Marc had been easy prey. She almost laughed out loud remembering how she'd duped him. He'd been on the rebound from a broken engagement, and after a few too many drinks and a sympathetic ear, seducing him had been child's play. And later, he'd actually believed she was pregnant. He'd insisted that no child of his would be fatherless and had done the honorable thing, exactly as she'd anticipated and counted on. After all, the Dureaux were raised to be Southern gentlemen.

But that was all in the past, she reminded herself. Marc had served his purpose. Now it was time to move on. Now she would show them all.

Weaving in and out of the crowd, Angelique searched the park area. Through the wrought-iron fence surrounding the green, lush square, she spotted Tony. He was seated on a bench not far from the huge statue of Andrew Jackson. "Old Hickory," as Jackson was known, sat astride his horse and dominated the center of the small park named for him.

Angelique waved and quickened her steps. Tony wouldn't let her down. Her father had always relied on him to handle matters that fell outside the realm of propriety. An older man, Tony was short and stocky, but he possessed an aura of power that made him seem much larger. His eyes, like the man himself, had always intrigued her. They were dark, sinister and mysterious. And each time they roved over her body, she could almost believe he wanted her. But she knew better. Theirs was strictly a business relationship.

As she approached him, she noticed he seemed oblivious to the impending storm and calmly continued his task of feeding the pigeons. That it was illegal to do so didn't seem to bother him. Angelique thought how appropriate his actions were in light of their plan. Together, they would feed the pigeons. The only difference being, their pigeons were of the human variety.

"Ah, Angelique," Tony said, standing up as she moved toward the bench. "How lovely you look." His dark eyes gleamed with appreciation, and he kissed her cheek.

"Sorry I'm late. Have you been waiting long?"

"No, not long, but I do have some business to take care
of and my associate is waiting for me in the car." He
smiled. "Now, what can I do for you?"

Once again, she felt the pull of his gaze and, as always,
his perusal made her uncomfortable. She glanced nerv-
ously around the square. The resident artists who lined the
square daily to display their paintings had already begun
packing up in anticipation of rain. The streets were fast
becoming deserted as the tourists sought shelter from the
fine mist that had begun to fall. Deciding her imagination was working overtime, she dismissed her uneasy
feelings about Tony. There were more important things to
worry about. She turned to face him. "What went
wrong?"

He shrugged his shoulders. "These things happen."

"But you promised me you'd take care of him."

Tony reached out and squeezed her arm. "Relax, and
keep your voice down. We'll find him," Tony soothed.
"This is just a temporary setback. You're not to worry.
My sources tell me a man fitting his description was spotted at a marina in Mandeville."

Angelique frowned. "That's where they keep the family boat. My God." Her eyes widened, and she took a
ragged, desperate breath. "He could end up anywhere if
he's aboard the *Jenny*."

"Yes, he could, but I have people watching and waiting all along the coast."

She reached out and gripped the sleeve of his suit. "You
know how important this is to me. I have to have that insurance money." She had to make Tony understand. She
couldn't be left destitute again. And time was running
short. With only one month left before the divorce was
final, she'd thought everything was at long last going her
way, but now—

"Tony, you have to do something."

Tony frowned. "Don't upset yourself, my dear. I told you I'd take care of things. Besides, if the worst happens and he escapes, your new love has enough to keep you in style."

"That's none of your business."

Tony held up his hands in mock defense. "Okay, okay. Sorry. I didn't realize you were so touchy about him."

"Just remember, he has nothing to do with any of this. Nothing," she repeated.

Tony's eyes narrowed as she whirled away and walked briskly toward the gate. He continued to watch her until she was swallowed up in the crowds hovering beneath the overhangs of the buildings surrounding the square. She was just as headstrong, just as arrogant as her father had been, but, unlike him, she had the guts to go along with the brains.

He shoved his hands into his pants pockets and slowly strolled across the park. Behind him, two men followed at a discreet distance. When he reached the front, he stepped down to the sidewalk.

A black limousine pulled up. It looked incongruous alongside the line of horses and carriages waiting for tourists' fares. The smaller of the two men following Tony rushed up and opened the door.

Tony turned to him. "I don't trust her," he said. "Something's wrong. Something's different about her. She's acting strange." He paused thoughtfully and patted his pocket. Instantly, the man whipped out a cigar and lit it for his boss. Tony puffed several times. "I want her followed day and night."

The man nodded, then motioned to the larger man. "Go with the boss. I got business to take care of."

The larger man waited for Tony to get in, slammed the door and slid in beside the driver.

"Sorry about the interruption," Tony said as he turned to face the man who had been patiently waiting for him.

"Do you think she'll be a problem?" his companion asked.

Tony shook his head and smiled. "I can handle her. As soon as Dureaux is taken care of, she'll have what she wants." He laughed. "It's really ironic in light of the fact that I have to get rid of him anyway." He shifted in the seat and crossed his legs. "While I'm thinking about it, make sure our contact at the police station is well paid. If the police spot Dureaux before we do, I want to know about it." Tony paused to relight his cigar and then continued. "I still haven't figured out how Dureaux knew about that meeting with Jackson. There shouldn't have been any witnesses." His eyes hardened. "Someone tipped him off, but enough of that. I'm not as worried about Angelique or her husband as I am about Congressman Landry. How's he holding up under the pressure?"

The man scowled. "When he heard Jackson had been murdered, he got rip-roaring drunk."

Tony cursed. "You better stay close to him. Don't let the press get near him until you're sure he's in control. We can't afford a slipup now."

The man nodded. "I canceled his speeches in Shreveport and Monroe and I've already issued a press release about how distraught he is over Jackson's death." The man glanced at his watch. "Unless there's something else we need to talk about, I should get back."

"Nothing else," Tony replied. "We'll drop you off, and I'll be in touch as soon as Dureaux is taken care of."

THE GULF STRETCHED OUT for miles before Samantha's eyes. The gray-blue water sparkled and shimmered under the morning sun and, she was pleased to note, caused her no distress. Her phobia seemed like a thing of the past. She breathed deeply and then tried, unsuccessfully, to stifle a yawn. The fresh air, along with the smell of frying bacon, teased her senses. The sound of Marc's whistling drifted up from the galley, and she chuckled softly when she caught herself humming along with the catchy tune.

With all her fears and suspicions of Marc resolved, she felt as if a tremendous burden had been lifted. And now, in the light of day, recalling the easy banter they'd enjoyed the night before, it was hard to believe she'd ever thought him capable of murder. Samantha scanned the northern horizon.

No. Marc wasn't a murderer, and if she were honest with herself, she'd never really believed he was. But someone was. A cold shiver ran up her spine. Someone was out there looking for him. They'd tried once and failed. Would they try again? And who were they? *If* Marc knew, he was keeping his suspicions to himself. It was almost as if he was trying to pretend that it had never happened.

He'd said the less she knew, the better. Was he still trying to protect her? Before she'd known the truth, reaching shore was all she could think about, but now...

The whistling stopped and Samantha glanced toward the companionway just as Marc's head appeared in the doorway.

For a man who'd been up most of the night, he looked fairly rested, and somehow different. In one hand he had a plate of food, and in the other he held a steaming cup of coffee. Samantha's mouth watered when she saw the bacon, scrambled eggs and toast. But even the mischievous twinkle in his blue eyes and his easy smile couldn't hide the faint traces of fatigue on his face. "You should get some sleep," she scolded. It was then she realized why he looked different. He'd trimmed his mustache and partially shaved, giving shape and definition to the beginnings of a full beard.

"I catnapped off and on last night." He held out the plate of food. "You'd better eat this before it gets cold."

"Where's yours?" Samantha accepted the plate and moved away as he took the wheel.

Marc patted his stomach and smiled. "Right where it belongs. I ate before I came up."

Samantha's eyes followed the movement of his hand and for a moment lingered. He'd changed into a brightly patterned cotton shirt; it hung loosely and was unbuttoned, leaving his chest bare. After only a few days in the sun, his skin had darkened to a golden bronze; the dark hair that generously covered the broad muscles of his upper torso had bleached to a reddish hue. Of course, she'd seen him several times without a shirt. But she'd had other things on her mind. Back then, he'd been the enemy, but now...Samantha quickly glanced away and tried to concentrate on her food. She was beginning to realize that her first reaction to him hadn't changed. She'd only suppressed her attraction to him because of the circumstances. He was still a beautiful, sexy specimen of a man. Just knowing he'd bathed and shaved made her aware of how grungy she felt. At least he had clean clothes to change into. She only had her bikini.

"Look! Over there."

The sound of Marc's excited voice broke through her silent musings. She turned her head in the direction he was pointing. Pure pleasure raced through her; all other thoughts fled.

"Dolphins," she whispered as she set her plate down.

Marc watched her face transform into delight as she spotted the large school.

"There are so many of them. Aren't they magnificent?"

"Magnificent," he repeated softly, but his eyes were on Samantha. He'd seen her display numerous emotions over the past two days, but none compared to this. It was exhilarating to watch her. Her eyes shone like polished emeralds, her cheeks were flushed, and the smile on her lips was one of pure joy. Her whole body seemed to vibrate with life, and he suddenly, joltingly, realized how attracted he was to her. She was so different from Angelique. That had to be the reason, he decided. That and the deprived libido of a man who had been without a woman for too long.

Marc looked back at the dolphins. For a moment it was as if a dark cloud had moved away to let the warm brightness of the sun shine through. But the moment passed and Marc was suddenly profoundly aware of the lonely void deep in his gut.

"Oh, Marc. They're heading this way."

In only a few moments, the boat was surrounded. The water burst into life, and the quiet peacefulness of the morning was shattered by the sounds of barks, clicks and whistles. Samantha's laughter rang out, the sound musically sweet and infectious. Despite his melancholy, Marc found himself laughing along with her as they watched.

"Over there." Samantha pointed to the bow. "Look how high he jumped. And there, that big one behind him."

"Sam, dolphins don't jump."

"Jumped, leaped, whatever." She waved vaguely, but only spared him a brief glare. Not the least daunted by his teasing, she pointed to yet another one. "Look at him. I swear he's laughing at us."

"He's laughing because he knows he has a captive audience."

"I think you're right."

"Of course, I'm right," he teased. "I'm the captain."

"Hmph!"

She flashed him an indignant look, but when she turned and motioned toward a baby dolphin off the bow, she was smiling.

Moments later, the dolphins began to leave, a few at a time, until only two remained.

"It's a good sign, isn't it?" Samantha spoke softly as she watched the final two follow the others.

"For hundreds of years, seamen have thought so," Marc answered slowly. "Yes, a good sign." And he hoped it was true. He thought about the unusual circumstances that had brought the two of them together; it had been a real twist of fate. And even though he worried about how it was going to end, he found himself strangely content for the first time in years.

Samantha glanced over her shoulder and noticed again the fine lines of fatigue that shadowed his face. "Why don't you get some sleep? I feel guilty for not taking a turn last night."

"Nag, nag."

Samantha raised an eyebrow, but Marc didn't hesitate to move away when she reached for the wheel.

"Maybe I will stretch out on deck for a while. It's too hot below. Wake me in a couple of hours."

Samantha couldn't resist. "Yes sir, Captain sir. Anything you say."

"Good," he grunted as he pulled his shirt off and threw it at her. "Just remember that when you see the galley." Marc climbed out of the cockpit up to the deck. "You can wash the dishes."

Samantha opened her mouth to protest as she clutched the shirt to her breasts, but the scent of spice and male filled her nostrils, and her retort stuck in her throat. Intoxicated, she breathed deeply. Several seconds passed before she came to her senses, but by then he'd already sprawled out on his stomach. The even rise and fall of his sleek back indicated he was asleep.

DOWN IN THE GALLEY, as Samantha grabbed yet another dirty dish and began to scrub, she wondered how one man could make such a mess scrambling a few eggs. Forewarned was forearmed, she decided. "I'm the captain," she mimicked under her breath. Next time she'd do the cooking.

She put away the last plate and closed the cabinet. She could feel the sweat trickle between her breasts, and she longed for a cool shower. But even more, she wished for a change of clothes.

Samantha made her way toward the forward cabin. After rummaging through several drawers, she found a clean pair of men's white shorts and another shirt similar to the one Marc had been wearing, only in different colors. She eyed the tiny shower stall as she stripped, but filled the sink with water, instead. A sponge bath would have to do until they reached land. Fresh water was too precious to waste.

Her skin was still tender in places from too much sun, and the cool water helped to ease her stinging flesh. A thorough search of the head turned up only a tube of first-aid cream. Samantha shrugged. First-aid cream was better than nothing.

Gingerly, she wrapped a towel around herself and padded back to the bed where she'd left the clean clothes. The towel slipped and fell into a terry heap at her feet as she began to rub the thick cream into her shoulders.

The sight of her naked back stopped Marc cold outside the doorway. His smile faded. Damp tendrils of her hair brushed her bare shoulders with each move she made. Her pink back was smooth and unblemished except for the white stripe from her bathing-suit top. Her hips curved outward from a waist so slim, he could easily span the distance with his hands. As she bent forward to step into a pair of shorts, she turned sideways, giving him an unobstructed view of one rounded breast. Marc groaned silently as his body automatically reacted to the tempting sight. He rubbed sweaty palms against his shorts, and quietly backed away, each step an agony. When he reached the companionway, he glanced down and swore softly. He'd always taken pride in his ability to control his emotions. He'd seen naked women before. Hell, he was married. Marc shook his head and squeezed his eyes tightly as he turned toward the ladder.

"Marc?"

The sound of her voice startled him and he jumped.

"Is something wrong?"

"Wrong?" His voice cracked and he cleared his throat. "No, nothing's wrong."

"I hope you don't mind that I borrowed some clean clothes."

Careful to keep his body and the evidence of his wayward desire out of sight, Marc turned his head to answer. Even the sight of her in his baggy shorts and oversized shirt knotted at the waist didn't dispel the memory of what he'd witnessed. If anything, the outfit made her even more appealing. Desire, hot and urgent, still burned within. Afraid his eyes would reveal more than they should, he turned away. "Feel free to use whatever you need," he replied gruffly, and quickly climbed the ladder.

Puzzled by his behavior, Samantha followed him. When she stepped into the cockpit, his back was toward her, and he was pulling on his shirt.

"Did you want something?"

"A cold shower," he mumbled.

"Me, too, but I was afraid we didn't have enough fresh water on board. How much longer do you think it will be before we reach shore?"

Marc didn't answer. He buttoned his shirt, and reminded himself she had no idea he'd been watching her.

"What's wrong, Marc?"

"Nothing," he answered as he reached and unleashed the wheel. "Nothing and everything."

Samantha stared at him. "Why did you come below?"

"I...ah...came to check on you, but...you were...ah...busy, and I didn't want to bother you."

"Oh..." Her eyes widened as understanding finally dawned. "I see, or should I say, *you* saw?"

Marc felt heat rush to his face. "I'm no damned Peeping Tom."

"I never said you were." Samantha knew she should have felt embarrassed or at least been a little outraged, but for some reason his reaction and his embarrassment struck her as funny.

LATER SHE WAS STILL smiling, and watched Marc open the rear-deck storage and haul out a small tackle box and an oblong sack.

He glanced up. "Fishing gear," he offered by way of explanation. "I thought I'd try, and with any luck, we might have fresh fish for dinner."

"Sounds good to me," she called out. "Just one thing, though."

"What's that?"

"You catch it and clean it, and I'll cook it. You make too big a mess when you cook."

"No can do." He shook his head. "I have this special recipe for panfrying and no female is going to ruin my fish. I'll catch it, you clean it—I'll cook it, and you wash dishes."

"Male chauvinist," she muttered.

"I heard that."

"I'm not cleaning up after you again. Did you hear that?"

"I heard."

But Samantha caught sight of his grin and the mischievous gleam in his eyes as he turned back to the tackle. In minutes, he had the gear rigged and had settled himself nearby. Expertly, he began casting.

"We should reach land tomorrow," he said.

"Any place I know?"

Marc shrugged. "If my piloting is correct, we'll be somewhere near Cedar Keys, Florida."

"And then what?"

"You finally get to go home."

Depression washed over her like waves along the shoreline. Relentlessly, one after another, they eroded the contentment she'd begun to feel. She watched as he reeled in the empty line. His news should have made her happy. Why, then, was she disappointed?

"Guess your family will be relieved to see you. As soon as we get near a phone, you can call them."

Samantha shrugged. "There's no one to call."

Marc glanced up; his eyes narrowed. "I know your parents are dead, but isn't there anyone else?" he questioned. "No husband, boyfriend?"

Samantha lifted her chin. "No. What about you? Is there a little wife waiting, or a girlfriend?" She could have bitten her tongue the instant she spoke the sarcastic words, but they'd just popped out. It seemed that every male she met assumed any woman past the age of twenty-five had to have a man to make her complete. Well, she'd had one, and all he'd done was cause her shame and misery.

Marc glanced at her and frowned. "I'm divorced. At least, in a month I will be," he amended, and turned away to cast again.

"Where have I heard that one before?" she said. When Marc jerked around to look at her, she realized she'd spoken the words out loud. Pain flashed in his eyes before they grew stormy.

"This time it happens to be true," he said. "I will admit it wasn't exactly my choice." He was only sorry he hadn't filed first. "She's the one who filed for divorce. It seems she's fallen in love with someone else, so I certainly won't stand in her way."

"Well, I wouldn't worry if I were you. It's been my experience that the husband and wife always end up back together. I just feel sorry for the 'other man.'"

Marc opened his mouth to tell her exactly what he thought about the "other man," but the tone of hurt mixed with bitterness in her voice and the defiant tilt of her chin stopped him.

When he turned back to his fishing and several minutes of silence had passed, Samantha began to feel distinctly uneasy. She shouldn't have taken out her frustrations on Marc, but when he'd admitted he was married, something had snapped within her and she'd lashed out at him. It certainly wasn't his fault she found him attractive and was having dangerous thoughts. He'd done nothing to encourage those feelings.

Samantha took a deep breath and sighed. A change of subject might help ease the awkward moment, she decided. "What will you do when we reach Cedar Keys?"

"If it's safe, I'll go home."

"And if it's not?"

Marc turned to face her. "I don't know. The people after me aren't just two-bit hoods. They're pros, and I'm the only one who can identify them. At first, I thought a congressman named Bobby Landry might be behind it."

"And now?"

"I'm not so sure. That phone call I received—"

"What phone call?"

Marc answered slowly. "That's right. You don't know about the call. That's why I was involved in the first place."

Exasperated, Samantha glared at him when he didn't continue. "Well?"

He blinked his eyes several times. "Oh yeah . . . the phone call." He paused, then suddenly slammed the rod and reel against the deck. "That's it! The phone call."

Marc jumped up, grabbed Samantha's arms and gave her a gentle shake. "A setup from the word go. I should have known. Landry had nothing to do with it, but someone sure wanted me to think he did, wanted me to report it that way."

She was stunned when his arms closed around her as he hugged her close. She could feel his heart pounding against her breasts.

"Sam, you're terrific!"

"But I didn't . . ." Her words died on her lips as he pulled away and held her at arm's length. As he stared down at her, the change in him was lightning swift. His boyish exhilaration faded as his eyes darkened. Samantha could feel desire emanating between them like a pulsing, living thing. His essence was salt and sea, musk and spice. A yearning began to build, a throbbing that begged for relief. His hands tightened on her arms, and for a moment she hoped—no, she wanted him to kiss her. Then he suddenly released her.

Samantha trembled with disappointment. Had it been only her imagination—wishful thinking? No. He'd wanted to kiss her, she was sure of it. She breathed deeply for control and watched him move away and bend to retrieve his fishing gear. It was happening again, and there was no use in denying it. Once again, she felt drawn to the forbidden—a married man. But this time she wouldn't allow it. This time she wouldn't be gullible; she wouldn't naively fall for the I'm-getting-a-divorce routine.

For now, the best thing to do would be to pretend the almost-kiss had never happened. She cleared her throat and tried to continue their previous conversation. "If Landry isn't behind the assassination, who is?"

Marc turned and stared at her, his eyes dark and turbulent with some undefinable emotion. "I'm not sure yet. I'll have to wait and see what kind of information my father comes up with."

She hadn't imagined his reaction—he had been affected; the physical evidence was plain to see. Samantha bit her bottom lip and glanced down to check the compass readings. The *Jenny* had veered off course by two degrees. Uneasiness crawled through her. Maybe she'd been wrong about him, maybe he wasn't the perfect gentleman he'd seemed, she thought as she adjusted the wheel. After all, she'd been duped once before and Clark hadn't been nearly as polished or worldly as Marc.

"Hot damn! I hooked one."

Samantha's head snapped up, and her eyes widened in disbelief. His rod was bent double. "Don't lose him," she shouted. "Give him some line."

"Who's catching this fish? Me or you?"

Samantha smiled. Even as he'd tossed the arrogant words over his shoulder, he'd released more line. She shook her head. All men were alike. None of them could ever admit a woman might be right about something. Why should he be any different? "Just remember," she called out. "I'm not cleaning up your mess."

IT WAS PAST MIDNIGHT when Marc entered the galley. Yawning, he eyed the cabinet top. It was still cluttered with dirty dishes and utensils. True to her word, Samantha had flatly refused to clean up after him. Marc chuckled, and as quietly as possible, he filled the sink with sudsy water. Still, she had surprised him with her offer to clean the fish. When he'd laughed, she'd called him sexist and proceeded to prove she could indeed clean, gut and fillet the large redfish.

Marc dried the last plate and stacked it in the cabinet. Samantha had several surprises in store for her when she awakened. Not only would she find the galley clean, but she would also discover they were no longer in the open gulf.

A stiff wind and strong currents had helped him make better time than he'd anticipated. Aided by a full moon and a star-studded sky, he'd successfully guided the *Jenny* into a small bay. If his estimations were correct and he hadn't lost his touch for navigation, the Cedar Keys were located a few miles south. There, he could take on fresh provisions, and he could contact his father.

Marc tiptoed to the doorway of the stateroom where Samantha was sleeping. The light from the galley dimly lit the room. He could barely make out her form on the bunk. He stepped inside the room and moved closer to the bed. Her deep, even breathing told him she was asleep. The air had cooled considerably, and since she was huddled into a fetal position with only his shirt and shorts for warmth, he pulled up the side of the comforter and covered her. Visions of her sleek, naked flesh appeared in his mind. When she moaned softly in her sleep, Marc froze, afraid to even breathe. But she only changed position, snuggling deeper into the warmth of the comforter.

His breath hissed quietly between his teeth, but his eyes strayed to her slightly parted lips. He knew he'd confused her earlier, but something had held him back, had kept him from kissing her even though she'd seemed willing. His present circumstances were not the stuff dreams were made of, and her sarcasm about "the other man" told him that at some point in her life, she'd been a victim, too.

Unable to resist, Marc bent forward and brushed his lips against the back of her head. She smelled fresh, and strands of her hair clung to his moist lips as he pulled away. Tomorrow, everything would change. For her safety, and for his own piece of mind, he'd send her home. It was better that way. Certainly better for her. She would be free to resume her life without any regrets. And just maybe, someday, he might look her up again.

Marc shook his head as he left the room. Who was he kidding? It was entirely possible he might not live to see next week, never mind someday.

CHAPTER SIX

PAIN. SEARING, THROBBING pain was the first sensation he felt. Tommy Bailey tried to open his eyes, but the light hurt, so he waited before trying again. Faint noises surrounded him: footsteps, clanging trays, beeps. But the sounds were muffled. One by one his nerve endings came alive and he realized something was wrapped around his head. When he tried to explore the bindings, his right hand refused to do his bidding, and he groaned with the effort.

"I think he's awake."

The feminine voice sounded close. Tommy tried again to open his eyes. This time he was successful. There was a woman in white next to his bed. And a man was looming over him. Tommy recognized him instantly.

"Young man, can you tell me who you are?"

Tommy tried to speak, but his throat was dry, and he had to swallow several times before the words would come out.

"Son, tell me your name."

"Come on, Doc," he croaked. "You know who I am. You've known me all my life."

The doctor chuckled. "But do you know who you are?"

Tommy sighed in disgust. "Tommy...Tommy Bailey."

"Good, good." The doctor smiled. "Now. Do you remember what happened to you?"

He tried to remember, but his head ached. A fine sheen of sweat popped out on his forehead, and he felt the doctor pat his shoulder.

"That's okay, Tommy. You'll remember in time. Don't push it for now."

"Doc, what's wrong with me? How did I get here?" Panic began to creep through him. He couldn't seem to move.

"You have a concussion and several contusions. Your right arm is broken, and three ribs are cracked."

"Is that all?" Tommy tried to laugh to cover his fear, but his chest hurt.

"Rest now, Tommy. Your folks will be in later. They've been pretty worried about you."

Tommy closed his eyes, but he didn't sleep. A million questions ran through his mind, but he couldn't come up with any answers. And there was something, something urgent, something other than the cause of his injuries that nagged at his subconscious.

For several moments, the room was quiet, then he heard shuffling footsteps. Blinking against the pain and light, he was finally able to open his eyes again. A nurse was checking his IV. Something about her struck a familiar chord in his memory, but then she turned to leave.

"Nurse? Wait." Like a ghost, the image of someone hovered but had no substance. If she would stay just a few minutes more, he could remember.

"Yes?" she asked, smiling. "Is there something you need?"

Tommy grimaced. "Nothing but a new body. This one's kind of beat up at the moment."

She laughed and shook her head. "I'm afraid I can't help you in that department."

Her hair was blond and came to her shoulders. She was slim, and beneath her crisp white uniform, she was well built. He guessed her age as mid-twenties. "What time is it?"

She looked at her watch. "A little past ten. Anything else?"

"I know this sounds like a line, but have we ever met before?" The moment the words left his mouth, a flash went off in his head. "Sam." The name hissed on his lips. "My God, Sam!" He groaned and closed his eyes. He could still see her as he'd left her, hovering over the stranger. Fear raced through his veins. How long had he been in the hospital? Was she still there waiting?

"What's wrong? No . . . you mustn't try to get up yet."

"You don't understand." Tommy pushed against the nurse's restraining hands without any success. He was too damn weak. "She's still out there."

"Mr. Bailey, please. You'll pull the IV loose. Calm down."

"Okay, okay." Tommy slumped against the pillow. "Get Doc for me." She didn't move, but picked up his wrist and began taking his pulse. Tommy jerked his hand loose. "I'm okay, just get Doc."

Slowly she backed away, frowning. "Don't try to get up again."

"Please, it's urgent. Hurry."

SAMANTHA TENSED as she opened her eyes. It was morning. Bright prisms of sunlight permeated the darkness of the stateroom. She was still on the *Jenny,* but something was different, something had changed.

Easing the comforter aside, she swung her legs over the edge of the bed. The comforter? She glanced down. She didn't remember covering herself the night before. In fact, the cabin had been so stuffy, it had taken her forever to fall asleep. Marc must have come in later and covered her. She stood up, her eyes still on the comforter. Her heartbeat quickened at the thought of him watching her sleep.

Still vaguely disquieted about Marc's intimate gesture, Samantha moved to the porthole and pulled aside the tiny curtain. Tears stung her eyes and threatened to spill as she squinted against the rising sun. Beyond the *Jenny,* the clear aqua water mingled with a grassy shoreline. Beyond that, marsh, sand and a solid wall of rich green foliage defined and outlined the shore.

It was over. She would soon be on her way home. Back to safety...back to loneliness. In the beginning, she'd begged Marc to take her home, but now...

Samantha stepped away from the porthole and headed for the galley. She swallowed to ease the tightness constricting her throat, but this time she knew her inability to breathe had nothing to do with her phobia. This time it was a fear of a different kind. Fear for Marc. Leaving the anonymity of the Gulf meant danger—possibly death—for him. Someone had killed four policemen to get to him. They'd try again.

Through the doorway, she could see Marc sprawled on his stomach. The sight of him increased her anxiety. So much had happened in such a short time. From the first, she'd felt drawn to him in a way she couldn't explain. Since then, her emotions had run the gamut from fear to desire where he was concerned.

She turned toward the cabinet and retrieved a mug. After filling it with water, she placed it inside the microwave. Her thoughts strayed back to Marc. Maybe her feelings were the result of a combination of factors. Since the fiasco with Clark, being alone in the world had been preferable to chancing another relationship. The humiliation and embarrassment had been too painful, but then she'd had Gram to lean on for comfort and reassurance. Now she had no one. Had she subconsciously transferred her dependence to Marc? And, because of his own situation, was he taking advantage of it?

True, he hadn't actually done anything—except the near kiss. But she was sure the desire was there. She hadn't missed the looks he'd given her when he'd thought she wasn't paying attention.

Being confined for days with someone who was in danger did funny things to a person, she silently concluded. It distorted reality. Reality was that she would have been concerned for the safety and well-being of anyone in Marc's situation. Reality was that he was married and didn't seem happy his wife was divorcing him. But his wife could change her mind, and Marc would take her back—just as Clark had reconciled with his wife.

The beeper sounded from the microwave. As Samantha filled a spoon with instant-coffee crystals, she decided she'd be wise to remember the realities instead of allowing her foolish imagination to play tricks on her, instead of repeating the painful mistake she'd made with Clark.

"Fix one for me, too."

Marc's voice startled her. The spoon shook and the crystals scattered.

"I thought you were still sleeping." She hastily brushed the wasted coffee from the countertop into the sink, and reached for another mug.

"Notice anything different?"

Different? she thought. *Everything* is different. Today she was going home. Today she would stop living in a fantasy world where a dark-haired pirate kidnapped her, swept her away on an exciting adventure and fell madly in love with her. Samantha glanced toward the doorway where he was stretching and yawning. With his sleepy, dreamy eyes, bare chest and tousled dark hair, he was one hell of a sexy man... sexy, dangerous and forbidden.

"Well?"

"What?" She blinked and lowered her gaze to the counter. Disconcerted, she mentally groped for an appropriate answer. "We've reached land," she finally said.

"Yes, and...?"

Puzzled by the disappointed tone in his voice, she slowly inspected her surroundings. Everything seemed the same. As always, the galley was spotlessly clean. After she'd glanced around, she stared at him and shrugged her shoulders.

Marc feigned a long-suffering sigh. "That's the trouble with you women. We give you what you want and what do we get for it? Not a word of appreciation, not even a thank-you." Suddenly, his hand sliced the air. "Forget it," he said haughtily. "If you don't mind," Marc moved to within arm's distance of her, "I'll get myself a *clean* mug and fix my own coffee." He eyed the spilled coffee crystals with mock distaste. "Messy, Samantha. You really must learn to clean up after yourself."

Samantha backed away a step as he reached for the cabinet door in front of her. Then it came to her. Her confused expression altered to one of exaggerated humility. "By all means, help yourself," she said, motioning toward the door. "And please accept my most humble apology. You did a superb cleanup job, Captain, sir. I couldn't have done better myself."

"Hmph!" he grunted in response.

Her lips quivered with suppressed humor. But the twinkle in his eyes belied his gruff response, and they both burst out laughing. Then, to her surprise, he reached out and pulled her into his arms.

"Oh, Sam. I'm going to miss you."

His voice was a husky growl that caused her stomach to contract. At his touch, her playful mood vanished. She was going to miss him, too. His sense of humor delighted her. His gallantry and concern for her safety touched her and, most of all, his willingness to treat her as an equal thrilled her. And now he'd proven he was not ashamed to express his feelings. His words made it easy for her to ignore all warning signals.

When his hands pulled her firmly against his lower body, she realized his gesture was deliberate and not just one of brotherly affection, and she felt the urge to press into the hard strength of him.

The microwave signaled the water was hot, and Marc slowly released her, then turned away. Samantha's insides churned with both disappointment and relief, leaving her more confused than ever and feeling curiously unsatisfied.

"Let's go topside while we drink our coffee," Marc said in a gruff voice. "I need to talk to you."

Samantha forced a smile and nodded.

A few minutes later, seated opposite her in the cockpit, Marc began to outline his plan. Still trying to regain her composure, she stared at the shoreline as she listened.

"We're only a few miles north of the Cedar Keys." He paused to sip some coffee. "There's a small marina there that should be safe enough, and there are plenty of stores around where I can get some supplies in case I have to sail again. Once I've contacted my father, I'll make the necessary arrangements for you to return home. You'll need some clothes to travel in, so if you'll write down the different sizes, I'm sure I can pick up some suitable things—"

Samantha twisted to face him. "Why can't I go with you?"

"I've thought about it and decided you'd be safer on the *Jenny*, out of sight."

"And just what am I suppose to do while you're off gallivanting around? Besides, you just said it should be safe." As the silence between them lengthened, Samantha became agitated. "What if something happens to you, then what?"

"Nothing is going to happen to me. And yes, I think it's safe, but I can't be sure. If someone is watching the marina, they'll follow me, and I'd rather not have to worry about you if there's trouble. And don't worry, nothing is going to happen to me."

Samantha frowned. "You don't know that." Marc's confident words failed to reassure her. She thought of Tommy. He'd promised to return, too. She had no idea what had happened to him, but she knew what could happen to Marc. Professional killers were after him. Maybe she should appeal to his sense of responsibility. "What am I supposed to do if you don't come back?" Her voice rose in desperation. "All I've got are the clothes on my back. No money, no ID."

"Sam, I promised you would get home safely, and I damn well meant it."

Samantha's chin jutted forward. "I'm not staying on this boat by myself. I'm going with you."

Marc counted to ten. "Sam, be reasonable. One of us needs to stay on board the *Jenny* in case someone gets it into his head to borrow her."

"That's bull and you know it."

"I was afraid that's what you'd say."

"Any other bright ideas?"

Marc glared at her. "Don't rush me. I'm thinking."

"Don't strain on my account."

Marc ran his hand through his hair, then grinned. "You're not going to let me play macho protector here, are you?" Samantha's complacent smile was his answer.

"Now that we've got that settled," she said, "what would you like for breakfast?"

Marc shook his head. "Oh, no, you don't. It's not that easy."

Her smile faded. "Whoever's after you is looking for a lone man, not a man and a woman," she said. "Less attention would be given to a couple." He was still shaking his head, but she ignored it and continued, hoping that by reemphasizing her points, he'd relent. "By yourself, you're going to stick out like a sore thumb. Together, we'd be less conspicuous."

LATER THAT AFTERNOON, Marc stood inside a café looking out of a window. Just beyond the walkway, rows of boats were sandwiched side by side in the small marina. People of all shapes and sizes crowded the dock area. But Marc concentrated on the *Jenny* and Samantha. Afraid she would try to follow, he waited. At that distance, he couldn't see the expression on her face, but he didn't have to. The stiffness of her stance, the way her arms hugged her body—she was madder than hell. And he didn't blame her.

He'd played a dirty trick on her. He'd asked her to change back into her bathing suit and shirt, knowing she'd think he had given in and decided to let her go with him. As soon as she'd gone below, he'd taken off.

Several minutes passed, and still she stood there searching the crowds milling around the harbor. Finally, she jerked around and disappeared down the companionway. Satisfied she wouldn't try to follow, Marc turned and eased out the side entrance.

He glanced at his watch and walked determinedly toward the main street of the small resort. Given the time difference and his father's penchant for having dinner each evening at precisely six o'clock, he was reasonably sure his father would be home.

The heat of the late afternoon was diffused by the overhanging trees that lined the street as Marc walked past rows of frame houses with porches. It was like stepping back fifty years in time. He'd discovered Cedar Keys on the maiden voyage of the *Jenny II*. Marc glanced around with interest. Except for a few boutiques and restaurants, the resort was much the same as he'd remembered. The phone booth on the corner was unoccupied. Marc slid the door closed and placed his call. After three rings, Dora answered. The familiar voice of the housekeeper caused a momentary pang of homesickness. More than just a housekeeper, Dora was part of the family, and the closest thing to a mother he'd ever had.

"Dora, it's Marc."

"Thank God! Are you okay? They didn't hurt you, did they?"

"No. I'm fine." Marc smiled, anticipating Dora's next reaction. And he wasn't disappointed.

"Well, it's a good thing." Her voice lowered menacingly. "I swear. I should have taken a cane switch to you years ago. Worrying everybody. Not a word from you in days. Not knowing if you were alive or—"

"Dora, I love you." As in the past, the three little words worked like a charm. Silence stretched across the miles, and Marc could picture the slim, middle-aged woman blushing like a schoolgirl. "Is Dad around?"

"Mr. Edward is in the library. I was on my way to tell him dinner is ready."

"I don't mean to rush you, but could you hurry and get him? I'm afraid the phone might be tapped, and I'm not sure how long I have to talk."

"Oh, goodness, of course." She paused, then, "Take care of yourself."

"I will," he answered and smiled. Dora might be somewhat unorthodox where he was concerned, but his father had always commanded her utmost respect. Once, in his early teens, Marc had suggested, in his naivety, that Dora marry his father. Not only had she soundly boxed his ears, but she'd told him in no uncertain terms that Mr. Edward was a gentleman, and she was the housekeeper— paid to do a job. She'd also warned him that if he ever so much as hinted at such a preposterous thing to his father, she'd resign. Her protestations had only confirmed what Marc had suspected for a long time: Dora loved his father, but because of their different stations in life, she'd never risk revealing that love. The click of the telephone extension alerted Marc before he heard his father's voice.

"Son, it's a relief to hear from you. I've been worried. You didn't sound so good the last time we talked."

"I'm fine, Dad, really. But I'm not sure how much time we have to talk—"

"Hold on just a minute."

Though muffled, he could hear his father shouting for Dora to hang up the foyer phone. Within seconds there was a firm click.

"Finally," Edward grumbled, paused, then cleared his throat. "Marc, they know about the woman—Samantha Bradford."

All the breath left Marc's body; his mind went blank.

"Son, are you still there?"

Marc gripped the receiver. "How?" he whispered harshly. "And who are 'they'?"

"She was reported missing by a friend of hers. He recognized you from a picture in the newspaper. He said he and the Bradford woman found you sick. That he'd gone for help, but had an accident and was unconscious for a couple of days. The newspapers are having a field day speculating why you kidnapped—"

"Kidnapped! My God." Marc ran shaky fingers through his hair. Frustration washed over him.

"That's just one version," he continued. "A Mississippi paper ran a story that she's some kind of zany heiress you've been having an affair with."

Marc's mouth dropped open and then snapped shut. "Sam? A zany heiress?" It was too absurd to be taken seriously.

"Is she with you?"

"Yes, but it wasn't my choice. It...it's a long story, and I don't have time to explain, but, Dad, I'm no kidnapper...and believe me, there's nothing zany about Samantha Bradford."

"None of that matters, but she is a complication."

Marc shook his head. "This whole mess is unbelievable. I thought I was protecting myself and her by refusing to take her back and now...I don't know. I was going to send her home today—"

"No. You can't do that. Whoever's behind this might figure she would know where to find you."

"But if they catch up with me, they'll—"

"I know. Still, she has a better chance with you than by herself. The damned police sure as hell can't be trusted."

Silently, Marc agreed. "Have you found out anything else?"

"Only that this thing is bigger than we'd originally suspected. From what my sources tell me, someone more powerful than Bobby Landry is behind it. They just used him as bait, figuring that since he's the fair-haired boy, he wouldn't be a real suspect after the deed was done."

"I'd already figured that out. It was a setup, and I fell for it. What I can't figure out is why they picked me to witness it."

"Part of the reason is your reputation as a journalist. No one would dispute your word, but there's more. I'm sure of it. I just haven't figured out the rest." Edward Dureaux paused. "I'm waiting for some information, but it's going to take a couple of days. I've been in touch with an old friend who's very interested from a professional standpoint. I don't have much to go on yet. But I can tell you I'd trust him with my life. He's going to help us."

"You can tell your friend to start with that little sleaze-bag snitch—Arnie Turner. He's the one that called me in the first place and told me about the governor and Landry's meeting. I should have known better than to trust him. He'd set up his own mother for the right price. You can bet Arnie works for whoever engineered this mess."

There was silence.

"Son, about Ms. Bradford."

Marc closed his eyes against the mental image her name evoked—long, blond hair and fiery, emerald eyes. "What about her?"

"Do you think you can trust her?"

"She won't be a problem," Marc answered quickly. At least, as far as trusting her, he added silently. But in other ways he was in for a hell of a time. He was finding it impossible to keep his hands off her and now... "How are... Angelique and my dear cousin Jean Claude taking this?" His throat was tight, and his voice sounded harsh even to his own ears. He didn't really give a damn what either of them thought of his situation, but for the moment he needed a diversion. Just thinking of Samantha caused a tightness in his groin and a heaviness around his heart. Several seconds passed before his father answered.

"Angelique is fine."

Marc turned sideways in the phone booth to lean against the opposite glass wall. "Has she moved out yet?"

"No... not yet, and I decided not to insist until your divorce is final, especially since... well, it didn't seem to matter since you weren't living here anyway—"

"Dad, it's okay. I understand." Marc shook his head. His father had always been too softhearted for his own good.

"Is she around?"

"No... she's out this evening."

Probably with Jean Claude, Marc thought.

"And would you believe," Edward continued, "even after all that's happened, that fool cousin of yours still insists he's going to run for governor." Edward gave a snort of disgust. "He claims all the publicity..." He paused again, then swore softly. "Never mind. You don't need to worry about him—he can take care of himself. I want you to call me again in a couple of days. I should have more information by then. Will you be safe where you are?"

Marc glanced around. The only place he truly felt safe was on the *Jenny,* but he didn't want to worry his father. "I'll be safe enough. I just hope they aren't able to trace this call."

"I don't think they've had time to put a tap on the line, what with all the bureaucratic nonsense they have to go through nowadays, but just in case, we'd better get off. Don't hang around there too long, and take care of yourself, Son."

"Dad..."

"Yes?"

"Thanks. I love you."

Marc held the receiver until he heard the phone disconnect, then slowly hung up. For several minutes he stared into the street as a myriad jumbled thoughts rolled in his head. But one thought above all kept returning. How was he going to tell Samantha? He'd promised her safety, and now...

He jerked the door open; the small rush of fresh air provided momentary relief from the heat. Deep in concentration, Marc headed back the way he'd come. With his and Samantha's names plastered in all the newspapers, he couldn't risk staying in the harbor for two more days. Whoever was after him would know about the *Jenny.* Even now, someone could have already spotted her and made the connection. And what if his father's phone had been tapped, and they'd had time to trace the call? Marc clenched his fist. He needed time to think, time to plan...away from Samantha. Visions of a dark cool bar and a tall icy drink spurred him on.

Halfway down the street, Marc stopped suddenly. Casually he glanced around, but saw nothing out of the ordinary, nothing to justify the strange pricking sensation along his spine. But still, he knew. He was sure of it. Someone was watching him.

CHAPTER SEVEN

EDWARD GLANCED UP to see his nephew standing in the doorway with a concerned look on his face. Something in his expression didn't ring true, but as always, he tried to give Jean Claude the benefit of the doubt.

"Was that Marc?"

Edward nodded.

"Is he okay?"

"He's okay, but I'm still worried. I feel so damned helpless, and I don't dare trust anyone."

Jean Claude stepped into the room. "Can't say I blame you." He shook his head. "Poor Marc. If I can do anything, you'll let me know, won't you?"

Edward wished with all his heart that Jean Claude was, for once, sincere in his concern for Marc. He'd learned over the years that his nephew had a jealous streak a mile long.

Edward took a deep breath and sighed. He'd tried to treat Jean Claude like another son. He really had. His nephew had been only eight years old when his parents had died and Edward had taken him in, but even at the tender age of eight, Jean Claude had had a chip on his shoulder as big as the Rock of Gibraltar. It was ironic, Edward thought. Marc, only five at the time, should have been the resentful one—after all, he'd never had to share his father's affections with anyone. But Marc had always looked up to Jean Claude and had accepted him as his brother.

Edward eyed his nephew with regret. It was a shame Jean Claude hadn't been as accepting as Marc. He cleared his throat. "Thanks for the offer of help," he finally said. "I'll let you know if there's anything you can do."

JEAN CLAUDE HURRIED from his uncle's home. He was late. He shouldn't have stayed for dinner, but Dora had insisted and for once his uncle seemed to need him.

He should have known better. His uncle had never needed him—he needed Marc. But in time that would all change. When he was elected governor, things would be different.

Even though it was eight o'clock, twilight still lingered. Jean Claude backed his Mercedes out onto the narrow, oak-lined street in the Garden District of New Orleans. With its eerie, old-world quality, it was an area steeped with tradition and history that few other places possessed. He'd grown up here and knew it like the back of his hand.

As he turned onto St. Charles Avenue, his thoughts turned to Angelique. She hadn't reacted well to his decision to run for governor, especially when he'd told her he couldn't risk seeing her anymore. But what had she expected him to do? After all, technically she was still a married woman. Jean Claude frowned. No. He couldn't risk a scandal now. With old J.H. dead and Bobby Landry under suspicion for his murder, the opportunity was too good to pass up. Even now he could see the headlines: Respected Attorney Jean Claude Dureaux Elected By A Landslide.

But Angelique worried him. He hadn't expected her reaction to be so... so dramatic. And now she was insisting she had to talk with him.

Thirty minutes later, he knocked on her door. As soon as the door opened, his breath caught in his throat and he forgot all his well-rehearsed words.

Angelique stood, naked from the waist up, her blouse and bra lying in a silken pool near her bare feet.

Slowly he stepped into the room and closed the door behind him.

Later, sweat-slicked and satiated, Jean Claude leaned back against the headboard of the king-size bed and lit a thin cheroot. He could hear the sounds of running water from the bathroom as Angelique showered. He remembered the first time Marc had introduced her as his wife. From that moment, he'd become obsessed with her and had wanted her for himself. He'd done some digging and found that her dark background, like her dark features, was fascinating.

The report of the private detective he'd hired had made fascinating reading. Angelique Marie St. Pierre had once been among the elite, had once been part of a fast-dying breed—the pampered debutante raised in the old Southern tradition to be a wife and mother. And, unlike many, she'd had the prestige and wealth to go along with her family name. The St. Pierres had settled in New Orleans, and there they had carved themselves out a place in society. Wise investments had kept them wealthy through several generations until Angelique's father, the last male heir, had lost it all. Jean Claude knew that nothing was left except the small French Quarter apartment, a secret place she fiercely protected.

Stubbing out the remainder of the cheroot, Jean Claude slid out of the bed; the smell of his and Angelique's spent passion still lingered on the sheets. He glanced thoughtfully toward the bathroom door as he pulled on his pants and wondered what she'd hoped to gain by seducing him. This one evening wouldn't make him alter his decision. He'd tried to explain it to her three days ago, but evidently she hadn't believed him.

He shouldn't have come, he decided as he headed down the hall toward the living room. He was risking everything by coming here. Somehow he was going to have to make her understand their affair was over. It had to be, no matter how much he regretted it. Jean Claude walked over to the liquor cabinet and poured himself a drink.

"I'll take one of those, darling," Angelique said.

Jean Claude turned, his drink suspended in midair. Damp tendrils of dark hair curled around her face. The white towel barely hid her generous breasts and gaped at the apex of her shapely legs. Once again he felt a tightening in his groin, but quickly turned his back and reached for an empty glass. He'd known it wouldn't be easy breaking off with her, but he hadn't counted on her being desperate enough to use her body as a bargaining tool.

"Why don't you slip on a robe?" he called over his shoulder. The carpet muffled the sound of her bare feet. When he felt her fingertip feather down his back, he stiffened, but couldn't control the shudder that racked his body.

It took every bit of willpower Jean Claude could muster not to give in to temptation. "No, Angelique!" He jerked away. "Go put on a robe, and then we'll talk...just talk."

Angelique opened her mouth to protest. Then she reached up to cover her ears. She shook her head, gritted her teeth and without saying a word left the room. When she returned, Jean Claude noticed she seemed unnaturally calm, and there was something about the glazed look in her eyes that made him uneasy. *Just my imagination,* he thought. *Be glad she isn't ranting and raving the way she did three days ago.* Maybe what he'd told her had finally sunk in.

He took a deep breath and began mixing himself another drink.

"If Marc was dead, would it make a difference?"

"He's not dead," Jean Claude answered, "so there's no point even speculating about it."

"He's supposed to be dead."

Jean Claude turned to stare at her. "What do you mean, he's supposed to be dead?"

Slowly her hand lowered and clutched the lapels of her robe. "Someone tried to kill him, so there's probably a contract out for him. Since they obviously didn't succeed, they'll try again, and when he's dead we can be together. I'll be a widow—a rich widow. He has lots of life insurance. And after a few months, we can get married and there won't be a scandal."

Jean Claude's stomach contracted; he suddenly felt queasy. Was it possible? Had she done something stupid like…he shook his head. No, she couldn't have. But still, that calmness about her bothered him, and her eyes…they seemed to glitter.

Angelique walked over to him and removed the drink from his hand. "I love you. I have since the first time we made love." She smiled slyly. "You remember, don't you, darling? The first time we made love."

"Yes, of course." How well he remembered. He still fantasized about that night. They'd been at his uncle's. After dinner, Edward and Marc had played a game of chess. It was hot that evening, and he and Angelique had walked outside to the edge of the veranda. He'd been angry with Marc over something he couldn't even remember now. Since Angelique had been giving him the come-on even though she was married to Marc, he'd decided to get even with his cousin. The air had been sultry with the scent of gardenias and her musky arousal. He'd pinned her against a column and had been surprised to find the only thing she was wearing beneath the silk dress was a lacy garter belt and hose. He'd also been pleasantly surprised when she'd been more than willing.

Jean Claude continued staring into Angelique's expectant eyes. Her hand was flattened against the center of his chest. Slowly she traced an erotic pattern up and down his skin. Again he got the feeling something was wrong, something he couldn't quite put his finger on. Sweat broke out on his forehead as he began to remember some of the rumors that had circulated when Marc married her. At the time, he'd dismissed the rumors as just talk. People had said she'd gone crazy after her parents' death, that she'd been committed to the state hospital for the insane.

Suddenly something else clicked in Jean Claude's memory. There had been a time period the detective hadn't been able to pin down. Was it possible? Had the rumors been true? And, worst of all, what if she was about to have some sort of relapse as a result of what he'd done to her?

When Angelique began combing her fingers through the hair on his chest, he backed away, out of reach. Guilt shivered through him. He'd used Angelique. At first, he'd only done it to get even with Marc. Later, he'd become so infatuated with her, he'd forgotten about Marc. All he'd been able to think about was Angelique, and along the way, somehow everything had backfired. He'd thought she understood that their relationship was strictly physical, but evidently she hadn't. Angelique had fallen in love with him and now... What the hell was he going to do?

CHAPTER EIGHT

SAMANTHA GLANCED toward the cluster of buildings surrounding the marina, but only shadows mingled with the streetlights. Seated with her back against the *Jenny*'s mast, she looked out at the water. A soft, balmy breeze whispered through her hair. Absentmindedly she reached up and brushed aside several strands, hooking them behind her ear. The marina had quieted. The soothing night sounds of lapping water, and pinging metal shrouds were occasionally interrupted by the footsteps and voices of other sailors returning to their boats.

It was growing late. Samantha yawned. The gentle rocking of the *Jenny* was making her sleepy. The emotional strain of waiting for Marc's safe return had stretched her nerves to the limit, leaving her exhausted. She closed her eyes.

PRECARIOUSLY BALANCING the sacks of supplies, Marc stepped onto the *Jenny*, then glanced over his shoulder. Was he being paranoid? Even though the earlier prickling sensation had diminished, he still felt uneasy. He placed the heavy sacks onto the deck and turned once more to scan the dock. Lights twinkled up and down the piers. The sound of distant music floated in the air. He saw nothing suspicious. Maybe he'd imagined it. Maybe he'd overreacted. Still, the sooner he was back in the open gulf, the safer he'd feel.

Marc looked around for Samantha. With her back to him, and the mast between them, he almost didn't see her. It took him a moment to realize she was asleep. Quietly he walked toward her, then stooped. "Sam." She jumped.

"Take it easy." He caressed her shoulders. Her shirt slipped a little and his fingers touched her satiny skin. "It's just me," he whispered.

"Marc." She tried to summon her earlier anger toward him but failed. Marc's hands moved to her neck; his fingers were wonderfully soothing as he kneaded and massaged her tense muscles. She closed her eyes and bowed her head. "Ah," she moaned. "That feels wonderful."

"It's the sea air and the sound of the waves."

"I suppose so," she answered, but knew better. His touch was pure heaven.

"Sam."

"Hmm," she murmured.

"About this morning—"

Samantha reluctantly pulled away. "I'd just as soon forget about this morning."

Marc held up his hands in mock defense as she faced him. "What can I say? I'm sorry. I shouldn't have sneaked off."

"It was a dirty trick."

"Yes, it was, but—" Marc scooted around to her back and resumed his massage "—at the time, I thought it was necessary, and I needed time to think...by myself."

"I finally figured that out when I saw you go into the bar." His hands stilled for a moment.

"That was you following me?"

Samantha looked up at him and nodded her head. "I intended to give you a piece of my mind for giving me the slip."

"Dammit to hell!" His hands tightened on her shoulders, almost painfully. "All this time that was you?"

Startled and confused, she jerked away. "You don't have to yell. I came straight back to the boat."

"Great . . . just wonderful." Sarcasm oozed from each word. "In the meantime, I'm looking over my shoulder every minute wondering when some bastard is going to nail me."

"You saw—you thought—"

"You're damned right." Marc shoved his fingers through his hair. "How was I to know you'd sneaked off the boat and were spying on me?"

Samantha went up on her knees; she doubled her hands into tight fists. "Me, sneaking? Spying? Why you . . . you . . ." She wanted to punch him and would have if she'd thought it would knock some sense into him. "You have a lot of nerve accusing me of sneaking anywhere. For your information, I was worried about you, though now for the life of me, I don't know why."

"Okay, okay." Marc held up his hands. "You've made your point."

Tight-lipped, Samantha glared at him.

"Would it help if I apologized . . . again?"

Samantha shrugged.

"Look, I'm sorry for blowing up." And he was. He was sorry for a lot of things, most of all for getting her involved in his problems. But there wasn't a hell of a lot he could do about any of it. And he still had to convince her to delay going home. He reached out, placing his hands on her shoulders. "Would you please sit down?"

When he pushed gently, Samantha eased back onto the deck, curling her legs beneath her. She crossed her arms over her breasts

With one hand on her shoulder, he tilted her chin with his other one. "Listen," he said, choosing his words carefully.

When she tried to move away, he increased the pressure against her chin, forcing her to look at him.

"There's something else we need to talk about. I know I promised you'd go home today, but we'll have to delay a little longer."

Samantha narrowed her eyes. "Why?" she asked.

"I talked with my father and circumstances have changed. The media knows about you . . . and me."

"I don't understand."

Marc reluctantly released her and rubbed his jaw. "Which version do you want? Kidnapping or zany heiress?"

Samantha's mouth dropped open, then snapped shut. "You're kidding."

"I wish I was. It seems your friend recognized my picture—"

"Tommy!" Samantha grabbed Marc's arm. "Is he okay?"

Marc stared at her. "I suppose so—"

"What happened to him? Why didn't he come back?"

"Sam, all I know is he had some kind of accident and was unconscious for a couple of days."

"Poor Tommy." Samantha released Marc's arm. "He didn't want to go in the first place."

"Is he someone special to you?"

The question hung between them for what seemed an eternity.

"Well, is he?"

She looked him square in the eyes. "Tommy Bailey is a college student who was always kind to my grandmother. He's my friend."

"Well, for what it's worth, I'm sure he's okay."

Marc turned away to stare out over the bay. Samantha swallowed her disappointment. He was a hard man to understand, and she'd be better off it she stopped trying. "I'd like to at least call Tommy and make sure he's okay for myself."

Marc shook his head. "That wouldn't be wise…at least not now."

Samantha frowned. "Why not?"

"My father said that whoever's after me probably knows you're with me, thanks to the newspapers…and your friend. It's too dangerous for you to go home or make contact with anyone. They might try to get to me through you, or through whomever you contact."

Goose bumps crawled up Samantha's arms. Until now, she'd only been concerned about Marc. She'd never considered the danger to herself or anyone else. After all, she was just an English teacher, an innocent bystander who happened to be in the wrong place at the wrong time.

"I'm supposed to call my father again in a couple of days. He has some sort of plan he's working on. You'll have to stay with me until then," Marc said.

"But what about the police? Couldn't they give me protection?"

Marc's head snapped around. "Like they gave me? Sure," he said, laughing bitterly. "They'll protect you."

"Yeah, I see your point."

Regretting his harsh words, he reached for her hand. He squeezed gently. "I'm sorry for getting you into this mess. I should have taken you back when you asked me."

Samantha forced a brightness she didn't feel. "Well, as Gram used to say, once the cows are out of the pasture, there's no use fussing about the open gate."

His lips curved. "Your Gram sounds like a wise woman."

"She was."

"Was?"

Samantha lowered her head to stare at their entwined hands. "Yes. She died . . . three weeks ago."

Marc placed a finger beneath her chin, lifting her face. Her sad eyes tore at his heart. He wanted to comfort her, to fold her in his arms and kiss away her sadness. But he couldn't. "Was she the one you lived with?"

Samantha nodded and tried to smile.

"You must have loved her very much."

"Yes . . . yes, I did." Then she did smile. "She was a wonderful lady. She would have got a kick out of me being labeled a zany heiress."

"How did they come up with that label?"

Samantha shrugged and her smile faded. "Gram left me quite a bit of money."

Something in the tone of her voice made Marc believe that something besides the money was bothering her. "Would you like to talk about it?"

Samantha was deeply touched by his concern, but she shook her head. "No, it's late. If I start telling you about Gram, we'll be up all night."

"Some other time?"

"I'd like that," she answered softly.

Marc stood and held out his hands. Samantha grabbed hold and he gently pulled, bringing her close. The small movement stirred the air between them. Marc breathed deeply, tempted to pull her even closer. The impulse was so strong he held her hands a moment longer than necessary. But common sense prevailed. Reluctantly, he released her and retraced his steps to the sacks he'd deposited on the deck

"I think we'd better leave first thing in the morning," he called over his shoulder.

Once they'd carried the groceries below, Marc shoved the companionway hatch into place and locked it. "Don't want any uninvited guests."

Just the thought was enough to make Samantha shiver. "Are you sure you don't want to leave tonight?"

Marc shook his head. "Early tomorrow morning will be soon enough."

Samantha rubbed away the goose bumps on her arms, feeling silly for being so apprehensive. "Well, good night then."

Marc waited until she'd slid the forward stateroom door shut, then walked slowly toward his own cabin. Once in bed, he found it impossible to sleep. It was too damn stuffy, and he kept recalling the brief moments he'd held Samantha in his arms earlier that morning. Fresh from sleep, her body had been warm and firm. It would have been so easy to forget everything, to lose himself in her sweetness.

He squeezed his eyes shut. He had to stop thinking about her. Not only was she forbidden fruit, but from what she'd told him, she was probably still in mourning for her grandmother, which made her emotionally vulnerable. Marc rolled over on his stomach and wondered how he was going to get through the next few days.

SAMANTHA'S EYES snapped open. She wondered why she'd awakened. The cabin was still dark, and it seemed as if she'd just gone to sleep. Then she heard them— footsteps directly above her head. Listening intently, she sat up slowly. It was very hot inside; maybe Marc had gone on deck for some cool air. She heard the footsteps again, but something sounded wrong. Marc would be barefoot or have tennis shoes on. Whoever was prowling on the deck was wearing hard-soled shoes.

The assassins! Samantha's heart pounded. She had to get to Marc. She eased off the bed. She had almost reached the door when the scratching began. The hair on the back of her neck stood on end, and for a moment she froze. The scratching stopped. Drawing a deep breath, she slowly reached for the door. Suddenly, it flew open. Someone grabbed for her as she lurched forward. She was seized in a viselike grip. When she opened her mouth to scream, a hand quickly clamped over her lips to smother the sound.

"Shh, Sam. It's me," Marc whispered in her ear.

A tremor rippled through her body as she sagged against him with relief. When Marc started to pull away, the scratching started again, and Samantha grabbed him.

"Hey, Mabel! Open the damn door." The loud voice was slurred and accompanied by pounding. "C'mon, Mabel."

"What the hell!" Marc jerked away, flicked on the light and started up the companionway.

"Who you got down there, Mabel?"

Samantha followed, just in time to see Marc shove the hatch open.

"You got the wrong boat, buddy," he said.

"Where's Mabel?"

"Look man, Mabel doesn't live here," Marc argued. "Get the hell off my boat before I throw you off."

"George, where are you?" A shrill voice barked out the words, easily carrying across the water.

"Mabel?" George turned toward the sound of the voice. "What'ar ya doing over there?"

"You damn drunk, you're on the wrong boat," Mabel shouted. "Get over here."

George turned back to look at Marc, shrugged his shoulders and stumbled across the deck toward the pier.

Marc watched just long enough to make sure George made it off the *Jenny* without falling overboard. Cursing under his breath, he backed down the steps, slammed the hatch shut and locked it. When he turned, Samantha was standing in the middle of the room wearing nothing but an oversized shirt. Her arms were crossed, hugging her body. Her hair was a tangled gold mass, and her eyes were huge against her pale face.

Marc stepped closer just in time to see two fat tears trail slowly down her cheek. "Sam. Don't." He opened his arms and pulled her against him, pressing her head against his shoulder. "He's gone," Marc crooned softly and felt the firm fullness of her breasts press into his chest as she released a shaky sigh.

"I thought it was them . . . that they'd found us," she whispered brokenly. "I was coming to w-warn you . . . and . . . God, I was so afraid it would be too late."

"It's okay," he said. Running his hands up and down her back, he molded her warm body to fit his. "It's over." Like a slow-burning candle, she seemed to melt against him and finally relax.

She slid her arms around his waist. He felt the need to keep her safe—to keep the world at bay if that was what it took. He pulled her closer and whispered, "Oh, Sam." He nuzzled her cheek with his. "You have no idea how important you are to me."

Under his gentle hands, she felt safe. His soothing ministrations had calmed her, and it was easy to forget about assassins and death. His soft beard felt like a thousand tiny feathers stroking and tempting. He turned his face a fraction and his lips sought out hers. How could any man's lips be so firm, so demanding, yet so gentle?

she wondered. Then he filled her mouth. His tongue teased, tantalized, explored, and Samantha groaned as tight desire made her squirm to get closer.

The outside world didn't exist. Here, together, on the *Jenny*, they'd created their own world.

And that was the real danger, Samantha thought with a start. For days they'd been thrown together under harrowing circumstances. Overreacting was understandable, but she couldn't let it get out of hand, and she definitely couldn't risk making the same mistake she'd made before.

She pulled away abruptly. "No...I mean...I'm okay now." She straightened her shirt and took a step backward.

Marc wanted her back in his arms. It had felt good to hold her, and for a moment she'd responded—she'd wanted him. He'd been sure of it.

Why hadn't she come along earlier in his life? he wondered. Why had she appeared at the worst possible time for involvement of any kind? He wasn't even sure he would live to see tomorrow. But more to the point, why had she pulled away?

"Sam, I think we need to talk. Both you and I realize what's happening between us...I mean I..." He closed his eyes. He felt worse than a blundering schoolboy as he searched for the right words. After all, he thought, words were his business. *Just say it and get it over with,* he told himself.

Marc opened his eyes. "I'm attracted to you, and I think the feeling is mutual. I want—"

Samantha held up her hand to still his words.

"Don't," she entreated, and for a moment she couldn't speak. Finally, she lifted her head and met his gaze. "I'll admit I'm attracted, too," she said boldly. "But as my grandmother used to say, wanting and doing are two different things. And I don't intend to do anything."

"I guess under the circumstances, I can't blame you, what with assassins chasing me and—"

"That has nothing to do with it." At his puzzled look, she sighed. "Don't you see? Being confined together on a boat for days does funny things to people. It's just our...our circumstances."

He vigorously shook his head. "I disagree. It's more than that."

"Maybe," she answered. "But there are other considerations." Samantha held up a forefinger. "One, I wasn't brought up to hop into bed with someone just to satisfy a physical urge. A lot more than instant gratification is involved. And two—" she held up a second finger "—you're a married man."

Swift, hot anger shot through him. "I'm not talking about instant gratification. I'm not after just a wham, bam, thank you, ma'am. And as far as my being married, I won't be in a month. I told you my wife has filed for divorce."

"Sure." She rolled her eyes upward. "Sure, you told me. And I told you I'd heard that one before. Besides, I got the impression you weren't overjoyed with the whole deal. In fact, I'd bet money you'd take her back in a minute with all forgiven."

"Is that what he did?"

"He?" she questioned, confused for a moment.

"The man in your past, your ex-lover."

Fury rolled through Samantha. "That's none of your business, but to set the record straight, I was engaged."

"Oh, that's rich." Marc sneered, and without thinking the words seemed to roll off his tongue. "You were engaged to a married man."

He wished he'd never opened his mouth as he watched Samantha turn pale. When her lower lip trembled, he felt like a heel. He stepped toward her. "I'm sorry, I didn't mean . . . I . . ."

She backed away, shaking her head. "You don't understand. I didn't know he was married. And when I found out, he said he was getting a divorce, just like you. Even then, I believed him." She made a sound of utter disgust. "It took his pregnant wife to convince me otherwise."

Marc swore. No wonder she felt the way she did. She'd not only been hurt, she'd been humiliated, too. "You can't possibly compare my situation to that jerk's," he said in an attempt to explain. "I can guarantee Angelique—that's her name—is not pregnant." He laughed harshly. "If you want to talk about deceit and humiliation, let me tell you what my dear wife told me during our last argument."

Samantha winced at his bitter sarcasm.

"She actually confessed she'd tricked me into marrying her. Knowing what a fine, upstanding gentleman I was, all she had to do was pretend she was pregnant. And guess what? I fell for it. No child of mine was going to be fatherless."

Samantha's heart ached for him. Still, what he'd said changed nothing.

Marc hadn't meant to upset her further. He'd only wanted to prove how wrong she was about him. But from the stubborn set of her jaw and her closed expression, he could tell enough had been said for one night.

Later, filled with too many churning emotions to sleep, Marc slipped off the bed and reached for his shorts. Once on deck, he raised the mainsail of the *Jenny* and watched as it caught an early-morning breeze. His conversation with his father and the scare with the drunk had made up his mind. In the predawn light, Marc guided the *Jenny* through the small bay into the gulf.

CHAPTER NINE

JEAN CLAUDE PACED the floor in his uncle's living room. He wondered why he'd been summoned so early. He paused before the mantel and stared at a snapshot of Marc and himself as boys. Edward had had it enlarged and framed. Jean Claude remembered the day it was taken; Marc had been five and he had been eight. Dressed in identical T-shirts, they'd been to the zoo. It had been an innocent time in his life, a time filled with boyhood dreams. All those dreams had been shattered that afternoon. Marc had run into the road and been hit by a car. His hip had been broken. Jean Claude learned then who came first and always would in the eyes of his uncle.

Jean Claude turned away when Dora entered the room carrying a silver tray of coffee and croissants. "Is Uncle Edward still on the telephone?"

Dora nodded and set the tray on the breakfront against the wall. "Mr. Edward said for you to wait," she answered sharply.

Jean Claude frowned, wondering who'd ruffled her feathers. She fussed with the contents of the tray for several moments, then walked toward the door. He noticed she'd brought three cups and saucers. "Is someone else joining us?" he asked.

"I wouldn't know. I'm only the housekeeper. Your uncle told me to serve coffee for three, so that's what I'm doing." She turned to leave, but stopped at the doorway.

Placing her hands on her hips, she faced Jean Claude. "Where is that wife of Marc's? She didn't come home last night, again."

Jean Claude shrugged. "How should I know?"

"Oh, you'd know all right."

Flashing her a mocking half grin, Jean Claude strolled to the table. "Never could fool you, Dora, could I? You always saw right through me." And it was true. Even if Dora called herself the housekeeper, she'd been much more. He respected Dora. Many times she'd intervened with his uncle on his behalf, and unlike his uncle, she'd never shown favoritism between Marc and him.

"I see enough. But that's between you and your cousin. You're both a couple of fools where that woman is concerned. The sooner that divorce is final and she's out of here, the better off this family will be." She took a step toward him. "And while we're on the subject, how do you think your uncle is going to react when he finds out about her and you?"

Jean Claude's grin faded. "He won't find out because there's nothing to find out anymore. Besides, it wouldn't have mattered anyway. You know how he feels about me."

Dora shook her head and said softly, "I know how you *think* he feels about you, but you're wrong."

Jean Claude glanced again at the mantel. "I don't think so." He motioned toward the picture. "Maybe if it had been me that day... if that car had hit me instead of Marc—"

He paused, closing his eyes for a moment. "Never mind," he said when he opened them. "It doesn't matter." He turned back to the table and poured a cup of coffee.

As he added a spoonful of sugar, he heard the rustle of Dora's dress. She placed her hand on his arm.

"Is that what's been eating you all these years? My God, you were just boys."

"That may be true." Pulling away, he stalked to the sofa. "But he's never forgiven me or let me forget that I was supposed to be watching Marc."

"That's ridiculous! He was upset that day. If the driver had been sober, he could have avoided hitting Marc and your cousin wouldn't have ended up with a broken hip. Besides, part of your uncle's anger was at himself—he knew you were too young to baby-sit Marc. And yes, he was hard on you, but he regretted it, and I've never heard him mention it again."

"Oh, he never *said* anything, but it was always there." Jean Claude couldn't stem the flow of bitter words that poured from his mouth. "Nothing I ever did was good enough for him, no matter how hard I tried. Not the grades, the college scholarship, the law degree...nothing. But Marc, Marc the jock, could do no wrong."

Dora walked over to him. "Nothing I say will convince you, but think about this." Once again, she placed her hand on his arm. "Right now Marc is running for his life. Yes, your uncle loves him. But it doesn't mean he loves you less. From the first day you came to live in this house, he's tried to treat you as another son. It's just that he loved your aunt almost more than life itself. She knew having a baby was dangerous—she was a delicate woman, but she insisted on going through with the pregnancy anyway. She died giving birth and Marc, having the same dark hair and blue eyes—to your uncle, Marc was a continuation of her."

Dora reached up and tilted his face toward her. "Right now, he needs *you.*"

"She's right, you know," Edward Dureaux said from the doorway.

Dora paled, then quickly excused herself and almost ran from the room.

"I do need you."

When Jean Claude swung around to face his uncle, their eyes locked in a silent battle of emotions and wills.

His vibrant, larger-than-life uncle seemed to have aged overnight. His face was drawn with worry, his wrinkles appeared deeper, more pronounced. He looked every one of his sixty years and more. But Jean Claude detected something else. It was there in his uncle's overbright eyes, in the defeated slump of his shoulders. This was the man he'd looked up to, had striven all his life to please.

How ironic, he thought, that now, because of Marc, his uncle finally needed him.

As their eyes met, Jean Claude nodded. From Edward's expression, he knew his reaction had been less than his uncle had hoped for, but then he never had been able to please him.

Edward was the first to turn away as he eased himself into a nearby chair. His movements were slow, as if the effort cost him dearly.

"We have to talk," he said and leaned his head backward to rest against the high-backed chair.

Jean Claude frowned and poured his uncle a cup of coffee. "Have you had more news of Marc?"

Edward accepted the coffee. "Do you really care?"

Jean Claude's face grew warm with embarrassment. "I only—"

"Never mind," Edward interrupted. "It doesn't matter. But to answer your question. No, I haven't heard from Marc again directly, but a friend of mine has been snooping around and I don't like what he's come up with.

In my last conversation with Marc, something he said disturbed me, so I passed it along to my friend. I asked him to check out certain things. He called me, but didn't want to go into it over the phone. He should be here any minute."

Jean Claude seated himself across from his uncle. "Just who is this friend? Can he be trusted?"

"He and I served together in the Korean War. He saved my skin more times than I care to remember. Now he works for the FBI."

At that moment, the peal of the doorbell sounded. "That's probably Patrick," Edward said. "You'd better answer it. I'm sure Dora's elbow deep in flour and taking out her frustrations on a lump of dough."

Jean Claude nodded and left to answer the door.

There was nothing extraordinary about Patrick O'Connor, Jean Claude thought, as he shook the man's hand and introduced himself. But once they were seated in the living room, he soon realized O'Connor's innocuous appearance was deceptive. Jean Claude shifted uneasily under Patrick's steely gaze; the man was shrewd, direct and to the point.

"Marc was damned lucky to escape alive," Patrick said bluntly. "One of the biggest fish in the barrel put out the contract on him."

Edward cursed and a cold hand squeezed Jean Claude's gut.

Edward's eyes locked with Patrick's. "Go ahead, Patrick. Let's hear it."

"The man I'm talking about is smart—he's got connections like you wouldn't believe. We've been after him for years."

"Who is he?" Jean Claude asked. "What's his name?"

For several moments, Patrick didn't answer. Unease crawled along Jean Claude's spine under Patrick's hard scrutiny.

"His name is Antonio Manchetti. Does that name mean anything to you, Jean Claude?"

It wasn't so much the question that took Jean Claude by surprise as the fact it was directed at him, as if there was reason to be suspicious of any answer he might give. "Of course, I've heard of him. Anyone in Louisiana who reads the newspapers knows who he is."

Patrick smiled grimly. "Of course."

"Just what are you getting at, Patrick?" Edward Dureaux asked pointedly.

"A couple of years back, some of our people were working on a case against Manchetti, and they stumbled onto someone who had enough knowledge of Manchetti's operation to put him away for a long, long time."

"What happened?" Edward asked as he leaned forward and placed his empty cup on the small table in front of him.

"We'd been talking with the man for days and he'd finally agreed to turn state's evidence. We were on our way to pick him and his family up, but when we got there he was gone. Something or someone must have spooked him. Later, when we found him...it was too late. There had been an automobile accident. Both he and his wife were burned almost beyond recognition."

"My God," Edward said, slumping back in his chair.

"But that's not all," Patrick continued. "This man had a daughter. She was supposed to be with them that night, but for some reason she wasn't."

Caught up in the tale of horror, Jean Claude leaned forward, his arms resting on his thighs, his hands clasped loosely between his knees. Patrick turned suddenly, staring directly at him.

"That they've let her live this long is a miracle in itself." Patrick twisted to face Edward again. "I'm sorry, Edward. That woman is your daughter-in-law."

LATER THAT AFTERNOON, ensconced in his plush downtown office, Jean Claude glanced at his watch. After the sixth ring he slammed the receiver onto the cradle of the phone. Where the hell could she be?

As he paced the floor in front of his desk, he eyed the stack of messages placed neatly beside a mound of files needing his attention. He'd tried to work, but found it impossible; there were too many questions that needed answers. His thoughts kept flashing to the previous night and the conversation he'd had with Angelique. The fact that Manchetti had put out a contract on Marc, and had had a connection with Angelique's father, seemed too coincidental.

Rubbing the back of his neck with one hand, Jean Claude paused at the window. With his other hand, he stretched open the blind slats and stared down at the traffic on the narrow street below. Then, with a resounding pop, he released the slats and resumed his pacing.

Damn Patrick O'Connor anyway, he thought. Somehow, the agent knew about his affair with Angelique. Jean Claude was sure of it. He figured that out of respect for Edward, Patrick had stopped short of making an out-and-out accusation.

But accusation of what? Having an affair with his cousin's wife? He was certainly guilty of that, but was there more? Only Angelique could give him the answers he needed.

Seated behind his desk, Jean Claude again reached for the phone and punched out a set of numbers. He waited through six rings and was on the verge of hanging up when he heard the answering click.

"Hello."

Momentary relief was quickly followed by a rush of anger. "Where the hell have you been?"

"I beg your pardon?"

"I've been trying to reach you for the past two hours. I have to see you."

"So soon, darling?" she taunted. "You mean you've changed your mind?"

"Something's come up and—"

"Oh, Jean Claude." Angelique's knowing chuckle vibrated over the wires. "You do say the naughtiest things."

"Cut it out! I'm in no mood for your games. This is important." For several moments there was complete silence and Jean Claude could well imagine her elegant, flawless face screwed up in a sultry pout.

"Where do you want to meet?" she finally asked.

Thoughts of O'Connor having him tailed ran through his head. Was he becoming paranoid? What reason would O'Connor have? None, he answered silently. He might not have been tailing me, he concluded, but he sure as hell had been tailing Angelique. That was the only way O'Connor could have known about their affair. And if O'Connor knew, others might, too. Sweat popped out on his forehead; he reached in his pocket for his handkerchief and blotted it away.

"Stay where you are," he finally answered. "I'll be there within the hour." Before she could agree or disagree, Jean Claude hung up the phone. It would be risky to talk to her with Dora and his uncle under the same roof, but it was preferable to giving O'Connor reason to suspect him.

Thirty minutes later, Jean Claude walked into his suite through the private entrance, then quietly made his way to the other side of the house. He rapped lightly on the door and waited, careful to keep an eye out for Dora.

After several minutes, Angelique answered his knock. He quickly stepped inside the small sitting room. Angelique closed the door and snapped the lock in place.

"It took you long enough," he said.

"What's got into you?"

Instead of answering her, Jean Claude loosened his tie and motioned at the drink in her hand. "Get me one, too, will you?"

"Sure," she answered with a shrug of her shoulders. "The usual?"

"Yes, and make it a double."

Angelique handed Jean Claude his drink, then seated herself in a nearby chair. "For heaven's sake, will you stop pacing and tell me why you'd risk meeting me here?"

Jean Claude halted in front of her. "Tell me what you know about a man named Antonio Manchetti." For a moment she paled, but said nothing. Then she seemed to compose herself as she took a leisurely sip of her drink.

"Why do you want to know?"

"An old friend of my uncle's stopped by early this morning. This friend just happens to be an agent with the FBI and he's been looking into this business with Marc."

Angelique's glass slipped from her hand onto the floor. The contents spilled and a dark stain spread over the carpet.

When she bent to retrieve the glass, Jean Claude grabbed her arm. "Then I was right. You do know something."

"You're hurting me. Let go."

Jean Claude tightened his grip, pulling her out of the chair. "Not until I'm finished. Do you or do you not know a man named Antonio Manchetti?"

Angelique glared at him. "What if I do?"

"How do you know him?"

She jerked her arm free and backed away several steps. "He was a friend of my father's and he's been kind to me since my parents' accident."

"Kind to you!" Was she naive or just plain stupid? Still, he needed to tread lightly. He took a deep, calming breath. He didn't want to scare her into silence. "In what way has he been ... kind to you?" The words almost choked him as he recalled what O'Connor had said about Manchetti.

"Nothing important," she answered, rubbing her arm. "Just a small gift on my birthday or at Christmas, and dinner once in a while."

"And what did he get in return?" His voice was harsh. "Did you invite him to your apartment a few times? Maybe to spend the night?"

Angelique rushed to Jean Claude. "No, no," she denied. "It's not what you think." She reached up to caress his face but he recoiled.

"Then maybe you did him some favors once in a while."

"Darling, please ... don't. He's old enough to be my father. You know I love you. I'd do anything for you."

Jean Claude's harsh laughter ran out. "Anything? Including murder?"

Her eyes grew dark and haunted and stood out as she paled. "You said even if I divorced Marc to marry you, the scandal would ruin your chances for governor. Don't you see? There was no other way."

"And you thought killing my cousin would solve everything?"

She clutched at the lapels of his jacket. "I did it for us," she cried out.

Jean Claude grabbed both her arms and shook her. "Not us, Angelique." He shook her again. "You did it for yourself. Why? Damn you, why? Was it the money, the insurance money?"

Mascara-coated tears streamed down her face, leaving dark, smudged lines. Her lips quivered. "I had to. As long as I had you, it didn't matter. When I filed for divorce, I didn't ask for a settlement. But when you...when...I couldn't be left without anything again. I have to survive. They said so, said I was to go after what I wanted, that I had to think of myself."

Jean Claude shivered. She was acting crazy. She wasn't making sense.

Angelique began to cry again, and for several moments he watched her. What she'd done sickened him. His own part in the whole sordid mess sickened him even more. The only comfort he could give himself was that he'd learned the truth. Maybe O'Connor would be satisfied. And maybe, if Angelique really was mentally unbalanced, he might be able to get her the help she needed.

Jean Claude closed his eyes against the pain twisting in his gut. Who was he trying to fool? Now that his little affair had grown into a full-blown fiasco—even if they couldn't prove accessory to murder and attempted murder, he could kiss being governor goodbye. The publicity alone would do him in.

He sighed heavily. And even if by some miracle they were able to stop Manchetti, the chances of his uncle understanding or forgiving him were nil. And God help him if Marc died. As surely as if he'd pulled the trigger himself, Jean Claude knew the shock would kill his uncle.

Angelique's sobbing subsided to an occasional sniffle. "You aren't st-still angry with me, are you?" she asked as she raised her head. Her voice was whispery soft and filled with uncertainty.

For several seconds he didn't answer. If he alienated her further, there was no telling what she might do. She might even deny everything she'd confessed; then it would be his word against hers.

"No, of course not."

"Then make love to me."

She pulled his hand to her soft, full breast, then slipped her arms around his neck. Her mouth covered his in a searing, demanding kiss.

Jean Claude untangled her arms and firmly pushed her away, his breathing harsh. "No...we can't. I can't. Not now," he amended quickly. "You get some rest, and I'll be back later." He abruptly turned and after fumbling with the latch, hurried out the door as if the hounds of hell were chasing him.

Back in his own rooms, he stepped into the shower and turned the cold spray on full force, hoping the water would help clear his head. But there was no getting around what he'd have to do. Delaying would just make it harder.

With an abrupt twist of the knob, he shut off the water, dressed quickly and left to find his uncle.

Jean Claude paused at the door of Edward's library. He raised his hand to knock, then lowered it slowly. A weakness washed over him. He wanted to run, to hide, anything but risk the inevitable confrontation. If only there was another way.

But there wasn't. Quickly, before he lost his nerve, he rapped on the door, then pushed it open.

His uncle was seated behind the huge antique desk that dominated the room.

"Ah, Jean Claude." He raised his head from an album spread out before him and smiled. "Come in, come in."

Jean Claude entered the room and a rush of emotions assailed him. The smell of cigar smoke and old books mingled with the lemony scent of the brand of furniture polish Dora had used for years.

"I've been going through some old photo albums." Edward motioned for him to come closer. "Look at this. It seems like only yesterday." He paused and flipped the page. "The years pass too fast."

When Jean Claude moved closer, he was startled to see his boyhood pictures staring up at him.

"You were only nine when this was taken." Edward pointed at a picture near the bottom of the page. "You were always such a serious little boy, too serious for one so young. But I always figured your parents' death had a lot to do with that."

Suddenly, Edward swiveled around to face his nephew. "You came in here for a reason."

Jean Claude swallowed hard. Everything he'd done, everything he'd achieved, had been to earn the approval of his uncle. With a sinking feeling, he realized that once he told Edward about Angelique, he might never be able to bridge the gap between them. He knelt at his uncle's knees.

"I have to tell you something." He placed a hand on either side of Edward's chair.

"About Angelique?"

Jean Claude bowed his head and closed his eyes. He took a deep breath. "Yes. How did you know?"

"I've known for months," Edward said. His voice sounded tired. "I kept hoping you would come to your senses and see her for what she is— No, wait." Edward placed his hand on Jean Claude's shoulder to keep him from moving away. "Let me finish. I don't blame you completely. At first, I was taken in by her, too. What red-blooded man wouldn't have been? When Marc told me he was going to marry her and why, I suspected then she was trapping him, but the prospect of finally having a grand-child colored my better judgment. He never really loved her, you know. He just wanted to do the right thing. Then when she lost..." Edward paused, then corrected himself. "When she *said* she lost the baby, well, I knew it was a lie."

Jean Claude looked up at his uncle. "Uncle Edward, there's more. There's something else you need to know."

CHAPTER TEN

SAMANTHA AWAKENED to the aroma of coffee drifting in the air. She yawned and turned over just as Marc knocked on the door.

"Come in," she called out. He entered carrying a steaming mug and still wearing the same clothes he'd had on the night before. He looked ragged and exhausted and Samantha had to quell the urge to reach out to him. Her gesture might lead to something more and she couldn't afford to forget all the reasons she shouldn't allow herself to become involved with this man. So instead, she asked, "What time is it?"

"Around seven."

"Where are we?"

"I found a deserted bay several miles north of where we were yesterday and anchored. We should be safe here for the next couple of days till we head back to Cedar Keys so I can call my father." Marc offered her the mug. "Coffee?"

"Mmm, it smells good," she said as she swung her legs over the edge of the bed and accepted the warm mug. "Have you slept at all?"

Marc shook his head. "Tried to, but guess I was too keyed up."

For a moment he focused on her bare legs, and when his eyes finally locked with hers, they were filled with the same desire she'd felt when he'd first entered the room. In a split second the look was gone, and she wondered if she'd imagined it.

Throughout the day, Marc napped and kept pretty much to himself. It wasn't until the following day that Samantha began to get concerned. Again, he'd kept away from her, but she started noticing other things. He was deep in thought. She could almost see his mind working, sorting and analyzing the data he'd collected about the murderers.

Uneasiness crept through her like dark shadows. The closer the time came for Marc to make the call to his father, the more apprehensive she grew. No matter how many times she told herself it would be perfectly safe to return to shore, the nagging fear that the killers would be there waiting was there to torment her.

LATER THAT AFTERNOON, Samantha stared at the scorched, gooey glob that was supposed to have been the evening meal. Uttering an unladylike word, she snatched up the skillet and dropped it into the sink. She twisted the faucet knob and realized, too late, she'd only compounded the problem. A cloud of acrid smoke billowed and filled the galley.

"Sam?" Marc peered down the companionway opening. "My God!" He bounded down the steps. "Are you okay?" He grabbed the fire extinguisher hanging near the doorway.

"No. Don't!" Samantha reached him before he could release the locking pin. "That's not necessary." She took the extinguisher, then snapped it back into the wall-mount bracket. "There's no fire—just smoke."

Marc glanced around until he spied the source of the smoke. He walked to the sink. Already the haze was dissipating, leaving only a burned stench. Wrinkling his nose, he turned to face Samantha.

"Was this—" he motioned toward the sink "—dinner?"

"Don't you dare say a word," she snapped.

Her hair was pulled away from her face and twisted into a knot at the nape of her neck; damp curls stuck to her forehead. Her oversized shirt was soaked with sweat and clung to her body, and the baggy shorts were at least three sizes too big. His gaze returned to her face; her jaw was set and her eyes defiant. She looked hot, sweaty, harassed and adorable. Unable to contain the grin that tugged at his lips, he smiled. "Just out of curiosity—" he stepped closer "—what were we going to have?"

"Hot dogs and beans," Samantha said through clenched teeth.

Marc grimaced. "It's just as well. I hate hot dogs and beans. Tell you what. How about if we return to Cedar Keys a couple of hours early, and I'll treat you to a real dinner in a restaurant complete with air-conditioning?"

Without a word, Samantha abruptly turned and clambered up the companionway.

"Sam, wait!" But she'd already disappeared. Marc turned back to glance at the sink, shrugged his shoulders and followed her.

She was sitting on the foredeck with her back to him, her arms wrapped around her knees, hugging them to her chest.

When Samantha turned her head to wipe her face on her shirtsleeve, she saw Marc approaching. He settled on the deck close behind her.

She stared out over the calm bay that emptied into the gulf, drinking in its beauty, trying to draw a measure of serenity from it. She'd wanted to be strong, but when he'd mentioned going ashore, she'd come unglued. If only they could just sail away, keep going, she thought. Surely there was someplace where they would be safe.

Samantha bit her bottom lip and closed her eyes.

"Sam." His voice was soft with concern. "Why don't we talk about it?"

Samantha buried her face in her arms for several minutes before she spoke. "I'm scared."

Marc pulled her to him, and without thinking, she snuggled close to his chest. "Want to know a secret?" He felt the slight nod of her head next to his heart. "Me too."

She looked up at him. "You?"

He gave her a small crooked smile, then tucked her head back against his chest. "Yeah, me." He pulled the pins from her hair and combed through the still-damp strands with his fingers; the texture reminded him of hot silk. "Women don't have a monopoly on that emotion, you know."

His fingers were wonderfully gentle as he continued his soothing strokes. She thought about what he'd said for a moment. "No, I guess not," she finally replied, and didn't fight the urge to snuggle closer to him.

"Sam?"

"Hmm?"

"About the mess in the galley."

Samantha pulled away to glare at him, but he was smiling.

JEAN CLAUDE GLANCED at the clock over the mantel in the library and then at his uncle, who was sitting at his desk calmly turning the pages of his newest acquisition, a one-hundred-year-old medical book. Any minute Marc could call. Jean Claude reached up to rub the bridge of his nose. God, he was tired. The past two days had been hell.

His uncle had barely spoken to him and when he did, disapproval had laced each word. Between the closeted meetings with O'Connor and Edward, and keeping tabs on Angelique, he'd begun to wonder if he'd ever sleep soundly again.

Telling Edward about Angelique had been one of the hardest things he'd ever done. If he lived to be a hundred, he would never forget the look on his uncle's face. There had been denial, then acceptance and pain. But fast on the heels of that pain had come anger. No one betrayed the family of Edward Dureaux and got away with it. No one.

Edward had called Patrick O'Connor immediately, but the information about Angelique hadn't surprised the agent. Only through O'Connor's urgings had Edward agreed to allow Angelique to remain in his home. And Jean Claude suspected that his uncle had allowed him to stay only because O'Connor had stressed to Edward how important it was for Jean Claude to continue to keep an eye on Angelique until they figured out exactly how to handle the situation. She was their key to Manchetti.

Once again, Jean Claude glanced at the clock. How would Marc react to his plan? Knowing his cousin, he reckoned Edward would have his hands full convincing Marc. Jean Claude closed his eyes. He didn't know how far Angelique had gone when she'd told Marc she wanted a divorce, but if she'd even hinted that he was the reason, that he was "the other man," they could all forget it. At the thought, his heart began to pound, and he rubbed his sweaty hands on his slacks.

The jarring ring of the phone sounded harsh in the quiet room. Jean Claude jerked around as Edward answered it.

Twenty minutes later, Edward hung up the phone and slumped back in his hair. As Jean Claude waited for his uncle to speak, his insides churned. Even though the room was air-conditioned, he felt his shirt cling to his back.

"He sounds madder than hell," Edward finally said.

"But he will go along with the plan, won't he?"

"Yes, but..."

Jean Claude's stomach knotted at his uncle's searing glare.

"I couldn't bring myself to tell him about Angelique's part in all this. He has enough to worry about without hearing that. I'm going to let him believe Angelique is really grieving for him."

Unable to face the disapproval on his uncle's face, Jean Claude walked over to the window. Obviously Angelique hadn't been crazy enough to tell Marc who she was divorcing him for, or Marc would have never agreed to go along with a plan Jean Claude had masterminded.

Jean Claude pulled the edge of the drapes aside. In another hour or so it would be dark, and by the following evening, there would be no turning back—everything would be set in motion.

SEVERAL HUNDRED MILES southeast of New Orleans, the setting sun was spectacular in the western sky and cast a pink hue over the small town of Cedar Keys. People meandered up and down the main street laughing and talking. No one seemed in a hurry and everyone had a smile on their face—everyone but Marc Dureaux.

It was minutes before he could move after hanging up the phone. Never in his life had he felt such confusion, such rage. The plan was drastic and risky, but he reminded himself that his father and an FBI agent had approved of it. Marc clenched and unclenched his fist. Just the thought that Jean Claude had masterminded it was enough to make him want to smash something. If he'd had one shred of proof—just one little piece of evidence—that his self-serving cousin was Angelique's lover, he would never have agreed to the plan. It wasn't that he still cared for Angelique, but the idea that his own flesh and blood, someone whom he regarded as a brother, could have betrayed him, filled him with rage.

After several moments, he took a deep breath and shoved open the door of the telephone booth. He headed for the dock. One block from the marina, he could see the *Jenny,* but the deck was empty.

Where was Samantha? he wondered. For a moment sweat blurred his vision. He reached up and wiped his eyes with the back of his hand. "Don't jump to conclusions," he whispered. As he looked up and down the dock, he remembered how afraid she'd been for them to return to make the call. He'd finally convinced her they would be safe, and had even persuaded her to come ashore and buy something to wear.

Maybe she was still in the boutique where he'd left her? Marc glanced over his shoulder at the small dress shop across from the dock and frowned. A Closed sign was in the window. Squinting against the sun's reflection off the water, he looked back toward the *Jenny.*

Then he finally spotted her. She was standing on the pier talking with two small boys carrying fishing poles. No wonder he hadn't recognized her, he thought as he stopped to stare. He'd never seen her wearing anything but her bathing suit or his shorts and shirts.

She'd swept her hair back into a sophisticated twist and loose tendrils hung carelessly along her neck. Large jade-colored hoops dangled from her earlobes. Her tanned shoulders were bared except for spaghetti straps. The bodice of the sundress—the same jade as the earrings—laced up the front, pulling the fabric taut over her breasts. It fit smoothly to her hips, then fell into a long, full sweep to just below her knees. She'd purchased a pair of low-heeled, leather sandals in the same color.

She looked magnificent. For both their sakes, Marc thought, he'd have to call on every bit of self-control he could muster to get through what they had to do.

"Sam," he called out to her.

She turned at the sound of his voice, then waved good-bye to the two boys. When Marc reached her, he took her by the hand. Just touching her—no matter how innocently—was better than nothing, he told himself.

"What happened?" she asked. "What did your father say?"

"Not here," he answered. "Later, after the dinner I promised."

Keeping her hand firmly clasped in his, Marc headed for the *Jenny*. Even though she didn't question him further, he knew she wouldn't be put off for long. He'd seen the determined glint in her eyes. But he needed time to deal with the anger he'd felt so he could discuss the conversation he'd had with his father rationally.

The minute they stepped onto the deck, Marc let go of her hand, but she grabbed his arm.

"Why can't you tell me now? Has something else happened?"

Marc shook his head. "No, there's nothing new—"

"But there is something, isn't there?"

"Can't we talk about this later?"

"I want to talk about it now. I'm in this, too, and deserve an answer. I—"

He only meant to distract her, and maybe shock her into silence, to stall her questions. But when he took her in his arms and his lips met hers, his good intentions disappeared. He forgot about Jean Claude and the drastic, dangerous plan. Only Samantha existed. Her fresh scent filled his nostrils. Her shoulders were silky smooth and he allowed his hands to linger a moment to savor the feel of her bare flesh. Her warm mouth was inviting, tantalizing. He had to taste further, take the kiss deeper. He slid his tongue along her lips, seeking entrance into her sweetness, and for a joyous second, she responded.

Then a sound penetrated his senses, and Marc reluctantly pulled away. "We have company," he whispered. "Your friends decided to follow you."

Samantha stared at Marc, and then at the two little boys standing on the dock grinning from ear to ear.

"See what they want while I take a quick shower and change clothes."

"But Marc—"

His finger touched her lips. "Not now, Sam . . . and by the way, I like your dress, especially the bow."

Samantha smiled in spite of herself as Marc disappeared below. He'd successfully avoided answering her questions. Placing both hands on her hips, she took a deep breath and turned to deal with the mischievous boys.

A few minutes later, Samantha entered Marc's cabin without knocking. He was standing near the closet, one towel slung around his neck and another loosely knotted around his hips. For a moment they stared at each other. Her first instinct was to turn around and leave, but her desire to know about his conversation with his father was stronger than her embarrassment.

"Where are your friends?" he asked.

"Back on their own boat with their mother," she answered.

"What did they want?"

"Oh, no, you don't," Samantha retorted and narrowed her eyes. "I want to know what your father said."

Marc made an exasperated sound and turned his back to her. "Right now, I intend to get dressed. Do you mind?"

Samantha felt her cheeks grow warm, but she stood her ground. "Not at all." She motioned with her hand. "Be my guest, and when you're finished you can tell me what your father said. I'll be right here waiting."

"Okay. Whatever you say."

With one hand he reached for a pair of slacks; with the other, he pulled the towel from around his hips and dropped it on the floor.

Muscles rippled in his back all the way down to his firm buttocks as he stepped into the pants. Samantha forgot to breathe until she heard the rasp of his zipper. A surge of heat burned through her body.

Marc stepped over to the small built-in closet. "My cousin has come up with a plan."

Samantha had to swallow several times before she could say anything. "Why would your cousin be involved? I thought you talked with your father."

"I did." Marc shoved the sliding door open and jerked out a multicolored shirt; the hanger swung wildly on the rod. For the first few moments of his shower, all he'd thought of was the kiss he and Samantha had shared, but soon the cold water had eased the lingering desires of his body. Then he'd recalled the conversation with his father, and not even the cold shower had been able to douse the white-hot anger he'd felt. He took a deep breath, hoping to gain some semblance of control. Tossing the shirt on the bed, he turned to face Samantha.

"My cousin Jean Claude has lived with us since I was five. He's like a . . . like a brother." Marc almost choked on the words. "Or at least that's what I thought until recently." He spat the words. "I'm not quite sure why he's involved, unless he thinks he has something to gain." Marc silently cursed his inability to hide his bitterness. "Sorry," he said softly. He ran his fingers through his still-damp hair. "I'm just so damned frustrated. I don't know if I can trust Jean Claude. The whole thing is so bizarre."

Samantha bent over and picked up the shirt. "Why don't you start from the beginning?" She held it out for him to slip into.

Marc shrugged into the shirt and began buttoning it. "My father answered the phone. He's called in an old friend—an FBI agent. This agent suspects there's a contract out on me—"

"Contract! By whom . . . and why?"

Marc glanced up. Samantha was staring at him, a look of horror on her face. He stepped toward her. "Sam, I saw the men who killed the governor. I can identify them. For some reason, my father's friend thinks they can be traced to a man named Manchetti."

Samantha's eyes grew wide. "Antonio Manchetti?"

Marc nodded.

"But he's . . . he's—"

Marc nodded again. "That part doesn't matter right now. What matters is they've got someone who might be willing to testify against Manchetti, but it's going to take time to get everything set up." Marc paused. "Maybe months, according to my father."

"Months. I can't stay gone months. I have a job, responsibilities—besides, what are we supposed to do in the meantime? Sit here and twiddle our thumbs until the killers find us?"

"I'm sorry about your job, but right now we don't have a choice." Marc grabbed both her hands. "And no, we're not waiting around for the killers to find us—that's the whole point of this plan. You and I are going to disappear permanently."

Samantha stiffened. "What do you mean, permanently?"

Now comes the hard part, he thought. How could he convince her to cooperate with such a far-out idea when even he found it hard to swallow? "Sam," he said, gently squeezing her hands, "they want us to sail the *Jenny* out in the gulf and set fire to her."

"What?"

"It's supposed to look like an accident . . . an accident in which we're killed."

For a moment she simply stared at him. "That's the plan your cousin thought up?"

"Yeah. It stinks, huh?"

Samantha pulled away and walked to the small porthole. She stared out for several seconds in thoughtful silence. Finally, she turned to face him and began nodding her head. "It makes sense in a weird sort of way."

It was Marc's turn to be amazed. "Makes sense . . . nothing makes sense . . ."

"Yes, yes it does," she insisted. "Don't you see the logic? If everyone thinks we're dead, then no one will be looking for us. . . ."

"I know all of that." Marc reached up to massage the back of his neck. "What doesn't make sense to me is my cousin being a part of any plan to save my hide."

"Oh . . ." Her voice trailed away. Since she didn't know the real situation between Marc and his cousin, she couldn't comment. But if Marc had reservations, he had to have a good reason. And then another thought struck her. "Marc, what do we do once we set fire to the *Jenny*?"

"We bring along a rubber raft."

"That's a relief. I don't think I'm up to a long swim. How far will we have to row?"

"To make it believable, we need to be at least ten miles offshore."

Her mouth dropped open. "Well, I hope you're up on your rowing. I can manage a couple of miles, but ten? No way."

Marc grinned. "Sam, haven't you ever heard of a trolling motor?"

"Of course, I have, but we don't have one."

"We don't have a raft, either. We'll have to buy what we need."

"And then what?" she asked. "Where will we go and what will we do until they convict Manchetti? What will we live on?"

Marc shook his head. "Slow down, Sam. My father and Jean Claude are working on the details, and money is no problem. For now, just think of it as an extended vacation. We can always hope for a miracle, that things will get cleared up sooner than they think. Right now, the best thing we can do is go for dinner."

Samantha wanted to work out all the details right then and there, but Marc was insistent.

Evening dusk had darkened to night. A full moon and a host of stars greeted them as they emerged from the companionway. Samantha stood still long enough to admire the spectacular sight. "It's so beautiful," she said with a sigh.

"Not half as beautiful as you."

"Marc, don't."

"Okay, okay, but it's true."

Samantha gave him an exasperated look as he steadied her while she stepped off the *Jenny* onto the dock.

"Did I tell you I like your dress?"

She glanced sideways at him, a suspicious glint in her eyes. "I believe you mentioned you especially like the bow."

Marc chuckled and draped his arm around her shoulders. "Bows fascinate me." They began walking toward town. "Does that one really work?"

Samantha stiffened and Marc reluctantly removed his arm and shoved his hands into his pockets. "The restaurant is just past the next block."

"Are you sure it's safe?"

Actually, he wasn't sure about anything. Too much was happening too fast. All he really wanted—just for one evening—was to forget everything and just enjoy being with Samantha. He deliberately ignored her question. "The last time I was here, their seafood platter was out of this world. Ah, here we are."

Samantha read the sign over the nondescript building. "Clever name," she commented, tongue-in-cheek. "The Seafood Platter," she read the name out loud.

The place was crowded, and since they didn't have a reservation, they had to stand in the foyer and wait for a table. Samantha hoped that the food would prove to be worth the wait. At least the air-conditioning was running full blast. Even with the crowd, it was blessedly cool.

At first Marc ignored the prickly feeling along his neck. But when the feeling persisted, he casually glanced around. Someone was watching them. *Are you sure it's safe?* Samantha's question reverberated in his mind.

Marc noted the people standing in line. No one seemed to be paying attention to Samantha or to him. Over to the side was a bar, deserted except for one man at the end nursing a drink. It was there Marc spotted the reason for his unease.

The bartender. He was staring straight at him. Marc stared back. The bald-headed man had the decency to glance away, but several minutes later Marc caught him staring again.

"Sam." Marc pulled her close. "Wait here. I'm going to get us a couple of drinks at the bar."

"Sounds good," she answered. "Vodka Collins for me, please."

Marc nodded, then made his way through the crowd and approached the bar. At first he thought the bartender was going to ignore him, but the man finally stopped polishing the glass he held and walked over.

"May I help you?"

Marc lowered his voice to a menacing level. "What's your name?"

The man shrugged. "Jack. Everyone calls me Jack."

"Yeah. Well, Jack, you can tell me why you keep staring my way."

"You're crazy, man. I ain't staring at nothing."

"Like hell." Marc grabbed the front of the man's shirt and pulled him across the bar until they were nose to nose. "How would you like me to rearrange your face, Jack?"

"Hey, man, okay, okay. Just back off."

Marc released him.

"Two guys came in about an hour ago showing your picture around, asking if anyone had seen you."

Marc's heart began to pound in his chest. "What did you tell them?"

The man threw up his hands in self-defense. "Nothing, I swear. How could I?"

"Where did they go after they left here?"

"How am I supposed to know?"

Marc reached into his pocket, pulled out a ten-dollar bill and shoved it across the counter. "You might have heard them say something."

Jack stuffed the bill into his pocket. "Yeah, well, they said something about checking out the other restaurants in town."

"Thanks, Jack." Marc turned to leave.

"Hey, mister. You might be interested in something else they said."

Marc turned back and reached into his pocket again.

Jack's eyes followed the bill as Marc laid it on the bar. "They said they'd be back in a couple of hours to check again."

Without a word, Marc headed straight for Samantha. He grabbed her arm, pulling her toward the door.

"Marc! What are you doing?"

"We're leaving."

"But why? It's almost our turn."

"Trust me. We have to get out of here now. I'll explain later."

Once outside, Marc was careful to stay in the shadows as they moved quietly down the street. When they reached the dock area, Samantha started across the street toward the *Jenny,* but Marc pulled her back. "Wait here." He gently pushed her into a small alley. "I want to check out the boat first."

But Samantha refused to release his hand. "If you think I'm going to stay here by myself, think again," she said. "No way, Dureaux. No way."

"Sam, we don't have time to argue—"

"Good, then let's get moving."

Marc muttered something about stubborn women, then stepped out of the alley with Samantha following close behind. They skirted the area around the *Jenny* then quietly stepped on board.

"Stay here," he whispered, motioning toward the corner of the cockpit. "And try to keep out of sight while I check below." Marc leaned over her for a second longer. "Keep an eye out for anyone approaching the boat."

Even though she nodded, Marc hesitated. For all her bravado, he knew she was scared. He could see it in her eyes. "I won't be long."

"Just be careful . . . and hurry," she whispered.

Marc searched the boat thoroughly. After finding it just as they'd left it, he returned to the deck.

"Everything's okay. I don't think anyone's been around." When she didn't respond, he knelt in front of her. "Sam?" He took her clenched hands in his. They were cold and clammy. Even in the dim light, he could see she was pale. He squeezed gently. "We have to leave now."

"They've found us, haven't they?"

"No," he answered, not liking the sound of her voice. It was too fragile, as if any minute she might break into a thousand pieces. "But Sam, they are here looking. We have to leave."

"How did you know?"

Marc released one of her hands to gently caress her cheek. "The bartender in the restaurant . . . I asked a few questions."

Placing his fingers beneath her chin, he tilted up her face toward his. The temptation to kiss her, to comfort her, was strong. Too strong. He couldn't resist and he didn't. Samantha pulled away. "Oh, Marc," she whispered. "What are we going to do?"

He stood up abruptly and answered her. "We have to get out of here as soon as possible," he said. "I need your help."

"What about the raft . . . and the trolling motor?"

"There's another small marina north of here. We'll pick up what we need there. Come on." He clasped her shoulders, pulled her up and gave her a little shove. "Go change your clothes and secure everything below while I get us out of here. You'll feel safer once we're in the open gulf." And so will I, he added silently.

CHAPTER ELEVEN

ONCE THEY'D CLEARED the harbor, Samantha did feel somewhat calmer. Seated on the deck with her feet dangling over the side, she watched the harbor lights grow dimmer. Even though the breeze was warm, she shivered. Then she recalled what Marc had said about feeling safer. But safety, like everything else, was relative, and human emotions were fickle, she decided. When she'd first met him, she'd suspected Marc was a murderer and she'd been terrified out on the open water. And now, he was her protector and that same open water was their only security against the real murderers.

Marc watched Samantha as she kept her silent vigil. She was so still and quiet, a lone silhouette against the soft glow of the starlit night. He wanted to go to her, wrap his arms around her and promise no harm would come to either one of them. But he couldn't. He'd already made too many promises he'd been unable to keep.

Samantha swung her legs around and stood up. Slowly she made her way toward the cockpit. "How much farther do we have to go?"

"Not far. I'll anchor just offshore near a small marina at Horseshoe Point. Later, I'll take the dinghy and buy what we need."

"Do you have enough money?" She rushed on before he could answer. "I mean...well...you've already bought supplies and given me money for the clothes and—"

"Sam." Marc held up his palm to silence her. "I have enough to get what we need for now. Jean Claude is supposed to make reservations at a motel farther north and wire me more money."

"Sounds like everything's been planned to the last detail."

"Yeah, sounds like it."

"I get the distinct feeling you don't trust your cousin."

Marc grunted his response.

"Something's bothering you. Want to talk about it?"

Marc glanced up to check the sail. "Jean Claude's bothering me. If you knew my cousin, you'd understand."

"Tell me about him," she urged.

Marc was silent for several minutes. Talking about Jean Claude was the last thing he wanted to do.

"Marc?" Samantha touched his arm to get his attention. "So tell me about your cousin."

Marc gazed out across the moonlit water. "For some reason, Jean Claude has always resented me." There was sadness in his voice as he talked about his relationship with his cousin. Finally, he shrugged. "Who knows what Jean Claude's problem was. All I know is that in the past, he's barely acknowledged I was alive, so why should he suddenly want to help me?"

"Is he older or younger than you?"

"He's three years older."

As they sailed into the night, Samantha took advantage of Marc's conversational mood. She learned about his mother, and got a glimpse of his boyhood years, which were a stark contrast to her own childhood. Even though he made light of his family's social status, she could picture what it meant to grow up a Dureaux. At first she laughed when he told her about Dora and his speculations about the housekeeper's feelings for his father. She couldn't believe there were people who still adhered to such a strict code concerning their stations in life.

"That's one of saddest things I think I've ever heard. Poor Dora."

"Hmph. Poor Dora my foot," Marc said as he began the task of lowering the *Jenny*'s sails. "She rules my father and his household with an iron fist. I figure he loves her and has for a long time. Why else would he put up with her bossy ways? Either that or he's blind, deaf and dumb. And believe me, my father's none of those."

As she listened to him talk about his family, something occurred to Samantha. Marc mentioned everyone but his wife. Was the subject too painful?

Crossing her arms beneath her breasts, she turned away and walked to the edge of the boat. The gulf stretched out, dark and forbidding, only stopping as it met the backdrop of what seemed to be a million stars winking at the edge.

As she watched him lower the anchor, Samantha thought about the things Marc had said about his family. He cared deeply about his father and Dora, and even in a way, Jean Claude. It was evident in the way he talked about them. And the night they'd argued, even though he'd sounded bitter about his wife, he'd never denied he would take her back if she changed her mind; instead, he'd changed the subject. That he'd married Angelique because she'd told him she was pregnant only proved he was an honorable man, a man of integrity. Would he always feel a sense of duty to the woman he had married? Would he always feel an emotional bond between himself and his wife?

Samantha heard him approach her from behind, but she continued to stare out over the water.

"Sam? Why so quiet all of a sudden?"

"Just thinking."

"Too much thinking can drive a person crazy."

"Maybe so."

Marc turned her to face him, his firm grasp holding her prisoner. "Are you nervous about tomorrow?"

"A little."

As if it were the most natural thing in the world for him to do, he pulled her closer and wrapped his arms around her. "You shouldn't be," he whispered against her hair.

It felt good to be in his embrace, and for a moment Samantha gave in and savored being cocooned in the safety of his arms. The temptation to encourage him, to give in to what they both wanted, sent a shaft of longing through her that bordered on pain.

Samantha pulled away. "Actually, I was thinking about your wife."

For a moment he just looked at her. A muscle twitched in his jaw and his eyes took on a distant expression. "Why would you be thinking about Angelique? She has nothing to do with any of this."

"I'm just trying to understand."

"Why? What's to understand?"

"I don't know why. All I know is that I'm confused. You never did deny you would take her back."

Marc cursed. "That bastard ex-boyfriend of yours did a real job on you, didn't he?"

Samantha stared at him. "See? You're doing it again."

"Doing what, for heaven's sake?"

"You're avoiding the question. And you want to know what I think?" Samantha didn't give him time to answer. "I think you avoid answering because it's true. I think that you can't talk about her because you still love her, and I'm not sure you'll ever be really free of her."

Marc glared at her. "I'll admit Angelique left her mark. And you're right—I'm not sure I'll ever be completely free of her. But..." Marc released his hold on Samantha and stepped away. He shook his head as if he didn't want to continue the conversation. "Like I said before, too much thinking can drive a person crazy."

EARLY THE FOLLOWING morning, it was the gentle swaying that awakened Samantha. For several minutes she remained motionless. How different, how strange, she thought. It seemed like a lifetime had passed since the first morning she'd awakened on the *Jenny*. As she looked around the small cabin, her chest tightened. Within hours, they would have to destroy the beautiful yacht.

Samantha kicked back the sheet, slid off the bed and groped through a drawer for shorts and a shirt. After hastily pulling on the clothes, she took one more look around the cabin, then walked toward the companionway.

Peering out of the door into the bright light, she saw Marc standing at the wheel leaning sideways over a map. After he'd veered the conversation away from Angelique, he'd been silent the rest of the evening. Silent and brooding. Maybe he'd had time to think about what she'd said.

"Good morning," she called out.

He turned his head and nodded. He motioned toward her. "Come on over here. I want to show you something."

When she was within touching distance, he pulled her closer and spread out the map over the wheel.

"We'll be there soon."

"Then what?"

"I'll take the dinghy ashore and get what we need."

"We're not going to dock?"

"No. If this thing is going to work, we've got to get in and out without drawing attention."

As Marc pointed out their present location and Horseshoe Point, Samantha offered up a silent prayer that he knew what he was doing. He slid his finger over the map.

"There.' He tapped the paper. "Right there is the halfway point to shore."

All she could see was a tiny dot. "That's an island?"

Marc laughed. "Just barely. It's the perfect place to stow the extra gas and clothes. After we torch the *Jenny,* we'll need to get away fast. The lighter the load, the faster we can go. Trolling motors aren't built for speed."

Later that morning, Marc rowed the dinghy to the small town and purchased what they needed. She helped him drag everything aboard and watched as he meticulously checked off each item he'd bought.

Chills of apprehension ran up and down her spine. The escape raft was no bigger than a bathtub. "Are you sure that thing will hold two people?"

Marc glanced up. "Getting nervous?"

"A little."

"There's no need to. You're letting your imagination get the best of you."

Samantha disagreed but she kept silent. Their lives depended on their pulling off the charade. She shivered. "Just tell me one thing."

"What's that?" Marc asked.

"Are there . . . sharks in these waters?"

Marc shrugged. "Probably, but they only bother humans if humans bother them." *Or was that snakes?* He didn't know the first thing about sharks and hoped Samantha didn't, either. Hell, he hadn't even thought about sharks. He'd been too wrapped up in planning their escape. And then there was afterward to think about, and he'd been giving that a lot of thought. If Jean Claude assumed he was going to calmly disappear, he was in for a surprise.

MARC'S PILOTING EXPERTISE guided them straight to the tiny island where they would store their supplies. Samantha stayed on the *Jenny* while he rowed the dinghy to shore. She watched him jump out and pull the small boat farther up on the narrow beach. He selected one of the larger clumps of bushes near the shoreline and unloaded the supplies. He then tied a bright red cloth near the top of the bush to mark the spot.

Marc pushed the dinghy back into the surf, and climbed in. A knot of fear lodged in Samantha's stomach, making her feel slightly sick. So many things could go wrong, she thought as his powerful strokes brought him closer and closer to the *Jenny*. Samantha took a deep breath. There was no use speculating or worrying about the dangers; their course had been set, and whether she liked it or not, she knew she had little choice but to see it through.

Once Marc was back aboard the *Jenny*, they lifted anchor. There was barely enough wind to fill the *Jenny*'s sails, and an hour passed before they reached their destination, an hour in which Marc had gone over the plan until Samantha was ready to scream. It was actually a relief to climb into the raft alone and putter away to the distance they'd agreed upon. But when she cut the motor and looked back at the *Jenny*, she began to shake. At the first sign of smoke, her throat tightened, and she gripped the sides of the raft to steady herself as waves threatened to swamp the tiny rubber boat. Then fire seemed be everywhere. The flames raced over the deck, along the sides and up the mast.

Squinting against the afternoon sun, Samantha shaded her eyes with her hand. It was too fast, it was happening too fast, she thought. The raft dipped precariously, making it difficult to concentrate on anything but keeping it steady. Where was Marc? He should have been in the water by now, swimming toward safety.

Suddenly, an explosion ripped through the air, the noise deafening as it reverberated over the water. Stunned, she stared as burning pieces of the yacht fell haphazardly all around. Then she heard another sound and realized it was her own voice screaming Marc's name.

CHAPTER TWELVE

BLACK SMOKE BILLOWED from what was left of the *Jenny*, but there was no sign of Marc. Samantha leaned forward, clutching the side of the raft. "Marc!" she screamed again, but there was no response.

In that split second, Samantha knew without a doubt she'd done the unforgivable, the very thing she'd promised herself never to do again—she'd fallen in love with a man who was committed to another woman.

Her eyes blurred. She covered her face with her hands. For a moment she fought to catch her breath, knowing if she became hysterical, she was doomed. He couldn't be dead, he just couldn't be. He was out there...somewhere.

She jerked her head up to search the area once more. Splintered pieces of wood bobbed up and down in the water as if playing hide-and-seek. Then suddenly his dark head broke through the surface. "Marc?" Her heart thudded painfully as he swam toward her. "Are you okay?" she called out. He continued to swim toward her; each stroke seemed to be a struggle. He didn't answer. "I th-thought you were—" Something was wrong.

"Hold on," she yelled out. "I'm coming." She turned, grabbed the starter rope of the motor and pulled. But it only sputtered. "Damn," she cursed after the third try and snatched up the paddle. Gripping it tightly, she plunged it into the choppy water. The muscles in her arms protested, but she ignored the pain. When she was finally within several yards of Marc, she noticed a trickle of blood along his forehead. She swallowed the lump of fear lodged in her throat. Blood attracted sharks, she thought, paddling harder. That much she knew.

Marc caught hold of the raft, and Samantha threw aside the paddle to help him in. After nearly swamping the small boat, he was able to heave himself aboard. For a moment he lay gasping for breath.

"What happened?" She lightly touched his jaw, tilting his head. Satisfied the gash was superficial and small in comparison with the blood flow, she turned her attention to the rest of him. She ran her hands along his arms, then started on his ankles, working her way up his shins.

Marc grabbed her wrist. "I'm okay." He sucked in a deep breath and struggled to sit up. "We're running out of time. We've got to get out of here before someone spots us. Change places with me."

"Are you sure? You're bleeding—" He crawled around her. "Marc! Watch out!" The raft tilted and more water slid over the side, filling the bottom.

"See if you can bail it out." He turned toward the small motor and jerked the pull rope. The second time he yanked it sputtered, then hummed to life. "Sam, the water—we'll never make any time with the extra weight."

Samantha glanced around for something to bail with.

"Use that." Marc gestured toward the canteen. "Hurry. And hand me the compass."

"But that's our drinking water."

He grimaced. "If we don't get rid of this extra weight, we won't need drinking water. We won't have enough gas to make it to the island."

With shaky fingers, Samantha dug in a plastic bag for the compass and handed it to him. After she'd untied the canteen, she twisted off the cap and offered it to Marc first. He poured some over his head, then lifted it to his lips and drank deeply. He handed it back. Samantha drank several gulps and emptied the rest over the side.

The task seemed impossible as she repeatedly filled and drained the canteen. Her arms ached with the effort, and though only a short time had passed, it seemed like hours before most of the water was gone. Then there was nothing to do but wait as the raft continued its snail's pace through the endless, choppy water. The heat of the late-afternoon sun was relentless, but Samantha tried to ignore her thirst, telling herself she felt its intensity only because she knew she couldn't have a drink.

Marc couldn't bear to look at Samantha. He'd botched the whole thing from the beginning. He closed his eyes against the pain of his splitting headache, and cursed softly.

"Marc?" Samantha touched his shoulder. "Let me see your head."

He shrugged her hand away. He didn't want her to be kind. He didn't deserve it. "Sam, it's just a scratch. I'm okay."

"You don't act like you're okay. What happened back there?"

"The stove," he muttered.

"What?"

"The stove, dammit! I forgot about the blasted butane stove in the galley." He turned to glare at her. "There, are you satisfied?"

"No, I'm not." She glared right back. "And don't yell at me."

Marc rolled his eyes upward. "Okay, okay. Just before I dived overboard, the stove blew. The force of the blast knocked me into the water. All I remember is junk flying everywhere, so I stayed under as long as I could."

"Well, you scared—"

Suddenly, Marc raised his hand. "Listen," he whispered. "Do you hear that?"

Samantha tilted her head, and she frowned. She could hear a faint noise. "What is it?"

"Look . . . over there."

Samantha twisted to where he was pointing. Shading her eyes against the glare, she saw the source of the sound near the smoking remains of the *Jenny*. "A helicopter? Do you think they'll see us?"

Marc shrugged. "I hope not. We should be far enough away. Hopefully, they'll just search the immediate area."

After several moments, she turned back to Marc. "How long will it take to reach the island?"

"Not long," Marc answered, and prayed his calculations were correct. There wasn't enough gas to veer too far off course.

An hour later as they spotted the island, the motor began to sputter. "Damn," Marc whispered.

"Would tilting the can help?"

Marc nodded. "Good idea. It's worth a try."

Samantha tilted the gas can, trying to get the most out of what was left.

Marc gritted his teeth. "Come on, baby, just a little farther." Several minutes went by, bringing them a little closer, then the motor died. Marc grabbed the paddle.

"Are you sure this is the right island? I don't see the marker flag. It doesn't look the same."

"Of course, it's the right one." But the closer they came, the less familiar anything looked. The trees and vegetation seemed to be thicker, the beach more narrow than he remembered. And she was right. The damned red marker flag was nowhere in sight.

As the momentum of the incoming tide carried the raft onto the shore, a faint noise rose above the sound of the waves and grew louder; Marc didn't have time to worry about the flag.

"Sam, the raft. Help me drag it into those trees. That helicopter is coming this way."

Just as they pulled the raft beneath the outer edge of the trees, the helicopter appeared over the horizon. Within minutes it zipped overhead.

Out of breath, Marc leaned against the trunk of a large palm. "That was close. Too close."

"Guess they've been searching for survivors all this time." Samantha was gasping, too. "Do you think they'll come back?"

Marc pushed away from the tree. "We're not waiting around to find out." He bent over and unlashed a plastic-covered bundle from the side of the raft. From the bundle, he pulled out a chart. After several moments of studying it, he glanced up at Samantha. "Look at this."

Samantha knelt beside him.

"This has to be the right island," he said, and pointed to a tiny dot. "The tide must have carried us to the opposite end." He refolded the chart, placing it back in the plastic bag. "Come on." He grabbed her hand. "We've got some walking to do."

As they walked along the beach, Marc's confidence grew; the terrain began to look more familiar.

"Marc." Samantha pulled him to a stop. "Over there." She pointed to a cluster of bushes. Tied to one was the red marker flag.

When they reached the supplies, Marc pulled out a canteen and gave it to Samantha.

She took a long drink, and handed it back to him. "I never knew water could taste so good."

Marc took a drink, then wiped his mouth with the back of his hand. After replacing the cap, he stuffed the canteen in the knapsack.

"Here, I'll carry that." Samantha picked up the bag. "You can carry the gas can."

Marc bent to pick up the gas can. "It's getting late, Sam." He began walking back the way they'd come. "We need to get to the mainland before dark."

Samantha shifted the knapsack to a more comfortable position and followed.

DENSE FOREST shaded either side of the two-laned country road. Except for the never-ending sound of the tree frogs, there was absolute silence.

Samantha stared at Marc's back. His shirt was stained from sweat, and he looked as exhausted as she felt. The trip to the mainland had taken longer than they'd expected. Trolling motors were definitely not built for speed, she thought. The walk along the beach had seemed endless, but luckily they'd found this paved road—a deserted paved road that she was beginning to believe led to nowhere.

"Let's stop and rest a few minutes," Marc said, and stopped abruptly.

Still lost in her thoughts, Samantha almost tripped trying to avoid bumping into him. "Next time, give me a signal."

"Next time, watch where you're going," he shot back.

Samantha ignored his testy response and limped over to a grassy area beside the road. Both of them were hot and tired. Arguing wouldn't make matters any better, she decided.

Once she was seated, she carefully removed her shoe. "Damned sand," she muttered as she examined the heel of her foot.

"What's wrong?" Marc walked over and knelt beside her. "Here, let me take a look at that." He grasped her ankle, his touch warm, firm, yet tender. He gently rubbed his finger over the puffy blister. "If that thing pops, it's going to burn like hell."

Samantha looked up and grimaced. "I think I'll try barefoot for a while."

For a moment his gaze held hers, even as he continued to hold her ankle. "I didn't mean to be such a grouch a few minutes ago," he said as his thumb continued a soft, stroking motion.

"Me, either," she whispered, moved by the tenderness of his touch.

When he leaned forward and brushed his lips against the blister, her breath caught. She forgot everything but the quick, urgent desire that surged through her.

"Apology accepted?"

Samantha couldn't have spoken if her life had depended on it; instead, she nodded.

"Good." He released her foot. "You should be okay barefoot for a while. The asphalt is probably not too hot underneath all this shade," he said as he stood.

Marc pulled a map from his pocket, and Samantha automatically began to unlace her other shoe.

"There should be a main highway a few miles farther up the road. I think we're almost there."

BY THE TIME they reached the main highway, it was dark. All Samantha could think about was how good it would be to soak her aching body in a tub of warm water.

"Damn mosquitoes!" Marc's harsh voice cut through the night as he slapped his neck.

The pesky insects had descended immediately with the disappearance of the sun. If she hadn't been so close to tears, Samantha would have found the situation funny. Every few seconds, like clockwork, Marc alternately cursed and slapped.

The sudden appearance of lights down the highway, accompanied by the sound of a diesel engine, interrupted her self-pitying reverie. If only they could hitch a ride.

"Say a little prayer," Marc said, and started toward the middle of the road.

Samantha grabbed his arm. "If it does stop, what will you tell the driver?" She glanced down the highway, then back to Marc. The headlights were getting closer. "A man and a woman out in the middle of nowhere are pretty conspicuous."

Marc shifted the knapsack, placing it on the ground. "Stop worrying." His hand squeezed hers. "The old ran-out-of-gas routine works every time."

"But what if you're recognized?"

"Sam, this is Florida. There's not much chance my picture made the papers here. And even if it did, it's so damned dark, my own father wouldn't recognize me. Besides—" he rubbed his bearded jaw "—I'm in disguise."

The eighteen wheeler slowed as it passed them, and Samantha held her breath. What if it kept going? she thought. It didn't.

"Come on." Marc grabbed her hand.

When they reached the truck, he opened the door and gave her a boost inside.

"You folks lost?"

The gruff, feminine voice came as a complete surprise. All Samantha could do was stare.

"No, ma'am," Marc answered as he pulled the door shut, plunging the cab into semidarkness. "Just out of gas."

"Name's Tiny."

The lady truck driver reached across and shook both their hands, but Marc didn't offer any names.

As tired as she was, it was all Samantha could do to keep from laughing. She'd only seen Tiny for a few seconds before Marc had closed the door, but a few seconds was all it had taken. The lady truck driver's image was indelibly planted in her mind, and Tiny was anything but what her name indicated.

Marc turned sideways, draping his arm across Samantha's shoulders. "How far you going?" he asked.

"Got a load to dump in Tallahassee," Tiny answered as she shoved the gear into first, checked her rearview mirror, then pulled back onto the highway. "Came all the way up from St. Pete." She paused. "Didn't see no abandoned car."

Samantha squirmed and Marc tightened his arm to still her. "We pushed it off the road behind some bushes. Can't be too careful these days."

"You got that right." Tiny glanced over and grinned. "Well, tonight was your lucky night. Next town is a good ten-mile walk."

"Yeah, we really appreciate the lift."

"Are there any motels there?" asked Samantha.

"Yep. The Starlight Inn. Ain't much to look at, but it's clean."

"That's great," Marc chimed in. "We can see about our car tomorrow."

As soon as Marc said "tomorrow," Samantha grew uneasy. How many tomorrows would they have? What if something went wrong?

All day, she'd purposely avoided thinking about her revelation that she'd fallen in love with Marc. She hadn't allowed herself to consider much past surviving each minute. Besides, she told herself, thinking about it wouldn't change anything. There was still Angelique. Even if Marc happened to return Samantha's love, there could be no promises of happily ever after. Not under their present circumstances. Anything could go wrong. The whole elaborate hoax could backfire. Samantha shivered. No, she decided, they couldn't count on having tomorrow. The only promise they had was the moment.

Fifteen minutes later, a bright neon star blinking like a Christmas light came into sight. As they waved goodbye and the eighteen wheeler roared down the highway, Samantha stared at the shabby oblong building and reminded herself that Tiny had said the motel was clean inside.

"Come on." Marc reached for Samantha's hand. "Let's get checked in."

"Marc." Samantha pulled him to a stop in front of the entrance. "Do you have enough money for us to stay here?"

Frowning, Marc turned to face her. "We can't use a credit card. They're too easy to trace. How much do you think a night here costs?"

Samantha glanced around. Usually motels like the Starlight Inn posted their rates on the outside. Across the parking lot, she finally located the small sign. Her heart sank. "How much do you have?"

Marc released her hand and dug into his pocket. He pulled out several bills. After he'd counted what looked like mostly ones, he said, "Twenty-four dollars."

The rate for a single was twenty. Samantha pointed to the sign. "You'd better go in by yourself. I'll wait out here."

Even in the dim light, she could tell he was embarrassed. He'd probably never had to worry about counting pennies.

When Marc returned a few minutes later, he was smiling. He handed her a brown paper sack. "What's this?" she asked, following him as he searched for the room number that matched his key. Each of the doors were painted a garish red.

"That, m'lady, is our evening meal, courtesy of the management."

Curious, she peeked inside. Wrapped in napkins were several powdered donuts. Underneath were two disposable cups.

"The old lady out front told me to help myself," he said as he stopped in front of a door numbered 113 and inserted a key. He shoved the door open.

The room smelled musty and was warm inside. Samantha walked in and turned on a lamp.

A soft glow filled the small room, helping to disguise the shabby furnishings. There was a scarred dresser, a black vinyl chair that had a rip in the seat, and a double bed covered with a black-and-red bedspread. Matching drapes hung precariously over the only window. Beneath the window was an air conditioner.

Marc twisted a dial and the air conditioner clattered to life. "Well, it's not exactly five-star, but it beats mosquitoes and sand."

Samantha decided she would reserve judgment until after she'd seen all the facilities. She deposited the sack on the dresser, then walked over to a door she assumed led to the bathroom. She groped around for the wall switch.

Harsh light filled the room, making her blink, but after her eyes had adjusted, she breathed a sigh of relief. The motel room itself might be shabby, but everything in the bathroom sparkled with cleanliness.

Immediately she went to the tub and turned on the faucets. By the time it was full, she'd stripped and stepped in. Groaning with pleasure, she closed her eyes as she sank into the warm water.

Marc heard the running water and the happy facade he'd tried to maintain faded into a self-deprecating grimace as he glanced around the room. This stinking motel was the pits. If he'd been by himself, it wouldn't have mattered, but Samantha deserved better. Not only that, but all he had left to his name was four dollars, four lousy dollars. Jean Claude was wiring money, but the motel they'd agreed on was at least a hundred miles north.

Resentment bordering on fury began to boil in his gut. From the very beginning, he'd been set up, used. Destroying the *Jenny* had been like cutting out his heart. Marc stepped over to the window and pulled the drape aside. Somewhere in the night, a car door slammed and muffled voices rose in a crescendo, then died. Except for an occasional splash of water and the hum of the air conditioner, all was silent.

One name kept bouncing around in his head—Antonio Manchetti. He was the bastard responsible. If—Marc corrected himself—when he got his hands on Manchetti, he intended to beat him to a pulp. And find him he would, he vowed silently. He'd thought about it a lot since his conversation with his father. No way could he sit idly by and wait and rely on Jean Claude. He had to go to New Orleans . . . and he had to go alone.

But what was he going to do about Samantha? If he told her, she'd insist on going with him. Taking her would only slow him down. By the time they picked up the money at the other motel, the newspapers would have reported the accident. Officially, they would be dead. When that happened, Manchetti would call off the search. According to the plan, he and Samantha were to wait at a condo Jean Claude had rented for them. Marc could take her to the condo. She'd be safe there. And once he got her settled . . . But until then he'd have to pretend to follow orders. He didn't dare risk her finding out. Over the past few days, he'd discovered he was far too vulnerable where she was concerned. In a moment of weakness, he just might let her talk him into something stupid . . . like taking her with him.

The sound of splashing water filtered through his thoughts. Marc released the drape. Turning, he stared at the bathroom door. Instantly, a picture of how she'd looked when he'd accidentally walked in on her dressing flashed through his mind. One thin, wooden door separated him from what he ached for.

Marc turned away, retreating toward the vinyl chair. Who was he kidding? he thought, eyeing the chair with distaste. A hell of a lot more than a door separated them. Samantha had some cockeyed notion he was still hung up on his wife. Somehow, he'd have to convince her that once he was legally free, there would be no going back. But how?

And would he ever be free?

CHAPTER THIRTEEN

"THAT'S A LIE." Angelique glared at Patrick O'Connor. For a moment the living room of Edward Dureaux's home crackled with silent tension. "Tony would never do such a thing. He was my father's friend."

"Angelique, every word Mr. O'Connor has told you is true." Jean Claude's quiet voice was laced with an edge of authority. He leaned forward, placing his cup on the table. "I've seen the reports. I've heard the interrogation tapes of your father."

Angelique shot him a disdainful look. "You must think I'm an idiot. If what he says is true, Tony would have been arrested and charged."

"Without your father's testimony, all our evidence was worthless."

Angelique ignored O'Connor's explanation and continued to stare at Jean Claude. Her eyes reminded him of a wounded animal's, half-crazed from pain. Then suddenly, the look was gone.

Easing out of her chair, she walked over to the breakfront. "I don't know why we're even discussing this," she said as she poured a cup of coffee. "None of it has anything to do with me."

When she turned, her smile gave Jean Claude an eerie feeling. It had a disquieting unreality he couldn't fathom.

O'Connor cleared his throat. "Mrs. Dureaux, we know about your association with Manchetti. We also know you plotted with him to kill your husband."

Except for a slight flare of her nostrils, Angelique's expression didn't change. She continued to smile. "That's the most ridiculous thing I've ever heard. Besides, Marc isn't dead." She laughed; the high-pitched sound bordered on hysteria. "Why on earth would I do such a thing, especially since we've already agreed to a divorce? A divorce that, I might add, I initiated."

"Stop it, Angelique. They know." Jean Claude rose from the sofa and started toward her.

She backed away a step, her smile fading. "There's nothing to know," she whispered.

He reached out to her. "I told them. I told them everything."

She whirled around to stare out the window. Her back was ramrod stiff, and her hands were clenched into fists. "It's your word against mine. You have *no* proof."

He lowered his arm. "Tell her, O'Connor," he said as he stepped away, halting in front of the fireplace. His gaze rested on the picture of him and his cousin.

"We've had a man tailing you for weeks. He witnessed your meetings with Manchetti. Our surveillance includes a tape of your last conversation with him in Jackson Square." O'Connor paused. There was no reaction from Angelique. She continued to stare out the window.

He took a deep breath. "As for motive, we've also discovered a hefty insurance policy you would benefit from and then there's also the affair you've been having with Jean Claude."

Angelique bowed her head, her shoulders slumped. "You did tell them everything, didn't you, Jean Claude?"

"I . . . I didn't have to. They already knew most of it."

"And you confirmed it."

"I had to. I couldn't be a part of a conspiracy to kill Marc."

"No, of course not," she whispered. Straightening, she turned, and looked directly at Edward. "Do *you* believe what they said about Tony, that . . . that he had my father and mother murdered?"

Edward nodded. "I heard the tapes and read the police report."

Jean Claude glanced at his uncle. He'd worried that the strain of the confrontation would be too much for the elderly man. But so far, Edward seemed to be holding up well. When Jean Claude and O'Connor had planned everything, he'd objected to his uncle's playing a part in it. Edward had overruled his objection, saying Marc's life could depend on the outcome, and he wanted to be there to make sure nothing went wrong.

O'Connor stood up and started toward Angelique. "Angelique Dureaux, I'm arresting you for conspiracy to commit murder. You have the right to—"

"For heaven's sake, O'Connor," Jean Claude said, stepping in between them. "Do you have to do that now?"

"You know I do," said the agent. "You, as a lawyer, should know how important details and technicalities are."

Jean Claude glared at him for a moment longer, then stepped aside.

"As I was saying . . . you have the right to remain silent. . . ."

As O'Connor continued, Jean Claude's thoughts drifted. He felt as if the burdens of the world had descended upon his shoulders, and he felt empty, so damned empty . . . and alone.

"What happens now?"

Angelique's question brought Jean Claude's attention back to the situation at hand.

"That depends," answered O'Connor. "I'm authorized to make you a deal, but you might want an attorney present—"

"What kind of deal?"

"Do you want an attorney—"

"Just get on with it," she interrupted. "What kind of deal are you talking about?"

The tension in his stomach lessened, but Jean Claude was careful to keep the relief from showing on his face. Hook, line and sinker, he thought. She'd taken the bait just as O'Connor had predicted.

The agent took a deep breath. "If you cooperate, every consideration possible will be given to you."

"What would I have to do?"

"Just show up at the trial."

Angelique shook her head. "No deal. What's to keep him from having me killed? You didn't protect my parents."

"He won't know you've agreed until the day you enter the courtroom. By then, it will be too late. All we've got now is conspiracy, but that's enough to put him away for a long time. And if you show up, he'll believe you're going to testify against him. Afterward, he wouldn't dare do anything. He'd go to the chair if he did."

"You can't guarantee he won't find out," she shot back.

O'Connor held up his hands to calm her. "No one but the four of us will know you've agreed to anything."

Angelique looked at her father-in-law. "Edward?"

"You can trust Patrick. He wouldn't lie to you." Edward averted his gaze to O'Connor. "Tell her the rest, Patrick."

Patrick glanced over at Jean Claude.

Jean Claude nodded.

"Sit over here. This will take some explaining." Patrick motioned to a nearby chair. When she was seated, he continued.

Jean Claude listened as O'Connor went over the plan. Persuading Angelique to cooperate was imperative.

O'Connor had been able to pull some strings and confirm that after her parents' death, she had been committed to the state mental hospital.

Now it seemed she had relapsed into a dangerous mental state. O'Connor, Edward and Jean Claude had agreed that she needed psychiatric help.

Since going through the courts would have been a lengthy process, the only recourse was to get her to voluntarily commit herself.

All of their plans hinged on Marc's cooperation. Although Marc had agreed, Jean Claude hadn't been convinced he'd actually follow through. And they couldn't confront Angelique until they were sure. Then, early that morning, the news had come.

Jean Claude closed his eyes, remembering Dora's reaction. She'd become hysterical when they had told her Marc was missing and presumed dead. It had taken both him and his uncle to calm her. Even now, she was in bed heavily sedated. He'd hated putting her through that, but O'Connor had insisted on absolute secrecy. He'd said the fewer people who knew, the less chance of a slipup. He'd also pointed out that there was no way Dora could express the required grief during the mock funeral unless she really believed the lie; Edward had argued with him, but in the end he'd reluctantly agreed to O'Connor's terms.

"Now let me get this straight...."

At the sound of Angelique's voice, Jean Claude's thoughts drifted back to the conversation.

"I'm supposed to be so distraught over Marc's death that I have a nervous breakdown and have to be institutionalized?"

"Not institutionalized," said O'Connor, shaking his head. "We'll place you in a private hospital, one that specializes in depression."

"How soon?" she asked.

"Immediately." O'Connor held her gaze. "Will you agree?"

Angelique took her time answering. Jean Claude held his breath, but his attention was on his uncle. Even though Edward seemed at ease, Jean Claude noted the subtle signs of stress—the twitch beneath his left eye, the set of his jaw. So much—everything—depended on Angelique's cooperation. Without it, she wouldn't get the help she needed, and they wouldn't have anything to hold over Manchetti. And as long as Manchetti was free, Marc and the Bradford woman would have to remain in a state of limbo—alive, but dead to the rest of the world.

Angelique shook her head. "Tony will never believe it. He knows that I've left Marc. And he knows how I feel about—" she looked over at Edward "—sorry, I shouldn't have said that."

Edward's expression never changed. With a shrug, Angelique turned her attention back to O'Connor. "He won't believe it," she repeated. "He'll know something is wrong."

"You'll have to convince him that you are doing it as insurance against suspicion."

Finally Angelique relented, but her agreement proved to be anticlimactic. Instead of relief, Jean Claude felt more uptight than ever as he stood at a window watching O'Connor and his uncle escort her to his uncle's car. There was so much to do and no time to waste. Before long, they would have the press to contend with. Then there were funeral arrangements to be made for Marc, and later, the funeral. Because of Dora, he dreaded the funeral most of all.

The back of his eyes burned and he doubled his hands into fists when the Lincoln pulled onto the street. Something inside him twisted as it drove out of sight. Nothing would ever be the same again.

CHAPTER FOURTEEN

As SAMANTHA AND MARC crossed the short, narrow bridge separating the island resort from the mainland, she welcomed the steady breeze from the gulf. The sun had disappeared in the west, and already the temperature had begun to drop, bringing relief from the relentless heat.

No automobiles were allowed on the small strip of land, so there were no roads, just paved pathways. Residents either walked, rode bicycles, or drove golf carts.

Stepping off the bridge, Marc paused before deciding to take the path to the right. Samantha couldn't resist teasing him. "Pretty dull looking if you ask me. The condos all look alike. At least the Starlight Inn had red doors...and a shuttle service."

Marc groaned. "Don't remind me. My butt still hurts from bouncing around in the back of that pickup."

"The other passengers didn't seem to mind."

Marc turned to glare at her. "You're pushing it, Sam."

Samantha burst out laughing. Earlier that morning the old lady who managed the Starlight Inn had offered them a ride to the next town. She'd told them her doctor lived there and her babies had an appointment for a checkup. The doctor turned out to be a veterinarian and her babies were four basset hounds—two of which she said got carsick if they rode in the back. So Marc and Samantha had shared the bed of the pickup with the other two.

After that, they'd hitched two more rides, and it had been well past noon when they'd arrived at the motel Jean Claude had specified. Marc gave his name as Marc Brown, and the clerk handed over an envelope. Over lunch, Marc had told Samantha they would be staying in a condominium while a friend of his father's conducted the investigation.

Samantha frowned as they walked past the first complex of condos and approached a second one. Each time she'd questioned him about the investigation, he'd been vague and promptly changed the subject. Without asking her, he'd canceled their reservations at the motel. He'd seemed in a hurry to reach the condo—too much of a hurry. She had a feeling he was keeping something from her, but what?

The second complex was made up of five two-level condominiums, built side by side, all facing a center courtyard that included a pool. Each unit was made of weathered gray cedar and had its own deck facing a private, sugar-white sand beach. Beyond, the blue-green water of the gulf stretched out endlessly.

"Nice place," Samantha commented when Marc stopped at the second unit.

"A client of Jean Claude's owns the one next door." Marc knocked on the door.

"A client?"

"My cousin's an attorney. He has access to this particular client's properties." Just as Marc raised his hand to knock again, the door was opened by a middle-aged woman wearing a maid's uniform.

"Hello, ma'am. My name is Marc Brown." Marc motioned to Samantha. "My wife and I are guests of Jean Claude Dureaux. I believe he called about us."

"Oh, yes. Mr. and Mrs. Brown. Wait just a moment."
She turned to retrace her steps, calling over her shoulder,
"A special delivery package came for you yesterday."

"What if your cousin's client shows up?" Samantha
asked.

"He won't."

Samantha wondered how Marc could be so positive,
but before she could voice her question, the woman returned. The package she handed over was a thin, brown
envelope. Marc tucked it under his arm. "Thanks."

The housekeeper nodded and closed the door. Marc
headed toward the neighboring condo with Samantha
following close behind.

"How can you be sure... about the client?"

Marc halted in front of the door. After loosening the
clasp on the envelope, he slid his hand inside. "The man
is on safari in Africa and not expected back for two
months." Pulling out a key, he unlocked the door. "Besides, this is one of his winter homes."

"It's not exactly the Starlight Inn, is it?" Samantha
followed Marc inside and strolled over to a painting
hanging behind an overstuffed sofa. Her eyes widened
when she recognized the artist's scrawled name in the
lower right-hand corner. Most of his paintings hung in
museums. She cleared her throat. "I don't think I'll have
any trouble staying here for a few days."

Marc didn't comment, and she turned to catch him
staring at her, a brooding expression on his face.

"Marc?" She crossed the room. "Is something
wrong?" When she reached him, he suddenly pulled her
into his arms. For a moment he held her tightly, crushing
her against him as if memorizing each curve of her body.
He took a deep, shuddering breath.

"Sam... Oh, Sam," he whispered.

His lips covered hers in a desperate kiss that was both wild and passionate. Startled at first by his intensity, she held back. Then his lips softened and his tongue slipped into her mouth. The sensation was erotic; the effect, instantaneous. She buried her fingers in his hair. She couldn't seem to get close enough.

Marc's hands slipped beneath her shirt; he kneaded her lower back and then, holding her slightly away from him, he worked his magic around her sides to just beneath her breasts. For an eternity he seemed to hesitate and she trembled with anticipation. Then slowly, ever so achingly slowly, he finally cupped each breast. She moaned when she felt his thumbs rub gently over her nipples until they hardened.

She was on fire. She wanted more. *If you give in now, it will be the same as before. You'll be second best, second choice, someone expendable.* Samantha groaned and tried to block out the thoughts, but there was another consideration, one that rose above anything else. She loved Marc far more than she'd loved Clark, which meant Marc had the power to break her heart. She couldn't. She just couldn't risk it.

Samantha turned her head. "No...please," she whispered as she tried to push him away. "I...I can't."

For a moment he held her; she could feel his heartbeat thudding in rhythm with her own. Then, with a resigned sigh, he released her.

Without a word, he walked out the front door.

SAMANTHA SAT straight up. Disoriented, she peered into the darkness. Where was she? She'd dreamed she was still on the *Jenny*. That was impossible, she thought. The *Jenny* was gone...gone forever. But why the strange dream? Why the feeling of loss? Just nerves, she decided as she became more fully awake and began remembering.

Marc had been gone an hour before she heard him return. Only then had she been able to drift off to sleep.

For several minutes, Samantha listened and tried to figure out why the nagging feeling that something was wrong wouldn't go away. The condo was quiet, too quiet, she decided.

She groped in the dark for the lamp. Squinting against the sudden glare, she picked up her watch. It was five a.m. For a moment she hesitated. Finally, she threw back the covers and stood up. She slipped on the robe she'd found earlier and started down the hallway toward the kitchen. As she passed the door to the other bedroom, she paused in the open doorway. The full moon shed a soft glow over the bed—the empty bed.

Her heart began to pound. "Marc," she called out. Only silence greeted her call. She raised her voice; there was still no answer. An urgency gripped her—an urgency she couldn't rationalize. She rushed through the house flipping on the lights. When she'd checked every room and found each empty, she hurried back to her bedroom.

Maybe he was on the beach. Yes, of course. He was on the beach. As she reached for her shorts, a flash of white on the dresser caught her attention. Slowly she picked up the fat envelope. Her name was scrawled across it. Funny, she thought, she'd never seen Marc's handwriting, but somehow she knew it was his. Her breathing grew painful, her chest tightened as she pulled out the contents. Money—a fistful of fifties and hundreds. And a note.

Samantha laid the money back on the dresser. Her hand shook as she unfolded the single sheet of paper. For a moment the words blurred and she could hardly read them He'd left— taken off without as much as a goodbye. Or had he? Had the kiss been his way of saying goodbye?

The note said he'd decided to do his own investigation, that he didn't trust Jean Claude. Suddenly, she wadded the note and hurled it across the room. With her other hand, she swept the money off the dresser top; it scattered, floating gently to the carpet.

After everything that had happened, everything they'd been through, how could he do it? How could he just pick up and leave? Shaking with fury, she bent over and picked up her shorts. If he thought he could take off without her, he had another think coming. Samantha searched the room for her shirt. She spied it crumpled beneath the bedspread. She'd follow him all the way to New Orleans if she had to. She had just as much at stake as he did.

When she'd finished buttoning her shirt, she snatched up several of the hundred-dollar bills and stuffed them into her pocket. She was going to need some fast transportation—a taxi. After a moment's hesitation, she gathered up the rest of the money. She didn't want to be caught short. She glanced around. Where was the telephone book? She headed for the kitchen.

Samantha figured Marc would probably travel the scenic highway that ran along the coast; he wouldn't chance the interstate. After opening several drawers, she took out the phone book. Thumbing through the Yellow Pages, she found the taxi listings, but changed her mind.

What the hell, she thought as she turned to the *L*s. She might have to go all the way to New Orleans. Samantha punched out the number to the only limo service in the area. After six rings, a sleepy voice finally answered.

"Lady, do you know what time it is?" was the man's reply after she'd told him what she wanted.

"Mister, I'll give you an extra hundred if you can be at the bridge in fifteen minutes." Patting her pocket, Samantha hung up.

MARC STUCK OUT his thumb, but the car whizzed by. He'd only had one ride and it hadn't taken him far. He glanced over his shoulder, then readjusted his knapsack and started walking again. For the most part, the road was empty. Too early yet, he thought, but traffic would pick up at daybreak.

The dark, lonely highway stretched out for miles with only a few stars and the full moon to light the way. His heart grew heavier with each step he took. He'd been so positive leaving Samantha behind was the right thing to do. Now he wasn't so sure.

Antonio Manchetti was a dangerous man. If something went wrong, if Manchetti somehow found out they were still alive, Samantha would be all alone, with no one to protect her.

Only two more cars passed before daybreak. One went by without slowing, and he missed the other one because he'd stepped off the road to take his canteen from his knapsack. His anxiety over Samantha was increasing by the minute. Up ahead, he could see the outskirts of a town. Several buildings lined the highway. Rising above one was the familiar logo of a convenience store. Marc quickened his steps. Convenience stores usually had pay phones.

As he approached the store, he noticed three cars parked in front. The long black limo in the middle looked incongruous between a beat-up Mustang and a Chevy truck. Maybe the limo was headed east and he could hitch a ride... back to Samantha.

Still smiling, he walked past the cars to the front of the store, pushed open the glass door and stepped inside. The blast of cool air was a welcome relief, and the smell of brewing coffee drifted in the air. Suddenly, he froze. His smile faded. Leaning against the checkout counter with her arms crossed was Samantha.

"What took you so long?" she asked.

Marc slowly lowered his knapsack to the floor. The look on her face belied her thin smile. That look meant trouble—big trouble.

"Here's your coffee, ma'am."

Marc narrowed his eyes when Samantha accepted a steaming cup from a young man dressed in a chauffeur's uniform.

"You did say two sugars?"

She smiled. "Yes, that's fine. Thank you, Bill."

Marc lifted one eyebrow. Bill?

"Anything else, ma'am?"

"No," she answered. "You can wait in the car. We'll be out shortly."

Car could only mean one thing—the limo. But how the hell had she managed to get ahead of him? He'd seen every car that had passed . . . except one. Marc stepped aside for Bill to get by, then turned his attention to Samantha. She was paying for the coffee. As she handed the cashier the money, she called over her shoulder. "Do you want anything before we leave? Some coffee? Something to eat?"

Marc walked over to the refreshment center. "Just coffee," he answered.

"Add his to the tab, too," Samantha told the cashier. "And don't forget the gas."

As Marc poured the coffee, he tried to decide how he was going to explain leaving her. From all appearances, he was going to pay and pay dearly. He hoped for Bill's sake the limo had a privacy window.

"Ready?"

Marc grabbed the knapsack and nodded.

"Where are we going?" he asked as he followed her into the back seat of the car. She didn't answer, but the limo pulled out onto the highway heading west.

Miles sped by in complete silence. It reminded Marc of their first day on the *Jenny*. She'd been mad as hell then, too. He glanced over at her, but she was sitting sideways, staring out the window. Her hair was pulled back and secured with a rubber band.

A slight movement of her hand followed by a suspicious sniff brought his attention back to her face. He tentatively touched her shoulder.

"Sam..."

Shoving his hand aside, Samantha jerked around to face him. "Don't touch me you...you... Just don't." Even though tears poured down her cheeks, her eyes were glassy hard.

"Will you at least let me explain? I was only trying to protect you. I thought it best if—"

"I don't give a damn what you thought. You didn't have to sneak off like some...some... Come to think of it, you're pretty good at sneaking off."

Marc tried to remain calm. "That has nothing to do with this."

"It has everything to do with this. That first day on the boat, I asked you to take me back and you refused. You had your chance and blew it. So from here on out, like it or not, you're stuck with me."

"Promise?"

"And if you think—what did you say?"

"I said, do you promise I'm stuck with you?"

"I...I..."

Marc grinned. "Just for the record, I stopped at that store back there to call you. I'd already decided leaving you behind wasn't such a great idea. And don't look at me like that. I swear it's the truth."

Samantha sniffed. "Then why didn't you say so in the first place?"

"Would you have believed me?"

"What makes you think I believe you now?"

Marc groaned. "Would an oath in blood help?"

"Probably not," she shot back. And then she smiled.

The sound of Bill clearing his throat caused both Samantha and Marc to glance toward the driver.

"Excuse me," he said.

"What is it, Bill?" Samantha asked.

Bill continued to face the front, but his eyes, bright with amusement, were clearly visible in the rearview mirror. "Now that you folks have finished your...ah...discussion, may I ask you something?"

"Sure," Marc answered.

"When Ms. Brown hired me, she didn't say exactly where we were going."

Raising one eyebrow in a silent question, Marc looked at Samantha. When she nodded, he smiled. "Home, Bill. Home to New Orleans."

SAMANTHA HAD BEEN to New Orleans several times over the years, but the most memorable was when as a child, she had come during Mardi Gras. What she remembered most were the colorful floats, the flashy costumes, and sitting on her father's shoulders being showered with glass beads and trinkets the natives called throws.

This time, there would be no Mardi Gras, no frivolous gaiety. This visit would be different—secretive and dangerous. Samantha shivered and glanced at Marc. He'd leaned forward to tell Bill which exit to take. Would his being here make any difference? He seemed to think it would. Or had he allowed his suspicions of his cousin to cloud his better judgment? If someone recognized him, the whole elaborate ruse would have been for nothing.

Marc leaned back and slipped his arm around her shoulders. "Having second thoughts?"

"No," she answered, and without thinking, automatically snuggled closer to the warmth and security his body offered. She turned her head to peer up at him. "Well...maybe a few," she whispered. "I'm not sure I understand what you hope to accomplish. What can you do that isn't already being done?" She paused. His beard had grown longer and was a little scraggly. Her fingers itched to smooth it out, but she clenched her hand into a fist instead. "What if someone recognizes you?" she finally asked.

"I'm not really sure I can do anything, except check up on Jean Claude. His sudden concern for my welfare makes me nervous. He's never done anything for me unless he stood to gain something for himself. As far as being recognized, this—" he reached up and stroked his beard "—should help. I've never worn a beard before."

Even though his explanations seemed logical, Samantha felt apprehension settle over her like a cloak of doom.

Once the limo exited off the interstate, Marc guided Bill through the narrow streets.

"Where are we going?" she asked.

"I have a friend, an old childhood friend, who lives near the Quarter. We'll stay with him."

"Won't that be risky?" She glanced at Bill, then lowered her voice to a whisper. "What if your friend lets it slip we're still alive? What if—"

Marc leaned over. "Stop worrying," he whispered back. "I trust Ray."

Within minutes, Marc had Bill stop the limo. "We'll walk from here," he explained.

Bill opened the door, and Samantha stepped out onto the almost-deserted street. A stale smell permeated the air, and although it wasn't offensive, it wasn't exactly pleasant. Samantha wrinkled her nose as she peered up at the two- and three-storied, time-scarred buildings, which flanked both sides of the street, making it appear even narrower than it was. Intricate wrought-iron balconies lined the upper levels.

Marc conferred with Bill for several minutes over his fee, then turned to Samantha. "You'll have to pay him. I only have a fifty. You have the rest."

Not until that moment had she realized Marc had left her most of the money. She'd accused him of sneaking off, of dumping her, but his unselfish gesture touched her. He really had been concerned for her safety. She was suffused with a warm feeling. Samantha dug in her pocket and pulled out the money, handing it all to Marc.

Marc counted out Bill's fee, adding an extra hundred. "Spend the night and see the city tomorrow," he said as he shook the driver's hand. "And thanks for everything."

Samantha added her thanks and watched until the limo pulled away from the curb.

"Ready?" Marc grabbed the knapsack, then took Samantha's hand.

"How far does your friend Ray live?" she asked as they crossed the street, lined on both sides with typical French Quarter apartments.

"About a block from here."

A few minutes later, Marc stopped in front of an oak-framed doorway and pushed the doorbell.

"What if he's not home?"

Marc glanced at his watch. "He should be. He got off work about an hour ago."

Just then a muffled voice called out, "Who's there?"

"Ray, it's Marc. Open the door."

"What the hell— If this is some kind of sick joke—" The door swung open.

Marc's friend was tall, blond, and built like an Olympic weight lifter. His size, along with the scowl marring his rough features, made Samantha unconsciously move closer to Marc.

"My God!" Ray grabbed Marc in a bear hug. "It *is* you," he said as he pounded Marc's back. "I thought—" He held him at arm's length. "You're supposed to be dead."

Marc grinned. "As you can see, I'm not. Can we come in?"

"You sure as hell better. You've got a lot of explaining to do." Then, for the first time, Ray noticed Samantha. "You must be that Bradford broa—lady."

"Her name's Sam." Marc stepped aside. "Sam," he said, motioning toward Ray. "Meet Ray Fielding, the best friend any man could have."

Samantha smiled and offered her hand. His grip was surprisingly gentle for such a large man.

"Guess I'll have to watch my mouth with a lady around," he said as he ushered them through the door. "Excuse the mess. I didn't expect company."

Ray's "mess" was due to the ongoing renovation of the small living room in his French Quarter apartment. Two of the walls were paneled, while the other two were covered with torn, yellowed wallpaper. Side by side were a recliner that had seen better days and a sofa still wrapped in protective plastic.

"So what's this stuff about you getting yourself blown up? Man, they're having your funeral tomorrow." Ray's eyes narrowed. "That damned business with the governor. It has something to do with that, doesn't it?"

Marc dropped the knapsack on the floor. "If you've got some coffee, I'll explain everything."

"Sure," he replied. "Come on out to the kitchen."

"Marc." Samantha touched Marc's arm. "Would it be impolite if I lie down somewhere? I know it's still early, but I'm really tired."

Marc looked at Ray. "Ray, we need somewhere to hang out for a while. Do you have a couple of extra beds?"

"You know I do," he answered. "This way, little lady."

Ray pointed out the bathroom as he led Samantha down a narrow hallway. "Just make yourself at home and holler if you need anything. Your bedroom is the second door on the left."

"Thanks... for everything," she replied.

He nodded, then turned to retrace his steps.

Samantha glanced around the spacious bedroom. It was sparse on furnishings but neat and clean. There wasn't a speck of dust anywhere; she wondered what kind of man Ray really was. Though a little intimidated by his size, he had a gentleness about him she liked, and she hoped, for Marc's sake, that he was right about his friend when he said Ray could be trusted.

A soft knock sounded at the door before it opened. Marc stepped in and handed her a neatly folded T-shirt. "Thought you might feel more comfortable sleeping in this."

"Thanks," she whispered, touched by his thoughtfulness. Clothes to sleep in, or any other kind, had been the farthest thing from her mind.

"You're welcome," he said, and before she had time to protest, he leaned over and kissed her. An unexpected shock wave of desire shot through her at the touch of his warm, moist lips, and she trembled. Everything they had been through flashed through her mind—the storm in the gulf, the scare the drunk had given them and the moment the boat had exploded. The reality of their situation—the fact that Marc could die—made her ache with a longing she couldn't control. Samantha knew that at that moment she wanted him more than anyone she'd ever wanted before. She wanted to feel the hardness of his taut body pressed against hers until there was no defining the two, until they were one.

As if Marc had read her mind, he pulled her into his arms.

They fit perfectly, she thought. From head to toe, as if they had been made for each other.

Marc tightened his hold on her. "Ah, Sam, let me hold you." He nuzzled her neck. "I need your warmth and your strength right now."

Samantha didn't protest or pull away. It no longer mattered that he might never be free of the hold Angelique had on him, and it no longer mattered he might never completely love her in return. The love she felt for him, the love she'd tried to deny, was strong enough for them both. At the moment she'd take whatever he could offer. If he needed her, she'd be there for him. Samantha wrapped her arms around his neck and threaded her fingers through his hair. She pulled his head up until their lips met again.

His groan of satisfaction vibrated through her as his lips pressed against her. Then she felt his hands slide beneath her shirt and she shivered in anticipation. His fingers cupped her breasts, and a shudder of pleasure rippled inside her when his thumbs began to stroke her nipples.

"Ah, Sam," he breathed against her mouth. "So soft, so giving." He trailed a line of kisses to the vee of her blouse. As if by mutual consent, she loosened her hold and slid her hands down the sides of his arms. With trembling clumsiness, she unbuttoned her blouse, then guided his head downward. His mouth fastened around one breast as his hand continued to knead the other. Her insides quivered and convulsed as he suckled, and all she could do was hold on to him while wave after wave of desire pulsed through her body.

When Samantha cried out, Marc pulled her hard against him and held her close. "Oh, God," he whispered. "More than anything, I want to be with you, inside you." His voice was ragged and breathless with his own need for release. He cursed softly and he held her for a moment longer. "I'm sorry," he said. "I shouldn't have let things go this far. But now is not the time or place, not with Ray waiting in the kitchen."

Samantha bit her lip in frustration as she felt the heat of embarrassment creep up her neck to her face. Marc was right. She'd forgotten all about his friend. And even though her body cried out for more, she knew she would have been mortified if Ray had walked in on them.

Marc stepped back and trailed his forefinger between her breasts. "You're one hell of a woman, Samantha Bradford."

She watched him leave the room, and for several moments she couldn't move or breathe; her skin continued to tingle where he'd touched her.

Later as she lay on the narrow bed, she could still feel a trembly sensation in the pit of her stomach, and she wondered if there ever would be a time or place for them.

CHAPTER FIFTEEN

MARC FACED a scowling Ray across the square oak table. After explaining the situation, he'd hoped Ray would help, or at least sympathize. But Ray hadn't been the least bit sympathetic. He thought Marc was being foolhardy and he tried every argument possible to persuade him to return to Florida. At one point, afraid their raised voices had disturbed Samantha, Marc had left to check on her. But she'd been sound asleep. When he'd returned to the kitchen, Ray had started in again.

"I don't like it, man," he said. "You're playing with fire. These are the big boys we're talking about—not the weak-kneed politicians you're used to dealing with."

"Ray, they think I'm dead. My God, the damn funeral is tomorrow."

Ray snorted. "I still don't like it. Let the feds handle it. Go back to Florida."

Marc shook his head. "I can't do that—"

"Yes, you can," Ray interrupted, his voice growing louder. "What about your lady friend in there?" He pointed toward the hallway. "Don't you care what happens to her? If those bastards get hold of her, she won't be worth burying. Have you thought about that?"

"You don't understand."

"I understand all right I understand you're stubborn and pigheaded"

The silence in the kitchen crackled with tension as the two men glared at each other, neither willing to concede his point. Ray was the first to break the impasse.

"Aw, hell." Ray shoved his chair back. He grabbed his and Marc's mugs and stomped over to the counter. "Do what you please. You will anyway," he mumbled, reaching for the coffeepot.

Marc took a deep breath, then released it slowly. Some of the tension of the past hour eased from his body. "Can we stay here?"

Ray walked back to the table and shoved a mug across to Marc. "What do you think?"

A slow smile formed on Marc's lips. "I think you're a foulmouthed son of a bitch with a heart as big as Lake Pontchartrain."

Suddenly, Ray grinned from ear to ear. "You always did have a way with words, Dureaux." He straddled a chair and took a swallow of coffee.

"Yeah, and I'd forgotten how you enjoy playing the devil's advocate."

For several moments, Ray didn't reply as he stared down at his mug. Then he shifted in his chair and looked up at Marc. "Have you told the little lady about Angelique?"

It was Marc's turn to lower his gaze. "Yeah, I told her." When he finally raised his head, his eyes reflected the anguish he felt. "Sam thinks I still care about Angelique, that I'll take her back." His voice was barely above a whisper. "What scares me is that I'll lose Sam."

For the first time since they'd begun discussing the situation, Ray's expression softened. "Have you told Sam you love her?"

Marc frowned "I don't know if you could call it love. All I know is I don't want to lose her. She makes me feel . . . well . . . as if life has meaning, as if there's more to life than just existing."

"Hell, man. If that ain't love, I don't know what is."

"Maybe," said Marc. "But I can't tell her anything yet, not until I do what I came here to do, not until this mess is cleared up."

Ray twisted and reached toward a bundle of newspapers stacked beside the table. Pulling one off the top, he slid out a section and handed it to Marc. "Then we've got our job cut out for us." He pointed at the paper. "Take a look at that."

Marc's eyes widened as he spotted the black-and-white picture of Angelique. The caption beneath the picture read: Angelique Dureaux, Wife of Journalist Marc Dureaux. A lengthy article about the socially prominent Dureaux family accompanied the photo. Then he read the final paragraph.

"Something's fishy here," Marc said as he read it again. The last paragraph stated that Mrs. Dureaux would be unable to attend the memorial services for her husband. It said that after finding out about his death, Angelique had suffered a mental breakdown and had been confined to Oakview Sanitarium in LeFay, Louisiana. Marc looked up at Ray. "This can't be right. I can't see my dear wife having a breakdown over losing me."

"I thought it was kind of strange, too, but then what do I know? Maybe they planned it . . . you know, to make things look more realistic."

"Maybe." Marc paused to stare past Ray's head. "But why Oakview? There are plenty of good hospitals in the city . . . unless . . ." Turning his gaze back to Ray, he said, "Maybe Jean Claude's been lying all along."

"What makes you think that?"

"My cousin's an ambitious man. He sees himself as the next governor. He's not above using any means he can to get there."

Ray shook his head. "I don't follow you. What does putting Angelique in a hospital have to do with that?"

Marc frowned. "I'm not sure yet. With the governor dead and Landry's chances possibly ruined by the publicity, Jean Claude would have a damn good shot at winning the election. What if Jean Claude was the one who set up the assassination? Since I'm the only eyewitness to the governor's murder, he might think I could trace the killers back to him."

Ray looked puzzled. "I still don't see what that has to do with Angelique?"

Marc twisted his mouth into a cynical smile. "I've suspected for a long time my dear wife has been having an affair. If her affair was with my cousin, then she might know too much. What better way to keep her quiet than to have her committed?"

"Jesus, man. I had no idea, I mean about Angelique having an affair. I'm sorry."

Marc waved away Ray's concern. "There's no way you could have known. Even now, I can't prove anything."

"And Manchetti? How does he figure into all this?"

Suddenly weary, Marc closed his eyes. "Damned if I know. I'm so tired, I can't even think straight anymore. Maybe things will make more sense tomorrow."

Ray pushed out of his chair. "Go on to bed." He bent to gather the stack of newspapers. "I'll put these outside in the garbage. No use worrying Sam."

"Thanks, Ray," Marc said as he stood up and stretched. "I really do appreciate all this."

Straightening, Ray walked to the kitchen door, then paused. "What are friends for?"

THE FOLLOWING MORNING, Marc eased out of bed. The night before, he'd been filled with unanswered questions about Jean Claude and Angelique; sleep had been a long time coming, and had been erratic at best. As quietly as possible, he tiptoed past Samantha's room.

Across the hallway, he could still hear Ray snoring. Marc went to the kitchen and started a pot of coffee. While it brewed, he checked outside the front door for the morning paper. After quickly scanning each page, he found what he was looking for. There was a short obituary, which included the date, time and place of his funeral. It also listed the survivors.

A noise in the hallway caused him to look up. Ray shuffled in and Marc grinned. "You always could smell coffee a mile away."

Just as he'd expected, Ray didn't answer. Over the years, Marc had learned the hard way that Ray was definitely not a morning person.

Marc shoved the paper toward Ray and pointed at the obituary. Ray scanned the notice but only grunted.

When his friend hadn't made a move to leave after he'd drunk a second cup, Marc glanced at the wall clock, then back to Ray. "Aren't you going to work?" Ray was employed by a company that designed and built the elaborate floats for Mardi Gras. Most people didn't realize the annual celebration took all year to prepare for.

Ray shook his head. "Nope. Started my vacation Monday. Took two weeks so I could work on the house and maybe get in some painting."

"Your stuff selling?"

Ray shrugged. "Some. Right now I'm working on a one-man show for Jade's on Royal."

Marc raised his eyebrows. "Jade's? *The* Jade's?" he asked.

"Yeah," Ray growled. "So what?"

"Nothing. That's great." Marc could have sworn Ray's cheeks turned red, but he knew better than to say so. Ray was sensitive about his art.

"What's great?" Samantha asked as she wandered through the doorway and made a beeline for the coffee-pot.

As Marc watched her cross the room, he smiled. She'd borrowed his clothes . . . again. "I like your shorts, Sam. They never looked that good on me."

Ignoring him, Samantha turned to Ray. "He likes to change the subject, too—when it suits him."

Ray chuckled. "Yeah, I know. But I have to agree with Marc. There's something about the way those shorts hang—"

"Great. Just great." Samantha groaned and rolled her eyes upward. "Now there's two of them."

Ray looked at Marc and they burst out laughing.

This time, Samantha ignored them both. "Is that this morning's paper?"

When she reached for the newspaper, Ray suddenly lurched forward and grabbed it, snatching it from beneath her fingers. "You can't read the paper. . . . I mean, you don't have time . . . that is . . ." He glared at Marc.

Samantha glanced from one man to the other, a puzzled expression on her face. "Am I missing something here? You two are acting kind of strange."

"Ray was just . . . ah . . . concerned. He thought you might get upset. They're holding my—a mock funeral for me today. And it's listed under the 'Deaths.'" Samantha turned pale and her hands clutched the back of a chair. Marc could have kicked himself. "They have to, Sam," he said. "It's the only way to make sure the whole setup is believable."

"I heard Ray mention that last night, but I didn't think... Will they do that... will I have one, too?"

Instantly Marc understood. "Oh, Sam." He stood up and pulled her into his arms. "I don't know, but I'll try to find out." He nuzzled the top of her head.

Samantha allowed herself the luxury of being in Marc's arms for a moment. She wished she had the right to be there always, but that right didn't belong to her, she reminded herself. She pulled away. "It's just that... well...now that Gram's gone, there's no family left to take care of arrangements for me." Samantha paused to take a deep breath. "Maybe Mr. Potter will handle things."

"Who's Mr. Potter?" Ray asked.

"Gram's attorney—my attor— Oh, no!" She glared at Marc. "Do you have any idea what this means? If everyone thinks I'm dead, what will happen to my inheritance?"

"Sam, Sam. It's okay. You're forgetting the FBI helped plan this. Later, when everything is settled, I'm sure they'll straighten it out."

Samantha stiffened. "They damned well better. I haven't spent a penny of it yet."

Marc chuckled. "That a girl. Give 'em hell."

Ray eased out of his chair, reached for the coffeepot and poured Samantha a cup. "Cream or sugar?" he asked.

Marc laughed again. "Drink your coffee, tiger. Then we'll see about some clothes for you."

MARC GLANCED from his watch to the phone. The Mass would be over by now. If only he could talk with his father, maybe he could get some straight answers. All morning, nagging doubts had plagued him. Until he'd read about Angelique, he'd almost begun to believe Jean Claude was trying to help him.

Marc walked to the kitchen window. The small enclosed patio overflowed with subtropical greenery and looked cool and peaceful. But it was an illusion. The temperature was ninety-eight in the shade. Had Jean Claude fabricated an equally effective illusion? Marc wondered. Had his cousin deceived him and everyone else all along? And how were Angelique and Manchetti tied in? Marc stared at the phone. He'd wait a few more minutes and then he'd call.

Marc cocked his head and listened. Except for the occasional muffled voices of Ray and Samantha, the house was quiet. Earlier, he and Ray had taken her to a small, out-of-the-way boutique so she could purchase clothes. Marc smiled, remembering the shopping expedition. She'd taken one look at the price tags and refused to buy anything. Instead, she'd insisted on going back to another shop they'd passed that advertised secondhand clothes. When Marc had protested, she'd called him a snob.

After they'd returned, Ray had excused himself, then disappeared upstairs to his studio on the second floor. When Samantha had learned Ray was an artist, she'd been delighted and curious. Against Marc's advice, she'd followed Ray. Marc had been surprised when she didn't return right away. Ray didn't usually allow anyone in his studio.

Again Marc glanced at his watch. He needed to place the call before Samantha returned. He stepped over to the phone and punched out the number. There was no use worrying her unnecessarily. She'd only ask questions he couldn't answer. After the fourth ring, Jean Claude answered.

"Where the hell have you been? I've tried calling the condo several times. Did something go wrong? The money? The key?"

"Nothing's wrong," Marc answered curtly. "Everything went as planned."

"That's a relief. Your dad's been worried sick."

"Let me talk to him."

"He's not here right now."

Marc scowled. "When will he be there?"

"I'm not sure. He and Dora are gone. Marc, we couldn't tell her the truth, and she's pretty broken up. Uncle Edward thought it would do her good to get away for a few hours."

"Jesus." Marc tightened his grip on the phone. "Why the hell didn't you tell her?" He could just imagine her reaction. "That was a damned cruel thing to do—"

"I know, I know. But O'Connor insisted. Said it would be more realistic. Besides, we can't chance a leak."

"Dammit!" Marc gritted his teeth. "She's family."

"Marc, will you calm down?"

He closed his eyes and took a deep breath. Losing his temper wouldn't give him the answers he needed. "So...why were you trying to call us?"

"Uncle Edward just wanted to make sure you and the Bradford woman were okay."

"Tell him we're fine." Marc paused. "Jean Claude, does Angelique think I'm dead, too?" Marc knew, according to the newspaper, she did, but he wanted to hear what Jean Claude had to say about it.

After several moments, Jean Claude finally answered. "Yes, she does."

"Well?"

"Well what?"

Marc gripped the phone tighter. "How did she react?"

"How do you think she reacted? She was . . . upset."

His cousin's voice sounded peculiar, and his answer had been hesitant—a little too hesitant. Out of curiosity, Marc decided to probe a little further, to see how much of the truth Jean Claude would tell him. "Where is she now?" he asked.

"She's safe—I mean she's . . . she's in a hospital. Just for a rest," he quickly added.

Several moments later, Marc hung up the phone. He was more convinced than ever his cousin was up to something. Could his suspicions about Jean Claude's involvement in the assassination be true? Jean Claude had definitely sounded nervous when he'd questioned him about Angelique.

"Marc? Who were you talking to?"

Marc turned to face Samantha. "Jean Claude," he answered.

Samantha stepped into the room. "Did you have an argument with him?"

"No. What makes you think that?"

"You look like you could chew nails."

"Jean Claude has that effect on me."

"Hmm, I see." She tilted her head and frowned. "Are you keeping anything from me? Has something happened I should know about?"

Marc reached up and rubbed the back of his neck. "I didn't want to worry you. Last night Ray showed me a write-up about Angelique. It said she was so bereaved over my, ah . . . death that she'd had a mental breakdown and had to be committed to a hospital."

When Marc saw Samantha's eyes grow wide with shock, he rushed on. "For one thing, Angelique is just not that type. If anything, she'd be out celebrating, especially if she thought she might get some insurance money.

And just now, when I asked Jean Claude about her, he admitted she was in the hospital, but he sounded nervous."

"In what way?" Samantha asked.

"I can't really explain it, except that he made a slip. He said she was safe. Call it instinct or paranoia, but why would he say something like that?"

Samantha raised her eyebrows. "None of that makes any sense. Why would she need to be safe? And from who or what?"

"I wish the hell I knew. From the beginning, this whole mess has been confusing. At first I thought it was a simple matter. I'd seen the governor assassinated and the man responsible for it put out a contract on me, and I thought that man was Manchetti. But now I'm not so sure. What if Angelique knew too much?"

"Knew too much about what? And why would your wife have anything to do with your cousin?"

Marc sighed. "Because I suspect my cousin is the man my dear wife is divorcing me for."

Samantha winced at his bitter tone. No wonder he'd been suspicious of Jean Claude's willingness to help. No wonder he didn't trust his cousin. Suddenly, a thought occurred to her.

"Marc. Do you know which hospital she's in?"

Marc nodded. "It was in the newspaper."

Samantha began to pace, then stopped in front of him. "Why don't you ask her?"

"Ask who?"

"Angelique." Without waiting for him to comment, she hurried on. "If there was some way you could get in to see her and talk with her, then you'd know."

"That's the craziest idea I've heard yet. Just how the hell am I supposed to do that? Do you know how many security guards they have in those hospitals?" He shook his head. "No, there has to be another way."

But there wasn't. The longer he thought about it, the more he realized Samantha was right. If he wanted to get to the truth, he was going to have to figure out a way to talk with Angelique.

CHAPTER SIXTEEN

MARC FROWNED at the eastbound traffic on the bridge; it was bumper to bumper. As he approached the peak, he shifted down to pass the eighteen wheeler he'd been tailing. His head was pounding, and through the open windows of Ray's Jeep, the diesel smell from the big truck was pungent, making him feel even more nauseated. Maybe he was having sympathy pains with Samantha, he thought.

Poor Ray had blamed himself and the spicy gumbo he'd prepared the night before. But Samantha had insisted she'd picked up a twenty-four-hour bug. She'd still been asleep when he'd left.

By the time Marc reached LeFay, his head felt better and the queasiness had passed. The small town was located in the middle of nowhere. Other than a café, a bank and a grocery store, the hospital and a chemical plant were the only means of support for the people living there.

For the next hour, Marc sat in the parking lot of the hospital and studied the layout of the grounds. By noon, the heat was unbearable, so he ventured inside the reception area. Large and comfortable, the room was decorated in soothing shades of green and peach and was a cool contrast to the heat of the parking lot. Near the entrance door, the receptionist sat in a small alcove behind a sliding glass window. Scooping up a magazine from a nearby table, Marc headed for a chair in a corner where he could just sit and observe without drawing her attention.

It didn't take him long to realize that getting in to see Angelique wasn't going to be easy. Security around the place was as tight as that of a prison. To protect their privacy, each patient was assigned a number, and only family and friends were given that number. Without it, the receptionist wouldn't acknowledge the patient even existed. It didn't matter that the whole world knew Angelique was there. An authorized visitor would be expected to know her number.

Marc leaned forward in the chair and stared at the glass window. If only there was some way to get a quick look at the patient list. But how? Another hour passed, and he'd just about decided he'd have to give up when a man wearing a utility belt walked up to the receptionist.

"Phone company," the man announced. "Heard you were having problems with line four."

"Bingo," Marc whispered between his teeth. Casually, he stood up, tossed the magazine on the chair and strolled out the front door. Glancing backward, he noted the evening visiting hours posted on a sign. By then there would be a different receptionist.

Marc immediately spotted the phone truck. Just as he'd thought, the vehicle was unlocked. Glancing toward the hospital entrance, he opened the passenger door. He couldn't believe his luck. On the floor was another utility belt. Quickly he grabbed it, shut the door and headed straight for the Jeep. Throwing the belt inside, he looked up in time to see the phone man emerge from the entrance of the hospital.

Marc slid into the Jeep and waited until the truck pulled out onto the highway and disappeared, then he glanced at his watch. He had about three hours to kill before evening visitation, and he needed to find a pay phone to check on Samantha. He started the Jeep, reversed out of the parking spot and headed for the café he'd passed earlier.

"SAM, Marc's on the phone."

Samantha threw aside the book she'd picked up to read and raced past Ray toward the kitchen.

"Have you see her?" she said the minute she'd snatched up the receiver. "I've been worried sick all day."

"Whoa, slow down, Sam. I take it you're feeling better?"

"I'm fine," she said. "Never mind that. What did she say?"

Marc groaned. "I haven't seen her yet, but I think I've figured out how to get in."

"Well?" When Marc didn't say anything, she made an exasperated sound. "I'm waiting. Tell me."

"Have you eaten anything today?"

"Yes. Some soup. Stop trying to change the subject."

Marc chuckled. "Just wanted to check on you and let you know I won't be back until late."

"Marc Dureaux, don't you dare hang up."

Grinning, Marc hung up the phone and headed for the café.

Three hours later, he checked the time and signaled the waitress for his check. Back at the hospital, he strapped on the utility belt, took a deep breath and headed for the door.

Marc approached the receptionist's desk and waited. At first, the young woman ignored him and continued typing. When he cleared his throat, she looked up.

"May I help you, sir?"

Marc gave her his most winning smile. "Phone company. Got a call that said line four was giving you problems."

The woman frowned. "I haven't had any problems with it."

Marc's heart began to pound. He had to get behind that desk. "Look, lady, it's no sweat off me. Whether I look at it or not, I'll have to charge you for the service call."

Still frowning, the woman stood up. "I suppose since you're here, you might as well check it. Go through the hall to the first door on your right. I'll let you in."

Marc met her at the door, then followed her through a short, narrow hallway. Once at the desk, he pretended to examine the phone and hoped the woman knew less about servicing a telephone than he did. Out of the corner of his eye, he spotted the patient list. But as precious seconds ticked by, he grew more and more uneasy. The woman stood beside the desk fidgeting like a guardian angel with ants in her pants, and he was running out of things to check. With her watching him, there was no way he could search through the list.

"Is this going to take long?" she blurted out.

Marc looked up. Her cheeks were tinged pink and she avoided his direct gaze. "Not too much longer. I think I've found the problem, but I just want to make sure."

"Could I ask a favor?" She quickly glanced at him, then looked away. "If anyone comes in, just have them wait until I get back. And if anyone asks...I mean like...well, just tell them I had to go the ladies' room." She began backing out of the alcove toward the hallway. "I'll only be a minute."

"Sure. No problem," Marc called out. The minute the door closed, he grabbed the list. The names were alphabetized. He flipped over to the Ds. Within seconds, he'd found Angelique's name, patient number and approved visitors. There were only three: Patrick O'Connor, Jean Claude Dureaux and Harold Caldwell. Marc recognized the last name as a prominent defense attorney. Grabbing a pen, he jotted down the patient number on a nearby notepad, tore off the sheet and tucked it into his pocket.

When the woman returned, Marc made a show of punching each of the lines again, then hung up the receiver. "That about does it," he said as he started down the hallway. "If you have any more problems, just give us a call."

IT WAS DUSK by the time Marc hit the New Orleans city limits. With most of the rush-hour traffic cleared, he made good time as he wove through the narrow streets toward Ray's.

When he let himself in with the key his friend had given him, he was greeted by silence. The house was dark except for a faint line of light coming from beneath the bedroom door down the hallway.

"Sam," he called out softly, but there was no answer. He walked toward the bedroom and eased open the door.

For a moment he stood there and simply stared. Lying against several pillows, Samantha was stretched out on the bed. Sound asleep, she still clasped an open book with one hand, but her other hand was lying palm up. In the warm glow of the lamp, she looked almost ethereal—a wraith beckoning him to join her.

Marc quietly closed the door behind him and walked over to the bed. He eased the book from beneath her fingers and laid it on the night table. Her lids fluttered, then opened, and she smiled.

"Marc."

Her voice was husky from sleep. She held out her hand. "I had the most wonderful dream."

He took her hand and knelt beside the bed. "Tell me about it."

Her gaze held his as she began talking. "I dreamed we were on the *Jenny* again, but this time no one was chasing us. We had all the time in the world."

Marc braced himself with his arms on either side of her shoulders. With the tip of his finger, he traced a line down her jaw to her lips, then closed his eyes for a moment. He wanted to tell her he would buy another boat, that the next time they sailed, they really would have all the time in the world, but most of all, he wanted to tell her he loved her and beg her to love him in return.

Marc sighed and pulled away. "The *Jenny* was a beautiful boat," he said instead, knowing he didn't have the right to tell her what was in his heart. His future was too uncertain for him to even dream of a life with her.

HAIR CUT and beard closely trimmed, Marc walked up to the receptionist. Dressed in a suit and carrying a briefcase, he hoped he projected the image of a successful attorney. "I'm here to see my client," he said. "Patient fifty-four eighty-six."

The woman looked up and smiled. "Your name?"

"Brown, Jack Brown of Harold Caldwell and Associates."

The woman flipped through the patient list, then frowned. "I have Mr. Caldwell listed, but your name isn't here."

"I'm sure it's just an oversight. We've had some problems with our new secretary. The woman is totally inept."

"Well . . . I don't know—"

"Look, if I don't get these papers signed—" Marc held out the briefcase "—Mr. Caldwell will be very upset. Is the administrator around? Maybe our client would be better off in another facility."

"Yes, sir... I mean no, wait just a moment."

Marc held his breath as the woman pressed a button and asked for an orderly. Within minutes, he was being led through a series of locked doors, then down a long wide hallway.

The orderly stopped halfway down. "You can wait in here." He motioned toward a door.

Marc glanced around the empty room as he entered. His stomach tightened in apprehension. Along one wall was an entertainment center complete with a television and stereo. The opposite wall was flanked by shelves of books. He walked to a nearby chair and seated himself. After several long minutes, he stood up and began pacing.

Suddenly, the door opened. Marc halted in midstride and turned to face Angelique. Her hair was disheveled; her face, unadorned by makeup, was pale and drawn. But her eyes were what held his attention. For a split second, they had a certain blank look about them that made his skin crawl.

"Marc?"

Hearing his name shook him loose from the eerie feeling. Marc rushed over, grabbed her arm and pulled her inside. "Don't say anything." He stuck his head through the doorway and glanced up and down the hall. Satisfied no one had heard her, he closed the door. When he released her, she surprised him by throwing her arms around him.

"Thank God," she sobbed. "I knew you'd come. I knew you'd see through his lies."

Marc frowned as he untangled her arms and held her at arm's length. "What are you talking about?"

Tears streamed down her cheeks. "I told him you wouldn't believe him and I was right." She wiped her nose with the back of her hand and sniffed. "You have come to take me out of here, haven't you?" She clutched at the lapels of his coat. "Well, haven't you?"

Marc began to feel sick. She'd been expecting him to come. But Jean Claude had said Angelique believed he was dead. Marc swallowed hard and tried to keep calm. Facts, he reminded himself. One of the first rules he'd learned as a rookie journalist was to get the facts before making judgments. "I think we'd better start from the beginning." He motioned toward a chair. "You'd better tell me everything."

When she was seated, he pulled a handkerchief from his pocket and handed it to her. "And cut out the sob routine. You know that doesn't work with me."

Angelique blew her nose, then clutched the handkerchief with both hands, twisting and turning it as she talked. "He put me in here to keep me quiet."

"Who did?"

"Why, Jean Claude. Who else?"

"Hold it. I'm confused here. So you knew all along I wasn't dead?"

"Of course, I knew. Like I said, he wanted to keep me quiet."

"And what would you have to keep quiet about?"

"I'll tell you, but first you have to promise to get me out of here."

Marc clenched his fist. "I think you'd better tell me anyway."

She glared at him. "Not until you promise." Then she added, "And don't even consider going back on your promise, or I'll tell them you were here, that you're not dead."

Marc smiled sarcastically. "Guess you've got me there. Go ahead, let's have it." Her smug, self-satisfied look didn't bother him in the least. She could tell the whole world for all he cared. Who was going to believe a mental patient who was supposedly distraught over her husband's death?

Angelique leaned forward and whispered. "Jean Claude is behind everything."

Marc shook his head. "That's not what he said. He and the FBI seem to think Antonio Manchetti is behind everything."

"He's lying. They're all lying, the bastards...."

Her voice faded away and for a moment she stared at him with a look of pure hatred. But the look was so fleeting, he decided he must have imagined it.

And then her eyes went blank and she continued in a dull, emotionless voice. "Tony was a friend of my father's, and...very powerful, and Jean Claude—he knew all about my friendship with Tony. Besides, he just told them about Tony so they wouldn't suspect him."

"Suspect him of what?"

"Why, of killing the governor and trying to have you killed, of course."

"Jean Claude is ambitious, but it's hard for me to believe he'd go to that extreme. And what about you?" Marc pinned her with a glare. "What have you got to do with all of this?"

Dark fury sparkled in her eyes. "I know everything, and he didn't have the stomach to kill me outright."

"Why would you know everything?"

She curled her lips in a feline smile, and something in the way she looked at him made him uneasy. "I told you,

Tony was a friend of my father's. Nothing goes on in this state without Tony knowing about it, especially anything political.''

Marc shuddered and couldn't help but wonder what else she had in her background that she'd kept from him, and why. Who was he to believe? Angelique? Jean Claude? He didn't trust either one of them. Marc closed his eyes and pinched the bridge of his nose.

"Marc?"

He opened his eyes and looked at her.

"I know you don't believe me," she said. "Jean Claude fooled me, too. But Marc, what reason would I have to lie, especially about something like this? I have nothing to gain."

She seemed sincere, but Marc remembered another time she'd seemed sincere, too.

"I can prove what I've told you." She paused to look around the room and then smiled. "But not as long as I'm in here."

Marc narrowed his eyes. "How can you prove it?"

"Take me to Jean Claude and I'll show you." Angelique's eyes took on a hard glint. "We'll both confront them all, face-to-face."

Marc was suddenly full of misgivings. "All?" he asked, confused.

Again, her eyes went blank. "I meant Jean Claude." Then she laughed. "Who else would I mean?"

Angelique was definitely acting strange. Just stress from being locked up, Marc decided. Still, the eerie feeling that something was wrong wouldn't go away. But, despite his misgivings about Angelique, everything she'd said had confirmed his own suspicions. Who knows? he thought. Face-to-face, either Angelique or Jean Claude might slip up, and then he'd find out which one was lying.

"Okay," he finally agreed. "I'll see what I can do. Frankly, I don't trust either one of you, but I don't relish spending the rest of my life hiding out or playing dead." He seized her chin, tilting her face upward. "You just remember this. If you're the one lying, I'll have you back in here so fast, it'll make your head swim. And I'll make sure they keep you here for a long, long time."

Angelique jerked her chin from his hold.

"You'll have to do exactly what I tell you. Agreed?" She nodded. "Okay," he said. "Give me a minute to think this through."

He turned away from her and began to pace. "I can't risk coming back tonight. The receptionist would recognize me. So it has to be now." He whirled around. "Are you free to come and go in this area?"

Again she nodded, and a peculiar little smile formed on her lips.

"Good." Marc paused. "Go back to your room and change into a dress, but wear flat shoes—no heels. Put on some makeup." He motioned toward her hair. "And do something with your hair. Then meet me back here. The only way to do this is to walk right out the front door before they realize what's happened."

When Angelique continued looking at him as if she was in a daze, Marc frowned. "Well, get moving," he snapped as he pulled her to her feet. "And hurry."

Every minute that passed seemed to drag as he waited for her. When she returned, she looked like a different person. She seemed calm and almost serene. "Ready?"

When she smiled and whispered yes, her eyes glittered. But Marc told himself it was from the tension, the excitement of the moment. Grabbing his briefcase, he took her arm and escorted her down the hallway.

"Here goes." He drew a deep breath. "Just keep quiet and let me do the talking." His heart pounded in his chest as he pushed the call button. Within minutes, the same orderly who had brought him in appeared.

"What's going on here?" he demanded.

Marc cleared his throat. "My client has an appointment. I've come to take her to it."

The orderly shook his head. "Those weren't my instructions. Mr. O'Connor specifically said she wasn't to leave under any circumstances. I'll have to check it out with him."

The orderly turned and reached for a wall phone above the call button. So much for bluffing, Marc thought with regret as he lifted his briefcase and brought it down hard against the back of the man's head. The orderly crumpled to the floor. Marc quickly bent over the man and checked his pulse. Satisfied he'd only stunned him, he unfastened the keys hooked to the man's belt.

"Come on." He grabbed Angelique's arm and walked swiftly toward the first locked door. His hand shook as he pushed a key in the lock. After the third try, he found the right one. On an impulse, he tried the same key in the second door. The lock clicked and he breathed a sigh of relief.

"Now comes the hard part," he said, turning to Angelique. "A Jeep is parked outside, near the entrance on the right. If the waiting area is clear, walk out the door when I signal you. If it's not, we'll play it by ear, but be prepared. We may have to run for it. Do you understand?"

Angelique didn't respond, but simply stared at him with vacant eyes. A sick feeling knotted in his gut.

He shook her arm and repeated, "Do you understand?"

She suddenly jerked her arm free, surprising him. "I understand perfectly," she answered.

The sick feeling began to spread, but Marc knew it was too late to turn back. He'd come too far to stop now.

When they reached the waiting area, Marc casually strolled into the room and glanced around. Since it was empty, he walked over to the glass window.

The receptionist was sitting sideways, engaged in an animated conversation on the phone. Marc signaled Angelique. As she passed behind him, he moved slowly along the window, hoping he would provide a partial shield in case the woman caught sight of her. He held his breath, but by the time the receptionist hung up the phone, Angelique was out the door.

Marc smiled at the receptionist. "Just wanted to thank you for your cooperation." Suddenly, the phone began to ring, then an earsplitting siren sounded. As the woman reached for the phone, Marc turned and hurried out the door. Once outside, he sprinted toward the Jeep.

"Duck," he commanded as he jumped inside and started the engine. Angelique slid down out of sight. It took every ounce of patience he could muster to keep from squealing out of the parking lot. Once on the highway, he pressed the accelerator till the arrow indicated they were traveling a little past the speed limit, and kept a watch in the rearview mirror for flashing lights.

During the drive back to New Orleans, Angelique's expression had been grave and, except to answer whatever he'd asked, she'd remained quiet. As soon as they hit the city limits, Marc began to notice a change. Every time he glanced at her, she was smiling. Marc grew more uneasy as each minute passed. When he turned onto St. Charles Avenue, she began to hum; her strange little tune gave him the creeps.

As he neared the Garden District, Angelique stopped humming. "I need a bathroom and I'm thirsty," she said.

"We'll be there in a few more minutes. You can wait."

She clutched his arm. "No, I can't. I need a bathroom *now*."

Marc removed her hand from his arm. "Okay, okay." He glanced around for a place to stop. "There's a service station. That will have to do."

"Fine," she replied. "I don't care where."

The minute he pulled in, Angelique made a move toward the door. Marc grabbed her. "Oh, no, you don't. If you think I'm letting you out of my sight, think again."

She glared at him, but Marc kept a firm grip on her arm anyway as he escorted her around to the side of the building; the bathroom was located on the back corner.

"I'll be waiting right here, so don't get any cute ideas," he said when they stopped.

Without a word, she walked in and slammed the door. Several minutes passed as Marc paced. He wasn't sure what alerted him, but suddenly he knew something was wrong. He twisted the doorknob, but it was locked. "Angelique, come out of there." He put his ear next to the door and listened. Then he heard it. A faint creaking noise.

He cursed and sprinted around the corner. Sure enough, there was a window, and Angelique was already half out of it.

"Oh, no, you don't," he said as he grabbed her around her waist and hauled her the rest of the way out.

Just as he was about to release her, she turned on him like a wildcat. The sound she made was that of a cornered animal. She clawed at his face. Instinctively, Marc tried to protect his eyes, and at the same time hold on to her, but the tip of one sharp nail caught him just below his eyebrow, drawing blood. Then she lunged at him and they both fell.

The breath left his body with a swoosh, and a searing pain ripped at the back of his head. For a moment he saw stars and then the world went black.

CHAPTER SEVENTEEN

MARC GROANED as he sat up. He gingerly touched the lump on the back of his head; it felt like it was the size of a table tennis ball. What the hell happened? he wondered as he glanced around him. A large chunk of concrete caught his attention.

Cursing, he stood, but as he'd expected, Angelique was gone. Hands on his hips and a disgusted look on his face, Marc slowly scanned the area surrounding the service station. She was nowhere in sight. Raw fury welled up inside until he thought he'd explode.

He'd been had.

He should have known better. He should have gone into the damned bathroom with her.

But on the fringes of his fury, fear gripped him with sharp talons, fear for Samantha and fear for himself. What if he'd been wrong about Jean Claude? What if the assassins had been hired by Manchetti as the FBI man had suspected? Angelique had admitted she was friends with Manchetti. If she somehow made contact with him, and he learned that the explosion was a hoax, he would come after Marc and Samantha and, quite literally, he would get away with murder. The world thought they were dead anyway.

Marc took off running for the Jeep. There was one way to find out. He jumped in and twisted the key in the ignition. Ignoring the blaring horns and fist-shaking motorists, he left a trail of black rubber across the service station driveway as he bullied his way into the traffic. He'd find Jean Claude, confront him face-to-face and beat the truth out of him if he had to.

Fifteen minutes later, hidden behind the trunk of an oak tree, Marc noted the cars parked in the driveway of his father's home. Jean Claude's Mercedes was there, along with his dad's Lincoln. But the third one, a white Ford, was unfamiliar. So he waited. By the time he'd turned onto St. Charles Avenue, he'd brought his temper under control enough to rationalize the situation. He couldn't just barge in. He didn't want to upset his dad until he knew the truth, and if Dora should happen to see him—Marc cringed at the mere thought of what the shock would do to her.

Just as he decided he'd waited long enough, the front door opened, then slammed shut. A man hurried toward the unfamiliar white car, and within minutes, the man and the car were gone.

Glancing up and down the quiet shaded street, Marc waited a moment longer before he stepped from behind the tree. Making a wide circle, he approached his father's house from a side driveway that led to the outside door of Jean Claude's suite. The door was locked as he'd expected, but he knew where to find the emergency key. Lifting a stepping stone leading to the backyard, Marc found what he was looking for.

He opened the door, then stopped to listen. The house was still, so he let himself in to wait. He'd rarely had the occasion to be in his cousin's rooms. He glanced around out of curiosity. Jean Claude's taste surprised him. He would have guessed his cousin would either go for stark, modernistic decor or expensive antiques. Instead, the rooms had a country hominess that didn't seem to fit Jean Claude's flashy image.

Suddenly, Marc tensed at the sound of footsteps—a man's footsteps. Moving quickly to the door, he flattened himself against the wall and waited. When the door opened, he held his breath. Jean Claude strolled into the room. His back was to Marc, so he didn't see him. When Marc reached out and pushed, the door shut with a firm click.

Jean Claude whirled around and automatically snapped into the martial arts stance of self-defense. His cousin was a second-degree black belt, but that didn't worry Marc in the least. He leaned back against the wall and crossed his arms. "Hello, Cousin."

Jean Claude paled. "What in God's name are you doing here?"

"Aren't you glad to see me?"

Jean Claude glared at him. "Who else knows you're here?"

Marc shrugged and pushed away from the wall. "Aren't you going to offer your dead cousin a drink?"

Jean Claude took a step to block Marc. "For heaven's sake, man, what's going on? Are you crazy? You're going to ruin everything."

Suddenly, Marc lunged. Grabbing Jean Claude by his shirt, he slammed him up against the wall. "You tell me what's going on. I want the truth and I want it now."

"What the hell are you talking about?"

"You can cut the crap. I've seen Angelique." Marc felt Jean Claude tense even more beneath his hands.

"How . . . when?"

"I walked into the hospital and had a nice little visit with her."

Jean Claude closed his eyes and sagged against the wall. His voice was barely above a whisper as he asked, "What did she tell you?" He shook his head, then stared past Marc with unseeing eyes. "Never mind. I can just imagine."

Marc released Jean Claude. Running his fingers through his hair, he turned away. "Was she lying? Did you hire men to kill me?"

Jean Claude pushed himself away from the wall and walked toward the telephone. "No. I would never do that. But you don't have to believe me." He picked up the receiver and punched out a set of numbers. "I should have known you wouldn't just sit back and wait. You never have," he mumbled. "But I never dreamed you'd think I was behind—"

Marc faced Jean Claude. "Who are you calling?"

Jean Claude held up a hand to silence Marc as he spoke low into the telephone. "Uncle Edward, we've got a problem. Marc's here. Can you come to my rooms?"

Marc felt his gut tighten. At that moment, he knew the answer to his question. With leaden feet, he walked to the nearest chair and sat down. Slumping forward with his elbows supported by his knees, he covered his face with his hands. "God, what have I done?" he whispered. All he could think about was that he'd put Samantha's life in danger. Several minutes passed, then Marc felt his cousin's hand on his shoulder. He looked up.

"Here." Jean Claude handed him a glass of amber-colored liquid. "Drink this. You're going to need it."

Marc accepted the drink and gulped down most of it in one swallow. The bourbon burned his throat and spread its warmth throughout his stomach.

Both men turned their heads at the sound of the door opening. Edward Dureaux stood for a second, his steely gaze resting on Marc alone.

For the first time in his life, Marc felt his father's anger and disapproval directed at him. As Edward stepped through the door, he slammed it closed behind him.

"It really is you. What the hell are you doing here? Have you lost your mind?"

"Dad, I—"

"There are no excuses, so don't give me any," Edward snapped, his voice rising. "Do you have any idea of the hours and hours of planning, of worrying? And now, it's all for nothing. All down the drain—"

"Maybe not," Jean Claude interjected.

Edward swung around to face his nephew.

"No one saw him but Angelique," he offered. "But who's going to believe her?"

Edward snorted.

Jean Claude's mouth tightened. "Just look at him. With that mustache and beard, even if someone he knew saw him, they wouldn't necessarily recognize him."

Marc shifted in the chair and finished off his drink. God, what a mess. He swallowed hard, then cleared his throat. "Angelique—"

"What about her?" Edward interrupted, glaring at him.

Marc felt his face grow warm. His stomach began to churn. "She—" He drew a shuddering breath. "I got her out of the hospital."

Deadly silence filled the room as long seconds passed. Somewhere outside, a dog barked and a truck roared down the street.

Jean Claude was the first to speak. "Where is she now?"

Marc met his cousin's gaze. His words were a mere whisper. "I don't know. I was bringing her back to confront you." Marc went on to tell them what had happened at the gas station. When he'd finished, he turned to his father. "I didn't know who or what to believe."

"Oh, God...God help us all." Edward Dureaux stepped to the nearest chair and slumped into it. "Get Patrick on the phone."

While Jean Claude tried to locate Patrick O'Connor, Edward told Marc what they had learned about Angelique's background and her connection with Manchetti. When he told him that she had plotted with Manchetti to kill him, Marc jumped out of the chair swearing.

"Why? I agreed to the damned divorce—that's what she said she wanted. Wait until I get my hands on her. She'll wish she'd never been born."

"Calm down, Son."

Marc looked at his father's worried face, but dark rage still raced through his veins.

"She's not responsible. She's ill."

"Uncle Edward's right," Jean Claude said as he hung up the receiver, then seated himself opposite Marc.

"Jean Claude," Edward said. "Tell him what you found out."

Jean Claude told Marc about the violent way Angelique's parents had died, and how she'd lost everything. He explained how the strain had been too much—she'd had a mental breakdown. Marc listened as his cousin described her reaction on learning Manchetti was responsible for her parents' deaths; some of the fury he'd felt a few moments earlier ebbed.

When Jean Claude finished, all Marc could do was stare at him. He began to remember the eerie feelings he'd experienced around her and knew his cousin's words were true. "I didn't know," he said. "I was the woman's husband, and I swear she never breathed a word of any of this. All she ever said was that her parents had died in a car wreck, and I . . ." His voice trailed away.

Jean Claude turned to his uncle. "O'Connor said that Marc should stay here out of sight. He insisted that under no circumstances was Marc to leave. He said he would get back to us if he had any news."

Marc arose from his chair and began pacing. "I've got to call Sam—Samantha Bradford. She's at Ray Fielding's." When his father frowned, he stopped pacing to explain. "We were staying at his place in the Quarter. She'll be worried if she doesn't hear from me."

Edward Dureaux rolled his eyes upward. "Is there anything else we should know?" He shook his head and waved toward the phone. "Never mind. Call her. Oh, and Marc. . ." He paused for emphasis. "Tell her to stay put."

The phone rang only once before Samantha answered it.

"Marc, what happened? Where are you?"

Her voice was like the eye of a hurricane—the calm center in the middle of a raging storm. Just listening to her eased some of his burden. Even her silence was comforting.

Marc went into detail about everything that had happened. The longer he talked, the more he longed to be with her. But that would have to wait. As he slowly replaced the receiver, he closed his eyes. Would he ever see her again?

IT WAS MIDNIGHT before they heard from Patrick O'Connor. During those long, agonizing hours, Marc worried. About Samantha. About himself. And yes, he finally admitted, even about Angelique.

The only bright spot of the entire evening had been the joy on Dora's face when she'd found out he was still alive, but then she'd immediately lit into his father and Jean Claude for keeping the truth from her.

One look from Patrick O'Connor as he strode into the living room confirmed the conclusions Marc had already reached. Patrick made no bones about his opinion of what Marc had done.

"You've screwed up this whole operation. Our only hope has vanished. We've checked the St. Ann Street apartment, but if she went there—"

"What apartment?"

O'Connor quickly glanced at Jean Claude, then back to Marc. "You didn't know, did you?"

Marc shook his head. It seemed there was a lot he didn't know about his wife.

"Don't feel bad. She kept it a secret just like her father did. It was the only thing left from her old man's estate that wasn't auctioned off or sold."

Marc reached up to pinch the bridge of his nose as O'Connor rattled off the address. How had he been so blind? But immediately the answer came to him. He hadn't cared. He'd never really loved her, so he hadn't cared. She'd used him from the beginning and deep down, he'd known she'd lied about being pregnant. But at that low point in his life, he'd been willing to stick his head in the sand and ignore the truth rather than face the reality of his stupidity or its consequences. Marc ran his fingers through his hair. Now was not the time to dwell on what he should have done. He faced O'Connor. "So what happens next?"

"I've got a man staked out at the apartment just in case. But my guess is she'll go after Manchetti. I've put a tail on him, hoping she'll show sooner or later, but all we can do is wait and pray we get to her before she gets to him. If he gets to her first, you and Samantha Bradford might as well drop off the face of the earth forever."

THE FOLLOWING MORNING, as the three men sat around the breakfast table, Marc reached for one of Dora's homemade biscuits. Usually he could eat several at one sitting, but this morning the thought of food turned his stomach. Still, he nibbled on it for lack of anything better to do and tried to concentrate on the stilted conversation between his cousin and his father. The tension between the two men seemed thick enough to walk on, and Marc wondered why.

The sudden jarring ring of the telephone made him jump. The three men waited anxiously for Dora to answer the call.

"Marc, it's for you. Mr. O'Connor says it's urgent."

Marc's first thoughts were of Samantha. Had something happened to her? Marc hurriedly blotted his mouth with a napkin and pushed away from the table. He took the receiver from Dora.

"O'Connor? This is Marc Dureaux. Have you got Angelique?"

Patrick O'Connor sounded weary when he answered and Marc wondered if the man had managed to get any sleep.

"No, not yet. But we've come across something else. About five this morning, two bodies were spotted floating in the river near the docks."

Marc tightened his grip on the phone and he felt his stomach heave. All he could think of was Samantha and Ray. "Who?" He almost choked on the word as he held his breath

"That's what we were hoping you can tell us. Both the men were shot through the head, execution-style. Whoever did it dumped them in the river late last night."

Two men. Marc released his pent-up breath. "Why would I know anything about them?"

"We ran their fingerprints and descriptions through the computer. There were no warrants on them locally, but get this—their descriptions fit the ones you gave the Baton Rouge police of the governor's assassins. And we're still getting info in from other states. So far, they were wanted for questioning in connection with murders in Chicago and New York. In both places a power struggle was going on between two underworld forces. I'm beginning to wonder if the same thing is happening here."

"What do you mean?"

"What if someone close to Manchetti decided he wanted to be number one? We've suspected for a long time that Manchetti pulled Governor Jackson's strings, so what would be the best way to get rid of Jackson and Manchetti and not leave any traces?"

Marc thought about it for a moment. "Yeah, I see what you're driving at. If Jackson was dead and Manchetti was convicted of hiring guns to do it, that would leave the field free and clear for someone else to step in. But who?"

"I'm still working on that, but getting back to the two stiffs. We're holding the bodies at the city morgue. I want you to take a look at them. I'll pick you up in thirty minutes. We'll be in and out of there before anyone knows we're around."

Marc glanced at his watch. It was ten a.m. "I'll be ready," he said, then he hung up the phone. For a moment he leaned against the wall. The morning of the assassination flashed before him with startling clarity; it seemed like a lifetime ago, but the faces of the two murderers were indelibly planted in his memory, along with the picture of the governor clutching his bloody head.

WHEN MARC EMERGED from the basement of the building that housed the morgue, he took a deep breath. The smell of downtown New Orleans was a far cry from the smell of fresh air, but right now it was as sweet as any mountain air after the room he'd just come from.

O'Connor motioned for him to get into the car. He closed the door and immediately rolled down the window. As O'Connor pulled away from the curb, Marc continued to take deep gulping breaths. He wondered if anything could erase the memory of the bloated corpses he'd seen.

O'Connor had led him to the far end of the room where two bodies were laid out on stainless-steel tables. When he'd looked at each man, it had taken all the control he could muster to keep from throwing up. But he'd identified them. They were the hit men.

"I wonder why Manchetti waited until now to get rid of them."

O'Connor's statement startled Marc back to reality. He frowned. "Since he thinks I'm dead, maybe he just wanted to get rid of any other witnesses who could tie him to the governor's murder."

"Yeah, maybe. But if that's true, he had to do the job himself. Somehow I can't picture him dirtying his own hands. He's not the type, and besides, it's just not his style. Then there's the matter of your wife. It seems he would have tried to get rid of her right away."

"He may still," Marc mumbled, but he wasn't thinking of Angelique at the moment. O'Connor was right. From what Marc knew of Manchetti, he would never stoop to doing a job himself, so that meant someone besides Manchetti had killed the two assassins. Then he suddenly remembered what O'Connor had said earlier when they'd talked on the phone. He'd speculated about a power struggle. But with whom? he wondered. Who was intelligent enough and had the power to pull off such an elaborate scheme?

Marc knew he had the resources to find out, but first he had to persuade O'Connor he would be better off staying at Ray's.

"Take me back to Ray Fielding's." When O'Connor started to object, Marc interrupted. "If Angelique contacts Manchetti and tells him I'm alive, my father's house is the first place he'll look. I'll be safer at Ray's."

O'Connor finally, reluctantly, agreed, and Marc breathed a sigh of relief.

"I'll take you," he said. "But if you know what's good for you, you and the Bradford woman had better stay put."

CHAPTER EIGHTEEN

IT WAS ALMOST NOON when Ray and Samantha returned to his home. Although she was exhausted, Samantha had to agree Ray's idea had been a good one. After spending half the morning anticipating that Marc would call, she'd told Ray that the waiting was driving her crazy. He'd promptly handed her a black, floppy hat and told her to tuck her hair up inside it. Dressed in jeans, tennis shoes and Ray's paint-splattered shirts, they'd blended in perfectly with the French Quarter artists who had lined the fence surrounding Jackson Square.

Samantha stood quietly as Ray unlocked his front door. They stepped inside and he immediately checked his answering machine. Samantha anxiously listened as he replayed each message, but Marc hadn't phoned.

"Think I'll take a nice long bath," she said and headed down the hallway.

"I'll be in the studio," he called out.

Samantha soaked until her fingers began to wrinkle, then reluctantly stepped out of the tub. After drying off, she slipped on some shorts and a loose shirt. Barefoot, she padded down the hallway and went into the kitchen for something to drink. She wandered out onto Ray's patio and sat down.

The enclosed patio was shaded, but the humidity and lack of a breeze made it as warm as any sauna she'd ever used. God, it's hot here, she thought, and a sudden wave of homesickness washed over her as she rubbed an icy glass of lemonade across her forehead, then lowered it to take a sip. She missed Gram's creaky old house, the white sandy beach and the steady breeze from the Gulf of Mexico. And she missed Marc.

"So here you are."

Samantha turned her head and gave Ray a wilted smile. "Did he call yet?"

Ray shook his head and motioned behind him. "Nope, he didn't call. He showed up instead."

Samantha knew she was grinning like a schoolgirl, but she didn't care. Then she saw the look on Marc's face and her grin faltered. He smiled at her, but it was an absent smile, one that acknowledged her presence but little more. A pang of hurt mingled with anger wedged near her heart. She'd been worried sick and now he was acting almost as if she didn't exist.

Ray pulled out two of the wrought-iron patio chairs and he and Marc sat down. Marc fidgeted for a moment, then he stood up and began pacing as he filled them in on what had happened and discussed O'Connor's theory of an underworld power struggle.

"After thinking about it," he said, "I have to agree with O'Connor. It's not Manchetti's style to do a job himself. I still believe Manchetti had the governor killed. What I can't figure out is why. It's a well-known fact he controlled the governor, but no one could ever prove it. Only someone close to Manchetti would know what he'd planned, and that same someone knew that a witness, especially an investigative reporter like me, could identify the killers and trace them back to Manchetti."

"So how does Angelique figure into the whole thing?" Ray asked.

Marc abruptly halted his pacing, and Samantha held her breath. A brief look of fury crossed his face. And then something—was it embarrassment?—caused his tanned skin to darken. He gave a rough laugh. "Other than the fact that she had Manchetti put out a contract on me, I'm not sure how the hell she figures into it yet."

Samantha cringed at his sarcasm.

Ray closed his eyes and cursed.

"Dad and Jean Claude say she's a sick woman—sick as in mentally ill," Marc added quietly, in a curiously flat voice. "I...I guess she's not totally responsible for her actions." He paused, then shrugged. "All I know is that for now, those two men were not killed by Manchetti. Someone else did the job. And I think that someone could be the same person who wants to take Manchetti's place."

Despite her own hurt feelings, Samantha reached over and touched Marc's arm in a comforting gesture. "What's being done about...about finding Angelique?"

He gave her a hard look and she felt his muscles tighten beneath her touch. She removed her hand.

"There's nothing to be done for now," he answered, still in the same flat voice. "O'Connor has someone tailing Manchetti in case she tries to contact him, and there's an agent staked out at her apartment if she shows up there."

Samantha raised her brows. "Apartment?" she questioned. "I thought she lived at your father's."

Marc took a deep breath and began to explain his wife's background, telling them about her secret apartment. Samantha could tell even talking about it disturbed him, but as she listened carefully, sketchy ideas of a plan began to form in her mind, and she made a mental note of the address.

"Enough about Angelique," Marc declared. "I've got to find out who's behind this mess." He stared off into space. "Maybe there's something in my files that would shed some light," he mumbled.

He turned to Ray. "All my out-of-state contacts are in my files. O'Connor mentioned that the two hit men had been connected to murders in Chicago and New York."

Samantha stared at Marc with new eyes as he continued to talk. She'd known he was a reporter, but as she listened to him talk about his contacts, she began to realize he wasn't just any reporter. It took years of experience for a journalist to make the kind of connections Marc had. He was obviously big-time.

"Ray, I need those files," he said. "I imagine the paper turned my stuff over to my father. If they didn't, could you go with him to pick it up? And bring it back here?"

"Sure," Ray answered. "No problem."

Samantha took a sip of lemonade and half listened to the men's conversation. She kept going over and over the things Marc had said, about Angelique, the hit men, and Manchetti.

She felt that Angelique's escape was partly her fault; if she hadn't persuaded Marc he needed to talk to her face-to-face, maybe the poor deranged woman would still be in the hospital where she belonged. Samantha glanced at Marc and wondered if he'd had the same thoughts, and if that was the reason he'd been distant.

Stop it, Samantha, she told herself. *The man has the weight of the world on his mind. Instead of feeling sorry for yourself, you should be trying to help figure out what to do about this mess.*

There was something they were missing, she rationalized as she reviewed everything Marc had learned. She remembered Marc telling her he'd first thought Bobby

Landry might be behind the assassination of the governor, but had dismissed that theory because of the phone call he'd received; he'd figured out someone had wanted him to think Landry was guilty. Samantha felt a sudden surge of exhilaration rush through her veins like a current of electricity. It stood to reason that the person Marc was looking for had also set up the phone call. Maybe that person could be traced to whoever had made the call.

"You're forgetting about the phone call," she blurted out. Both men looked at her in surprise.

Suddenly Marc's eyes began to dance with excitement. He turned to Ray. "She's right. That phone call has bothered me from the beginning."

"Do you know who made it?" Ray asked.

Marc grinned. "I sure as hell do. The little snitch's name is Arnie Turner and I think I know just where to find him."

The enthusiasm between the two men was evident, and Samantha began to feel like the odd person out. If only *she* could do something, she thought, something that would help. If she could somehow find Angelique and talk with her, she might be able to convince her that for her own safety, she needed to return to the hospital. *And maybe you're just kidding yourself, Samantha. Why would Marc's wife, a woman who is mentally ill, listen to you, a complete stranger?* Samantha knew it was a long shot, but she also knew she had to try.

"Sam. Did you hear me?"

Marc's impatient tone startled her, and she blinked several times. "Ah, no... sorry. What?"

"Ray and I are leaving. He's going to get my files and I'm going to try to find Arnie Turner. Stay inside while we're gone." He emphasized each word as if he were talking to a child. "Don't go wandering off."

Samantha simply stared at him. His attitude toward her not only hurt, but rankled, as well. *Yes sir, Captain, sir.* The sarcastic retort was right on the tip of her tongue, but she forced herself to smile instead. "I'll be fine," she answered. "You go ahead."

She watched the two men disappear inside and her mind began to race. With Marc and Ray gone, it would be the perfect time to do a little investigating on her own.

AN HOUR LATER, Samantha walked slowly past Angelique's apartment. She could feel her heartbeat quicken and an attack of nerves caused her to shiver in the midafternoon heat. Within minutes after Marc and Ray had left, she had changed back into the clothes she'd worn earlier to the French Quarter, but it had taken much longer than she'd expected to actually locate the address Marc had rattled off. She'd had to stop several times and ask directions.

She glanced up and down the narrow street, but continued walking. According to Marc, O'Connor was supposed to have an agent watching the apartment, in case Angelique returned to it, and she figured since there was no one else hanging around except a wino sitting in the gutter, he had to be O'Connor's man. She reached the end of the block, turned the corner and stopped. From where she stood, the wino's back was facing her, so she decided to stay where she was and wait.

As the afternoon grew longer, Samantha began to doubt her reasons for being here. Every time a car drove down the street she tensed. Maybe this wasn't such a great idea, she thought as she adjusted the floppy hat and continued her vigil. She'd heard some pretty unsavory stories about the streets of New Orleans. Even the wino had left. Several people had strolled by during the afternoon, but no one had entered the apartment.

Samantha figured that by now, either Marc or Ray would have returned. Since neither of them knew what she'd planned or where she'd gone, she decided she at least owed them a phone call to let them know she was okay.

Two blocks farther down the street, she found a pay phone where she could still keep the apartment in sight. She dug a quarter out of her jeans pocket, deposited it in the coin slot and punched out Ray's number. On the third ring, Marc answered.

"Marc, it's me," she said.

"Sam! Thank God. Where the hell are you? I thought I told you to stay put. You were supposed to—"

"Did you find Arnie Turner?"

"No," he almost shouted. "And that's beside the point. I told you to—"

"I'm down the street from Angelique's apartment—"

"What the—" Marc cut in. "What in the name of all that's holy do you think you're doing? Come back here right now."

The phone line crackled with angry tension, and for a split second Samantha considered hanging up on him. Then she sighed. Coming to Angelique's apartment hadn't turned out to be such a great idea anyway; she might as well leave for all the good she was doing, she decided. "Okay," she finally answered, and perversely added, "But I want you to know it's not because you *told* me to."

"If you're not back here in twenty minutes, I'm coming to get you."

Samantha slammed the receiver onto the cradle. The man could be a real jerk at times, she thought as she glared down the empty street.

Just as she started to turn away, she caught a glimpse of a taxi turning the corner. It slowed in front of Angelique's apartment, then stopped. Samantha held her breath for a moment, then released it. The instant the dark-haired, petite woman stepped onto the curb, Samantha knew she had to be Angelique. There was a certain regal air about her that spelled money and finishing school.

The cabbie handed the woman a white sack, and within seconds, she entered the apartment and the taxi drove away. Samantha remained by the phone and tried to work up enough courage to do what she had set out to do. Talking to Angelique had seemed so logical, but now that the time had come, she wasn't sure she could go through with it.

But she had to try, both for Marc's sake and to salve her own conscience. Samantha raised her chin and commanded her legs to move. The short walk seemed like miles and each step felt as if she were walking in freshly poured cement.

She stopped in front of the door and reached up to push the doorbell. She hesitated, then swallowed several times to ease the dryness in her throat, and finally pushed the small, white button.

The door opened almost immediately.

"Tony— Oh." The woman looked at her curiously. "You're not Ton—never mind," she said. "What do you want?"

Samantha tried to smile. "Angelique?"

The woman frowned and a wary look crept into her dark eyes. "Do I know you?" she asked.

Samantha shook her head. "No, but if you're Angelique, I need to talk to you," Samantha answered softly, and for a moment she feared Angelique would slam the door in her face. But she didn't. Instead, she continued to stare, and Samantha began to feel uneasy under the other woman's scrutiny.

"Could I please come inside?"

Angelique looked at her for a few more seconds, then, with a shrug of her narrow shoulders, she swung the door wider and motioned Samantha to enter.

"Only for a moment, you understand. I don't have much time. I'm expecting a dinner guest," she added.

Samantha froze inside as she followed Angelique into the living room. Tony...Antonio Manchetti...dinner guest. Was it possible? She glanced toward a small dining table in the corner of the room; it was set for two, and in the middle was the empty white sack and cartons of what looked like Chinese food. A cold shiver ran through her. What had she got herself into?

"Well?" Angelique's impatient tone snapped Samantha out of her shock.

"Who..." she cleared her throat and tried again. "Who is your dinner guest?"

Angelique's dark eyes flashed and took on a hard glitter. "What business is it of yours and who the hell are you, anyway?"

The peal of the doorbell interrupted their conversation and Samantha watched in amazement as a change came over Angelique. The hard glitter in her eyes disappeared and was replaced by a blank stare.

Her lips barely moved as she spoke in a singsong voice. "Someone's at the door," she said. "Would you please answer it?"

She *is* crazy, Samantha decided. And I've got to get out of here now.

Samantha nodded, turned and walked slowly toward the doorway. She figured once she reached the door, she'd bolt for the outside and run like hell.

"No. Wait," Angelique commanded.

Samantha abruptly stopped.

"I've changed my mind," she said. "I'll answer it."

"Okay. Whatever you want," Samantha said. "And ah . . . since you're having a guest, I'll come back another time."

"I don't think so."

Samantha felt something hard and blunt pushed against her back. Her legs suddenly felt weak and trembly.

"Turn around."

Samantha slowly turned and found herself staring down the barrel of a small revolver.

"Sit over there." Angelique waved the small gun toward a nearby chair. "And stay out of my way. I have some business to take care of. Then you can leave."

"Why don't we both leave?" Samantha suggested in a quivery voice and tried to smile. She glanced around. "We could go out the back door."

"Don't be stupid," Angelique snapped. "I can't leave yet, but...you know what? I've changed my mind again—you go ahead." She waved the gun toward another doorway. "There's a back door in the kitchen. But hurry before Tony sees you." She slipped the gun in her skirt pocket and Samantha almost fainted from relief. "He thinks we're having dinner," she said as if to explain, then turned and walked toward the narrow entrance hall.

Angelique wasn't making sense, but Samantha was too scared to do anything but head for the door. She figured if she could get to a phone, maybe she could get some help.

Just as Samantha reached the doorknob, she heard Angelique's voice.

"Tony, come in."

"My dear, you look simply radiant," he replied.

Samantha didn't wait to hear more. She jerked the door open but immediately halted. She gasped.

A large man stood in her path. And he had a gun pointed at her. Her heart began to race as her gaze traveled the distance from the gun to the man's face. He held his forefinger to his lips and shook his head.

The FBI agent. He had to be the man O'Connor had tailing Manchetti, she decided, taking in his three-piece dark suit, white shirt and dark tie. Samantha nodded in understanding, and felt some of the tension leave her body.

As Samantha backed away, the man slipped inside and eased the door shut behind him. It was when he quietly slid the dead bolt in place that she began to feel uneasy. Why would he lock the door?

She didn't have long to wonder. He shoved the gun in her ribs and clamped his free arm around her neck. Samantha reached up and grabbed his arm to try to loosen his grip so she could breathe. She opened her mouth to scream, and the man shoved the gun harder into her side.

"Just keep quiet," he whispered, barely loud enough for her to hear. "Or I'll kill you now."

Samantha was aware of the voices in the other room and wondered why they couldn't hear her heart pounding; she thought it would surely beat right out of her chest.

The man half pushed and half dragged her toward the doorway, and Samantha could hear Angelique, loud and clear.

"I have a big surprise for you, Tony," she said.

"Put that gun away, Angelique," Manchetti's voice was calm.

"I can't, Tony."

"At least, let's talk about it," he said, his voice still smooth and low.

"Okay," Angelique answered. "But not for long. Dinner will get cold."

"Dinner? What the hell are you talking about?" he shouted.

"Don't yell. It's not polite," she shouted back. "Now sit down, you bastard, or I'll shoot you right now."

"Okay," Manchetti soothed. "Just don't get nervous with that gun."

Samantha tried to swallow, but her throat felt as dry as dust. She hoped Angelique wasn't the only one who didn't get nervous with a gun.

"I know all about what you did, Tony."

"And what am I supposed to have done, my little pet?"

"Don't call me that, you son of a bitch. You had my parents murdered, or maybe you did it yourself."

For long moments, Samantha didn't hear anything but her own thudding heart. Then Angelique screamed at Manchetti.

"Did you? Did you do it yourself?"

Again there was silence. Samantha closed her eyes and prayed that Marc would keep his word and come after her.

"No, I guess not," Angelique answered her own question. "A coward like you would have someone else do your dirty work."

Manchetti's voice came out like a roar. "I'll show you, you bitch"

A shot rang out, quickly followed by another one, and Samantha gave a muffled squeal of terror. Her captor suddenly lunged, dragging her with him.

Manchetti's eyes grew wide with surprise when they first entered the room.

"What the hell—" But Manchetti didn't have time to finish.

Samantha's captor removed the gun from her ribs, pointed it at Manchetti and fired.

Samantha flinched. Her ears rang from the roaring noise, and she knew she had to do something, and do it fast. As Manchetti crumpled to the floor, Samantha felt the man holding her momentarily relax, and she decided if she was going to die, she was going to go down fighting.

The sudden pounding at the door caught them both unaware. The man cursed. Samantha recognized Marc's muffled voice shouting her name, and the sound gave her the extra courage she needed. She sagged against her captor's arm and he loosened his grip. At the same time, she brought her elbow back as hard as she could, catching him in the groin with the blow. He released her instantly, doubling over in pain, and as she ran for the kitchen, she screamed, "Marc! He's got a gun!"

Knowing she'd only momentarily disabled the man—he was already beginning to straighten—Samantha frantically searched for anything she could use as a weapon. She had already decided there was no use running out the back door; bullets could travel a lot faster than she could run. Her only chance was to fight... or hide, she thought, spying the pantry door. More shots rang out and Samantha made her decision. She slipped inside the pantry and pulled the door shut, plunging herself in darkness. She immediately heard footsteps running through the kitchen, and she held her breath, afraid the slightest noise would be detected. A loud crash sounded, followed by cursing, the snap of the dead bolt, and the slamming of a door.

Then there was silence. Absolute silence.

Samantha bit back a sob. Should she stay put or leave? Was Marc dead or was Manchetti's murderer dead?

"Sam! Where are you?"

Marc's voice, Samantha thought. *That voice was Marc's and he's alive.* Sobbing with joy, Samantha shoved open the door. "Here, Marc," she answered. "I'm here."

Within seconds, he rushed through the kitchen door and she flew into his arms. "Oh, Marc," she cried. "I... thou-thought he... he'd killed you. He shot Manchetti, and he... he was going to sh-shoot me."

"Hush now," he soothed as he squeezed her tightly against his chest. "You're safe," he whispered.

Samantha pulled back a little. "What about... Angelique... and Manchetti?"

Marc slowly shook his head. An anguished look crossed his face. "Dead, Sam. They're both dead."

Angelique's face flashed through Samantha's mind and she closed her eyes. "Oh, no," she moaned. "Poor Angelique. It's all my fault. God forgive me. It's my fault."

Marc opened his mouth as if to contradict her, but unexpected voices in the living room startled them both speechless.

"Dureaux, where the hell are you?"

Samantha tensed.

"It's okay, Sam. That's O'Connor." He released his hold on her and yelled out, "In here. Sam and I are in the kitchen."

O'Connor reminded Samantha of a crazed grizzly. He roared into the room, growling and attacking.

"What the hell are you doing here? I told you to stay put. Good Lord, man, I've got two dead bodies out there. Your father and Jean Claude have been on my tail since I got this call—"

"Shut up, O'Connor, and give me a chance to explain."

But O'Connor ignored Marc and continued his tirade. "What is this?" he asked with an ugly sneer on his face. "Your cousin's out there crying over his lover—your wife, and you're in here with your lady friend. What's going on?"

Samantha's gaze flew to Marc. His face drained of all color. What Marc had suspected was true, she thought. Jean Claude was the reason Angelique had filed for a divorce.

Samantha watched as Marc narrowed his gaze. "That's enough," he said in a low, warning voice.

O'Connor shook his head. "Enough? No! That's not nearly enough. Do you have any idea how this looks? If I didn't know better and Manchetti wasn't lying out there with a gun in his hand, I'd think you and this woman killed your wife."

Marc made a move toward O'Connor, his hands balled tightly into fists, but Samantha stepped in front of him. "No, Marc," she pleaded. "Please don't."

He gave her a hard look, and she shivered from the sheer force of his anger. Without a word, he jerked around and marched out of the kitchen.

Every fiber of her being raged as she turned on O'Connor. "You're despicable," she spat out. "How dare you say such things to him. You're supposed to be on his side." She glared at him. "For your information, one of your own men shot Manchetti, and if it hadn't been for Marc, he would have killed me, too."

A puzzled look crossed O'Connor's face. "Whoa, back up here a minute," he said as he grabbed Samantha by the shoulders. "Calm down and run that by me again. You're not making sense."

Samantha shrugged away his hand. "I said it was one of your men who killed Manchetti. He came in the back door, held a gun on me and after Manchetti shot Angelique, he shot Manchetti."

O'Connor began shaking his head. "That's impossible. Both of my men are outside. One is dressed like a wino and the other one is out back, nursing a split head, which I assumed Marc gave him."

Samantha shook her head. "Marc couldn't have. He came in through the front door."

O'Connor seemed to deflate before her very eyes. "Then someone else *is* involved in this mess. Just as I thought."

MARC HEARD Samantha yelling at O'Connor and then their voices faded into quiet murmurs, but at the moment all he could think of was that everything he'd suspected about Jean Claude was true. His cousin had betrayed the very family that had taken him in.

Marc entered the living room. He noted that his father was there, standing near the front hallway, then he shifted his gaze to the rest of the room. Suddenly, his knees felt weak. "Dear God," he whispered as he looked around him. He'd seen the bodies when he first entered the apartment, but he'd been too concerned about Samantha to really take notice.

At the sound of his voice, Jean Claude looked up from his crouched position near Angelique's body. Marc had to blink several times to clear the dizziness from his head. For a moment he just stood there, his gaze riveted on the lifeless body of his wife. Marc took a step closer, and Jean Claude rose and backed away. Slumped sideways on the floor in an overturned dining-room chair lay Angelique. A shudder ran through Marc and he turned to look at the other body.

Antonio Manchetti was curled up, with a pool of blood spreading beneath him.

"She's dead and that son of a bitch killed her," Jean Claude said, his voice breaking.

Marc looked at his cousin. A blaze of red-hot fury began to build and build. Marc recalled the running, the hiding and the danger. His whole world had been turned upside down because of Jean Claude, Angelique and Antonio Manchetti. And the other man, the man who had killed Manchetti . . . and had almost killed Samantha.

Suddenly, the building fury burst into blinding rage. Angelique and Manchetti were dead, but Jean Claude was alive.

He lunged at Jean Claude, catching him totally off guard. They both hit the floor, and Marc slammed his fist into Jean Claude's face. Over and over, he felt his knuckles sink into his cousin's flesh, as all the pent-up frustration of the past two weeks found release.

Samantha and O'Connor heard the commotion and charged into the living room. "No, Marc!" she screamed. "Stop it. You're killing him."

Marc felt hands pulling at him. He heard his father's shouts and Jean Claude's groans as if in a dream. And he smelled blood, Jean Claude's blood.

She watched in horror as O'Connor, the wino and the two burly policemen pulled Marc off his cousin. He continued to strain against the hands that held him and she rushed over to him. "Don't," she pleaded. He was wild-eyed and breathing harshly and her insides began to quiver with fear and anguish. "He's not worth it. Angelique wasn't worth it. Too many people have died already."

Marc suddenly went still. He glared at her, his eyes still dark with fury. His voice sounded like the snarl of a wounded animal. "Just keep out of it, Sam. You shouldn't have been here in the first place."

His words hit her with the force of an earthquake, and she felt as if her heart were bursting from the aftershock.

And worse, she felt like an intruder. An intruder who had made a fool of herself. Wanting to salvage some of her dignity, she bit her lip to keep it from trembling, raised her chin and backed away.

CHAPTER NINETEEN

AN HOUR LATER Samantha sat at Ray's kitchen table and sipped her coffee as she absently thumbed through the stack of Marc's files Ray had brought in. The scene in Angelique's apartment weighed heavily on her mind and on her heart. Although she'd known all along that a relationship with Marc was hopeless, she'd once again allowed her emotions to overrule her common sense, and she'd fallen in love with him...just as she'd fallen in love with Clark.

Nothing under the sun really changes, she thought as she set down the mug and pulled out another folder. Her love for Clark had caused her humiliation and grief. Even if she'd wanted to—and she hadn't—there had been no way she could have competed with Clark's pregnant wife. With Marc, there was no way she could compete with his dead wife, nor could she compete with the memory of everything that had taken place in the French Quarter apartment.

Samantha sighed. As soon as Marc had calmed down and realized what he'd said to her, he had apologized. And even though she knew he'd been sincere, the memory of his harsh words still lingered...and still hurt.

Her hands tightened on the file folder. She had to stop thinking about it and concentrate. Just before O'Connor had hustled her into his car, Marc had asked her to go through his files and find the names of his contacts in New

York and Chicago; he'd said it was a long shot, but they might be able to dig up something that would give O'Connor a lead.

At the sound of shuffling feet, Samantha glanced up to see Ray walk into the room; he was shaking his head as he sat down.

"It's all so hard to believe," he said. "Whoever is responsible, whoever masterminded this whole thing is still out there somewhere."

Samantha shivered. O'Connor had wanted to put her in protective custody, but she'd flat out refused. She was grateful Marc had defended her refusal. He'd told O'Connor that after his experience, protective custody wasn't worth spit. He'd insisted she'd be safer with Ray. They'd argued, but O'Connor had finally agreed, saying that once she'd rested, he'd personally come by the next morning to escort her to the police station so she could go over some mug shots; he hoped she could identify the man who had held her hostage and killed Manchetti.

All the most recent articles and pictures in Marc's files were about the governor's election. Samantha remembered when she'd learned about the assassination. It had been her first night on the *Jenny*. Marc had been so ill that night, and she'd been tired and frightened.

Samantha blinked several times as tears threatened. How was Marc feeling tonight? she wondered. The press had gotten wind of the killings and were clamoring for interviews. Edward Dureaux had insisted he needed to consult with his son first, and O'Connor had readily agreed. From that point on, things had begun to escalate like a tidal wave. She'd gone one way and Marc had gone another, and now, each time she thought of him, a sea of misery threatened to engulf her. *Oh, Gram,* she cried silently. *How I wish you were here. I need you to tell me what to do.*

The scraping of Ray's chair brought her out of her reverie.

"I'm going to check the locks again," he said. "Just sit tight."

Samantha gave him a tremulous smile and pulled out a package of pictures labeled Landry's Campaign. She shuffled through the mountain of photos taken at various campaign functions; one in particular caught her eye.

Samantha stared at the picture in disbelief. Bobby Landry was standing on a platform shaking the hand of another man. She leaned closer and her heart beat faster. There, in black-and-white, was the man who had held her hostage and who had cold-bloodedly shot Antonio Manchetti.

Her hand trembled and she dropped the picture as if the mere touch had burned her.

"Ray!" she screamed. "Ray, I know who he is."

Ray bolted into the room. "What's wrong?" he asked.

"There." Samantha pointed at the picture. "That man with Landry—he's the one who killed Manchetti." Her voice sounded shaky to her own ears, and although fear raced through her veins, she felt a ripple of exhilaration begin to build. "We've got to call Marc and tell him," she said.

Ray picked up the picture and his brows lowered in concentration. "I don't recognize him, but you can bet Marc can identify him." Ray reached for the kitchen phone. After a few seconds, he said, "Dora, it's Ray. Sam—I mean Ms. Bradford needs to talk to Marc."

Ray handed Samantha the phone. Almost immediately Marc's voice was on the line.

"What is it?" he asked and she thought she detected a frisson of fear in his voice. "Is something wrong? Are you okay?"

"I'm fine," she assured him. "I was going through your files and I found something." Samantha could hardly contain her excitement. "There's a picture in your files of the man who killed Manchetti."

"Whoa, slow down, Sam. Are you absolutely certain?" Marc asked.

"I'm sure," she answered. "He's shaking hands with Bobby Landry and they're on some kind of platform."

For long moments Marc said nothing and Samantha began to wonder if he was still on the line. "Marc? Did you hear me?"

"Yeah...I'm thinking—listen, I can't leave." His tone grew hard and distant. "Damned reporters are everywhere, and I'm afraid they would follow me, but I'm going to send O'Connor after that picture."

An hour later, O'Connor showed up at Ray's front door.

"There's no doubt in your mind that this is the man?" he asked, pinning Samantha with an eagle-eyed glare.

Samantha raised her chin. "He's the one all right."

O'Connor shook his head. "Dammit to hell, woman. That man is Joe Dietrich, Congressman Landry's campaign manager. You'd better be absolutely certain before I go after him."

Samantha clenched her fists. "I'm sure," she insisted, glaring right back at him.

SAMANTHA GLANCED at the clock hanging on Ray's kitchen wall and resumed her pacing. It was midnight; it seemed ages since O'Connor had come and gone, and Marc hadn't called. Ray was in his studio and had cautioned her to keep away from the windows. The waiting was driving her crazy.

The sudden ring of the phone made her jump and she grabbed it. "Hello," she blurted out.

"Sam, it's me."

At the sound of Marc's voice, Samantha let out her breath in a swoosh of relief.

"O'Connor got him."

Samantha closed her eyes and gave a silent prayer of thanks.

"At first he denied everything, but when O'Connor showed him the picture and told him you positively identified him, he broke down and confessed. Sam, I..." Marc's voice broke and Samantha heard him take a deep, shuddering breath.

"Marc, it's okay. It's over."

"No, it's not okay. It won't be long before the press learns where you are. I...well, I've put you through enough as it is without you having to contend with the press, too. I keep thinking if only I'd handled things differently, Angelique might still be alive, and if only I'd taken you back to shore that first day, you wouldn't be caught up in this sordid mess."

Samantha searched for the right words. What she longed to tell him was that she loved him and that she wanted to ease the pain. But she couldn't, not under the present circumstances, and probably not ever, she thought as her chest tightened painfully. She didn't have that right and never had. Angelique had always been there, hovering between them—at first, as his wife, and now, as a burden of guilt they would both have to learn to live with.

There was nothing she could say to make things better. If she told him she loved him, she'd only make the situation more complicated for him.

But there was one thing she could do for him, one last act of love. She could get out of his life and save him the embarrassment of having to deal with a woman who, through no fault of his own, had fallen in love with him.

"Marc, don't worry about me. I'm fine."

"Sam," he interrupted, his voice intense. "You have to leave. The press is everywhere. Believe me, I know what they're capable of. They'd hang you out to dry for the whole world to see."

For moments, Samantha couldn't speak. Although she'd already made up her mind to do just that, hearing Marc telling her to leave was like a sudden slap in the face. And it was almost more than she could bear.

Obviously she'd misunderstood his intentions all along. She'd mistaken his physical desire for love. He'd told her he wanted her, that there was an attraction between them, but then they'd been confined on the *Jenny* running and hiding for their lives, and now the danger was over, and the *Jenny* was gone. And she'd fallen in love with the wrong man again, a man who had only wanted her for the moment.

Fierce pride welled within her, making her voice cool and distant. "You don't have to worry about me. I can take care of myself."

"Not where these people are concerned," he shot back. "Don't forget, I know how newspeople operate. Go somewhere for a few weeks. By then, the sensationalism will have died down, and they'll have someone else to chase after. I . . . I can meet you later, then—"

"No," she almost shouted. Samantha closed her eyes. "There's no reason for you to do that. I'm not Ange-lique. You don't have to do the right thing. Nothing happened between us, so you don't have to feel obligated to take care of me. As I said, I can take care of myself."

Deadly silence hummed over the phone line.

When Marc finally spoke, his voice was low and menacing. "In the first place, I never—I repeat—never, for one moment, thought you were Angelique." His voice became even more forceful. "And in the second place, doing the right thing is not the issue here. I don't feel obligated to take care of you. Obligation has nothing to do with how I feel about you. I tried to tell you on the *Jenny*, but you refused to listen. I love—"

"No, don't...don't say that." She rushed on before she lost her nerve and her pride. "Right now, things are too confusing. Being thrown together the way we were does funny things to people. With everything that's happened, you can't be sure of how you feel, and neither can I. Angelique was your wife. You—"

"Angelique is dead," he almost shouted. "Neither of us wished that on her, and I'm sorry as hell. She was a sick, tortured woman, but she had nothing to do with how I feel about you."

"Oh, Marc." She groaned and wiped at the tears rolling down her cheeks. "Don't you see? She had everything to do with how we both feel. If I hadn't encouraged you to go, to talk with her, if I hadn't interfered, she might still be alive. You're too mixed up right now to know what you want, and so am I. I have to go—"

"Don't hang up—"

Samantha hung up.

Almost immediately the phone rang again, but she ignored it and headed toward the bedroom.

All she could think of was getting away, getting out of New Orleans, going home. O'Connor would just have to get his answers from someone else. If she stayed, she might give in. And if she gave in, they'd eventually regret it.

Samantha swallowed back her tears and tried to think as she stood looking around the bedroom. She needed shoes and money, and a cab. She'd take the rest of the money Marc had left, she decided. Later she'd pay it back, by mail. If she was lucky, she could sleep in her own bed tonight.

Samantha grabbed her shoes. Sitting on the edge of the bed, she shoved the left one on, yanked the laces tightly, then tied a knot and a bow.

"What are you doing?" Ray appeared in the doorway.

"Putting on my shoes," she snapped. "What does it look like?" She grabbed the other shoe.

Ray eyed her warily. "And then what?"

Samantha spared him a brief glance. "I'm going home."

Ray frowned. "Samantha, be reasonable. It's late. At least wait until morning."

Samantha glared at Ray. "I'm leaving now."

Ray sighed. "Your mind's made up?"

"Yes. I'm going home to Pass Christian."

"Sorry, I can't let you do that yet."

"You can't stop—" She jerked her head up when he slammed the door. Samantha ran and grabbed the knob, but she was too late. It wouldn't twist. She couldn't believe it. He'd locked her in. She began banging on it. "Ray Fielding, open this door," she shouted. "If you don't, I'll scream."

Ray's voice was muffled and low from the other side. "If you scream, I'll tie you up and gag you."

"You wouldn't dare." She stepped back from the door.

"I'd sure hate to, but believe me, I'd do it. I can't let you leave. That was Marc on the phone again. He was afraid you'd do something like this, so I promised him I'd keep you here until he could come."

"And then?"

"And then you're going to give him a chance to explain before you run off half-cocked. The man loves you."

"He doesn't know what he feels right now," she retorted. "And I am going home tonight," she whispered as she walked toward the window.

Ray's voice stopped her dead in her tracks. "And just in case you get any ideas about going out the window, it's been painted so many times, you'd never get it unstuck."

"Damn you." She clenched her fist, then stepped to the window anyway.

"Just remember, I'll be right down the hall." His muffled voice began to fade.

As quietly as possible, Samantha eased open the drapes and pushed aside the sheers. She twisted the window lock, then grabbed the sash and heaved. Sure enough, just as Ray had said, it was firmly stuck. She tried again, but it didn't budge.

"There's got to be a way," she muttered as she ran her finger along the frame. If she could cut through the solid layers of paint, she could work the window open. A knife, a razor, or maybe a hammer and a chisel would be perfect. She glanced around the room. She'd take anything she could get. Even a nail file would be a welcome sight.

Samantha spent the following fifteen minutes searching the room. It was while she was standing on her toes, running her hand along the top closet shelf, that the solution hit her in the face—a coat hanger. She could straighten the rounded end and use it.

Within seconds, she was hard at work pushing and probing the inside edges of the window. Progress was slow, but at last she began to see results; finally, she lay the hanger aside. Placing the heel of her hand firmly against the sash and clamping her fingers over the top, she began to push and pull. Perspiration beaded her forehead and her arms ached, but she didn't stop until she felt the window begin to give. Encouraged, she shoved hard. Suddenly, it flew up and Samantha fell forward.

Hanging half in and half out, she breathed the humid outside air of freedom. But time was of the essence. Squirming back into the room, she ran to the bedside table. In the top drawer was the money. Samantha stuffed it all into her shorts pocket. With one last look around the room, she climbed through the window. Once her feet touched the ground, she didn't look back as she sprinted down the dimly lit street.

Samantha could see the corner. Just a little farther, she told herself, and she could flag down a taxi.

Suddenly, a man stepped out from a doorway. Samantha cried out in terror, but the huge man clamped his hand over her mouth and dragged her into an alley.

His hand held firmly, but Samantha continued to struggle, fear lending her strength. She kicked, clawed and twisted, but the man was too strong.

"Ms. Bradford . . . Ouch! Please, ma'am. I'm with the FBI."

Samantha continued to struggle, then quieted as what he'd said finally broke through her fear.

"If you promise to be quiet, I'll let you go. Promise?"

She nodded as best she could, and slowly the man released her. She whirled around and stepped backward. "Show me some I.D.," she demanded. In a flash, he produced a badge. "I guess you know you just scared two years off my life," she said.

"Yes, ma'am. I'm real sorry about that, but could you keep your voice down? We don't want to attract any unnecessary attention."

Samantha glared at the man. "What's this all about?"

The agent took her arm and began walking toward the end of the alley as he explained. "Patrick O'Connor assigned me to watch out for you. He was afraid you might try to leave, and he didn't want any reporters to talk to you until he did. I think we'd better go see him right away."

IT WAS ALMOST DAYBREAK when Samantha arrived home. After the agent dropped her off, she headed straight for her bedroom. Her mind was still overflowing with everything she'd been told, but her body was exhausted and demanded rest. Patrick O'Connor had met her and had taken great pains to fill her in on everything.

Most of what he'd said, she'd already figured out for herself. Joe Dietrich had been the one trying to take over Manchetti's underworld territory. The facts were still being gathered, but O'Connor told her they suspected that Manchetti had become disillusioned with the governor and he'd assigned Dietrich to groom Bobby Landry for the job. Manchetti had figured he'd hire a couple of out-of-state hit men to assassinate the governor and the coast would be clear for Landry; he hadn't counted on Dietrich having ambitions of his own. Dietrich had known about Manchetti's plans and had realized that if an eye-witness identified the hit men, the police could trace them to Manchetti.

One thing had still puzzled Samantha. Where did Angelique fit in? When she'd asked, O'Connor had just shaken his head. "Pure coincidence," had been his answer. She'd had no connection to Dietrich. When she'd filed for a divorce, she hadn't asked for alimony and Marc had stipulated that she not be given any settlement. Then Jean Claude had broken off with her, and the fear of ending up penniless had pushed her over the edge of sanity. The only solution in her tortured mind was to have Marc killed before the divorce was final and, as his widow, collect his insurance money.

O'Connor had wanted to make sure Samantha understood she wasn't to talk with any reporters until after an official news conference had been held. He'd said that since the whole thing had started with the governor's assassination, they wanted to be particularly cautious about what the press reported, especially since a congressman's aide was involved.

Samantha had readily agreed. She had no desire to speak with anyone. But she had agreed only on the condition that O'Connor would tell no one where she'd gone—especially Marc.

Try as she might, Samantha could not fall asleep. Each time she closed her eyes, Marc's blue eyes stared back at her. Finally, she decided a walk along the beach might help her unwind.

A few moments later, she stepped out of her shoes and her feet sank into the warm sand. A cool breeze caressed her face. The early rays of daylight were just beginning to spread over the horizon. Caught up in the beauty of the pale pink hues, she stood and watched until the glowing sun finally burst forth from the edge of the earth to begin its journey across the sky.

As Samantha turned away from the glorious spectacle, another sight caught her attention—a white sail growing larger and larger as it moved toward the shoreline. Suddenly, she felt her heart began to beat as if she'd run a fifty-yard dash, and her legs grew weak. Her eyes burned and filled with tears. With her arms wrapped tightly around her middle, Samantha sank to her knees in the sand as everything came back with a force that left her

breathless. She remembered it all, from the first time she'd
seen Marc until her flight out of Ray's window. All of it
pounded at her, steadily crumbling the protective wall
she'd thrown up around her emotions, like the surf erod-
ing the shore. The worst blow was realizing how deeply
she'd fallen in love with Marc, and how final their sepa-
ration had to be.

Samantha had no idea how long she sat there, rocking
back and forth, nursing her fractured dreams and broken
heart, but when she finally found the strength to pull
herself up, she knew she had to get away. She couldn't
even stay at Gram's—not until she could come to terms
with the emptiness she knew she would have to face for the
rest of her life.

So after only one day at home, Samantha packed her
suitcases, called a taxi, and left for the nearest airport.

A MILLION BEATING DRUMS pounded in his head. Marc
groaned and tried to open his eyes. Morning sunlight
poured through the window on the opposite side of the
room, making the task painful and almost impossible.
Squinting against the brightness, he turned his head
slowly from side to side, and for a moment he wondered
where he was. Then he realized he was in one of the guest
rooms in his father's home. And it all came back. Angelique had been killed the day before. Marc shuddered and
tried to push the gruesome scene from his mind. But even
the slight movement made his head pound again. It was a
hangover to end all hangovers, he thought.

Other memories floated into his mind. Ray had assured him he would watch over Samantha until Marc
could get free to talk some sense into her, and Marc had
returned to the library where a bottle of bourbon waited.
He'd been furious that Edward had allowed Jean Claude

to return home, but he'd had to respect his father's wishes. Marc thought about the previous morning, and the tension between Jean Claude and his father at the breakfast table. Edward must have known about Angelique and Jean Claude.

But everything has a price, Marc thought. Jean Claude would eventually pay his.

Several minutes later, he was still feeling groggy when he stepped into the shower. The blast of cold water was a shock he welcomed. It helped clear his head. He had generously soaped his body and was rinsing off when he remembered something else.

The press conference. He still had to face a damned press conference.

Marc closed his eyes and groaned. The only consolation was that once it was over, he could go to Samantha. Convincing her he loved her was proving to be almost impossible. Once she got something into her head, she could be infuriatingly stubborn.

Marc turned off the faucet and grabbed a towel. While he still had time, he decided he'd better check up on her. Dripping wet, he wrapped the towel around his waist and headed for the nearest phone. He dialed Ray's number. On the fourth ring, Ray answered.

"Ray, it's Marc."

"Well it's time you called. Past time. I've been trying to reach you all morning, but the damned phone has been busy."

"Sam? Let me—"

"She's gone."

Marc froze. "What do you mean, she's gone?"

"I mean gone, as in vanished, disappeared."

Marc picked up the phone and paced the length of the cord. "What time did she leave and how?"

"Aw, hell. I don't know."

"What do you mean, you don't know?"

"Well, I . . . I . . ."

"Come on, man. Spit it out."

"Last night I locked her in her room—"

"You did what?" Marc shouted and slammed the phone back onto the table.

"You heard me," Ray shouted back. "I locked her in the room and she climbed out through the window. I thought it was painted stuck, but somehow . . . Anyway, when I went to check on her this morning, she was gone."

Marc was speechless. It was all too incredible to comprehend. He'd asked Ray to keep her there until he could get free of O'Connor and the press, but he'd never dreamed his friend would go to such lengths.

What must have gone through her mind? And where was she? Cold chills crawled up his spine and goose bumps popped out on his arms. Samantha wasn't familiar with New Orleans. She didn't know what could happen to a lone woman walking the streets in the middle of the night.

"Ray, I've got to find her. God, if anything's happened—" Marc choked as a knot of fear lodged in his throat. For a moment he couldn't speak. The back of his eyes burned, then filled with tears. He squeezed his eyes shut and pressed his thumb and forefinger against them. Then he drew a deep breath and cleared his throat. "Did you look for her? I mean did you check the airport . . . the bus station . . . ?" His voice cracked and he couldn't go on.

"I checked. I even called all the cab companies. It's weird, man. Almost like she disappeared into thin air."

Angelique had disappeared and shown up dead. Marc shuddered and pushed the thought from his mind. Samantha wasn't dead, just missing or hiding.

"Keep checking for me, Ray. As soon as I can get loose here, I'll start looking myself."

"Sure thing...and, Marc? I'm sorry, man. Real sorry."

"Yeah. Me, too."

JEAN CLAUDE'S PRESENCE added to the irritation Marc felt as he listened to O'Connor brief them on the scheduled press conference. He wanted the conference over so he could find Samantha.

He wondered if Ray had turned up anything. Since he'd talked with his friend, he'd remembered a couple of people they could call. Mr. Potter, her attorney, was one, and then there was the beach boy, Tommy Bailey.

"Marc, have you heard a word I've said?"

Marc had been staring off into space and O'Connor's question caught him off guard. It surprised him to realize there was no one left in the room but him and O'Connor. "I'm worried about Samantha Bradford."

"Well, I wouldn't worry if I were you. I've already contacted her attorney and explained everything to him. If she shows up, she won't have any problems."

If she shows up? Marc stared at O'Connor. How could the man be so unconcerned, so blasé about Samantha? And come to think of it, not once had he asked about her or even mentioned her. The more Marc thought about it, the more puzzling it seemed. "What do you mean, if she shows up?" he asked, his voice growing louder with each word. "How did you know she was missing? Do you know something you're not telling me?"

"I'm sure she's just fine. After all, she's a grown woman, fully capable of taking care of herself."

O'Connor's voice was matter-of-fact; the expression on his face remained bland, revealing nothing. Marc was sure he was lying, but he also knew Patrick O'Connor wouldn't tell him a damned thing unless he wanted to. "You know where she is, don't you?"

"I think we've covered just about everything—"

"Where is she?"

"Hey, what's all the shouting about?" Edward rushed into the room. "Marc, what's going on?"

Marc's eyes never left O'Connor. Except for a slight twitch in the muscle along his jawline, O'Connor's expression still hadn't changed. He realized it was useless to question the agent further.

"Ask your friend," Marc answered. "But don't expect to get any answers out of him."

"Marc!" Edward shouted. "I won't have you being rude—"

Marc held up his hand. "Sorry, Dad, but this is personal."

Marc didn't stay to explain. Ignoring his father's protests, he stalked out of the room.

The first thing he did was call Ray.

"I've contacted everyone I could think of and come up with nothing," Ray said.

"I appreciate it, Ray." Marc gave a frustrated snort. "Could you make a couple of more calls for me?"

"Sure, let me get something to write on."

Marc heard a crash, then heard Ray let loose with a string of curses. He rolled his eyes upward.

"Okay, I'm back."

"Two people," Marc said. "One is Sam's attorney. You remember, she talked about him. Potter is his last name. I don't know his first. And the second one is a college kid who rents catamarans on the beach. His name is

Tommy Bailey. I'm not sure exactly where they live, just that it's somewhere along the Mississippi Gulf coast between Bay St. Louis and Gulfport."

"All we can do is try. Hell, I feel like it's my fault anyway. I should have—"

"Don't, Ray. No one deserves the blame for this but me. And another thing. Wherever she is, I think she's okay. I'm sure the FBI agent, O'Connor, knows something but he won't talk."

Ray cursed. "Why the hell not?"

Marc sighed wearily. "I can't figure it out. But with or without his help, I'll find her."

"Damned straight," replied Ray. "Don't you worry. We'll find her."

IT WAS LATER in the evening before Marc was able to sneak away. The trick was getting out without reporters following. Ray had offered to pick him up, and they'd decided the cemetery two blocks over was a good place to meet.

Marc glanced over his shoulders as he paced the sidewalk while he waited for Ray. It had proven quite easy to slip out the back way undetected. He'd kept close to the neighbor's fence and followed it to the street. Within a few minutes, he'd walked another block to the cemetery.

The cemetery was enclosed by a high brick wall. Some of the above-the-ground tombs dated back to the 1700s and had crumbled, leaving wide gaping holes. The spooky place gave him the creeps.

"Damned vultures," he muttered. He wouldn't have to sneak around in his own neighborhood if the reporters would go away.

He was learning firsthand what it felt like to be on the receiving end for a change. And he didn't like it one bit.

Even after the press conference, the situation had not improved. He'd felt like a freak on display for the world to see. Cars had lined the street in front of his father's home. Reporters had milled around on the sidewalk and in the driveway. The police had cleared them away several times, but they always came back; the whole spectacle had almost made him ashamed that he was a member of the profession.

God, he wished Ray would hurry. He should have already been there. Marc leaned back against the trunk of the tree and closed his eyes for a moment. Almost immediately, the familiar sound of Ray's Jeep reached his ears. He stood up. As he stepped from behind the tree to make sure, Ray steered the Jeep over to the curb.

"Am I glad to see you," Marc said as he climbed inside.

"Sorry I'm late," Ray said and pulled back onto the street. "I was working and lost track of time."

Marc settled back and fastened his seat belt. "I really appreciate this. It's been one hell of a day."

"Did the funeral director show up to discuss the arrangements for Angelique's funeral?"

"Yeah, he showed." Marc stared out the window.

"Bad, huh?"

"Bad enough."

"I remember going through all of that when my mom died. Hope your man wasn't as money hungry as the one I had to deal with."

"Actually, he was nice enough. I felt like a hypocrite the whole time he was there. Don't get me wrong. I'm sorry as hell Angelique is dead, and I feel her death was somehow my fault. But I can't seem to... you know... grieve for her."

Ray reached over and squeezed Marc's arm. "Hey, this is your old buddy. You don't owe me or anyone else an explanation."

No, I don't, Marc silently agreed. But he knew that for the rest of his life he would have to live with the guilt over the part he had played. "We're not sure when we'll be able to hold the funeral. O'Connor said it might take a week or so for the coroner's office to release her body."

"How are your folks holding up?"

Marc shifted in his seat. "Dad and Dora seem to be doing fine. Dad's been a rock—"

"Hey!" Ray interrupted. "I almost forgot. I finally located Sam's attorney in Mississippi."

A quiver of excitement rippled through Marc. "Did you talk to him?"

Ray shook his head. "Nope, but I left a message with his answering service. Told them that Ms. Bradford had purchased a painting from me while she was in New Orleans, and since I couldn't seem to locate her, I thought maybe he would know where she was."

"You old devil," Marc said, chuckling. For the first time since Ray had told him Sam was gone, he felt there was hope. "That's great. Think he'll call back?"

"Guess we'll find out tomorrow."

CHAPTER TWENTY

IT WAS A LITTLE past eight the following morning and Ray had just handed Marc a mug of coffee when the telephone rang. Marc tensed as Ray answered the call. The previous evening, he'd wanted to leave for Mississippi to talk to Samantha's lawyer, but Ray had persuaded him to wait until they knew something more definite. Marc listened intently to Ray's end of the conversation, but couldn't tell much from the monosyllabic answers.

"Well, who was it?" he asked expectantly when Ray hung up the phone.

"Potter."

"What did he say?"

His friend didn't answer right away, but scribbled something on a notepad, tore off the sheet, then seated himself across from Marc. "Nothing you want to hear. He gave me his office address to ship the painting to." He handed Marc the paper. "Said he'd see that she got it. When I told him I'd agreed to deliver it in person, he told me that was impossible, that Ms. Bradford would be unavailable indefinitely. I think he was suspicious."

Marc glanced at the address. "Is that it? Nothing else? What did he mean 'indefinitely'?"

Ray held up his hands. "Take it easy. At least it's something to go on. She's not a stupid woman, Marc, but she seemed to be a pretty private person—she wouldn't want the press hounding her."

"Or me tracing her," Marc added.

Ray shifted uneasily and stared at his hands wrapped around his mug.

"I have to find her, Ray. I have to try." Marc leaned back and sighed. "Then if she tells me to get lost...well, I'll cross that bridge when I come to it."

SINCE HIS OWN CAR was at his father's, and there were still reporters hanging around, Marc was forced to rent a car. All the way to the small town of Pass Christian, Mississippi, he thought about what he was going to say to the attorney. In his heart, he knew the most effective explanation was the simple truth—that he'd fallen in love with Samantha Bradford and they'd had a misunderstanding.

By the time he located the address, it was close to noon. Keeping his fingers crossed, he entered the small brick building. The receptionist—a trim woman who looked to be in her late fifties—was busy clearing her desk.

Peering over the top of glasses that had slipped halfway down her nose, she looked up at Marc. "Sorry, sir. We're closing for lunch." She opened a bottom desk drawer and pulled out a typewriter cover.

"Is Mr. Potter still here? All I need is a minute of his time."

The woman shook her head as she slid the cover over the typewriter. "He left an hour ago. Won't be back for two weeks."

"Two weeks! But I can't wait two weeks."

The woman pushed her glasses back into place as she slowly turned to face him. "Don't see as you have much choice, young man. If it's an emergency, I can recommend another attorney."

"No!" Marc shoved his fingers through his hair. "You don't understand. I have to talk to Potter. It's about Sam—Samantha Bradford."

The woman stiffened and her lips thinned into a disapproving narrow line. "Are you a reporter?"

"Yes—I mean no. My name is Marc Dureaux. Sam— Ms. Bradford and I were involved—"

"Mr. Dureaux, I'm well aware of what Ms. Bradford was involved in. I do listen to the news. And as far as you or anyone else is concerned, she is unavailable indefinitely."

"But you don't understand. I have—"

The woman stood up and grabbed her handbag. "I understand it's past my lunchtime. Now if you'll excuse me, I have to lock up."

AN HOUR LATER, Marc parked his car beside the low concrete seawall that ran along the narrow beach bordering the Gulf of Mexico. For a while he sat and stared out over the blue-green water. Two weeks, he thought. Two weeks of waiting before he could even talk with Potter, and then it might not do any good.

Marc opened the door and slipped off his shoes and socks. After he'd rolled his pant legs up, he quickly crossed the hot sand to the water. Stuffing his hands into his pockets, he began walking. He needed to think, to figure out what to do next.

It seemed every time he got close to locating Samantha, someone was there to throw up a barrier. He'd gone to the local newspaper office thinking if he could see some of their back issues, he might come up with an address, but the office was locked up tighter than a drum. The next place he'd tried had been the library, but a Closed For Lunch sign had hung on the door. Kicking at a mound of sand, Marc fought back a groan of frustration. If only he could talk with her.

Marc didn't know how far he'd walked, but when he glanced over his shoulder, the rental car was no longer in sight. He figured that enough time had passed for everyone to have eaten their lunch. Just as he turned to retrace his steps, a movement out over the water caught his attention. The bright red, yellow and blue sail of a catamaran skimmed by swiftly.

Marc shaded his eyes and watched the small boat. Samantha's young friend, Tommy Bailey, rented out catamarans somewhere along the beach. If he could find Tommy…Marc knew it was a long shot, but it was worth a try, he thought. Any hope was better than none.

Keeping the sails of the boat in sight, he began to jog along the wet sand. But the little boat moved swiftly over the water and was soon just a speck in the distance. For a moment Marc hesitated and wondered if he should return to his car; then up ahead, he spotted the bare masts of three more boats. By the time he was within several yards of the small fleet, the one on the water had turned around and had headed toward shore.

Breathing hard, Marc slowed to a walk and watched as the boat, manned by two young men, glided smoothly onto the beach. One boy jumped off and pulled it farther out of the water; the other boy seemed extremely angry.

"You idiot!" he shouted. "You almost turned us over out there."

"Cool it, man."

"Cool it, my rear end." The boy on the boat waved a cast-encased arm at the boy in the water. "I'm not supposed to get this thing wet. Hell, my mother'd kill me if she knew I went out. Here, help me off, will ya?" He held out his good arm. "Easy man, my ribs are still sore."

"Hey, guys," Marc called out as he approached the two boys. He motioned toward the mastless boats. "You rent these things?"

The boy with the cast grunted as the other one helped him off the boat. "Sure do, mister," he said. "Twenty-five dollars an hour."

"What's your name, son?"

The boy with the cast held out his other hand. "Tommy. Tommy Bailey." He shook Marc's hand. "And this is my cousin Charlie." He tilted his head in Charlie's direction, then held up the arm with the cast. "Got bummed up, so Charlie's helping me out. What can we do for you?"

A grin spread across Marc's face, and he slapped Tommy on the back. "Well, Tommy, I'm sure glad to see you."

Tommy looked at him and frowned. "Do I know you?"

Marc began to laugh. "Kind of." He smoothed his hand down his beard. "It's the beard. We never were properly introduced, and it's been a while, but you do know me."

LATE THAT NIGHT, Marc returned to New Orleans. He stayed with Ray until the day of Angelique's funeral, then went home with his father and Jean Claude.

The news media had long lost interest in him; their attentions were focused on a hurricane named Bertha that was wreaking havoc along the east Texas coastline. Instead of moving inland and dying out, the storm had moved back into the Gulf of Mexico and was situated a hundred miles southwest of New Orleans. As it sat in the warm gulf waters, building momentum, some predicted it would come straight up the mouth of the Mississippi

River; others said it would hit farther east, along the Mississippi state coastline. Either way, New Orleans was destined to get high winds and flooded streets.

Together, Marc and Jean Claude helped Edward and Dora prepare for the worst. Edward took Dora to stock up on canned goods, and Marc and Jean Claude cleared the yard and boarded up all the windows.

Marc couldn't help but notice the change in his cousin during the week he'd been gone. Jean Claude had lost weight, and from the dark circles beneath his bloodshot eyes, he wondered if his cousin ever slept. Jean Claude hadn't talked about Angelique, which suited Marc fine. But her presence was there, between them, causing a palpable tension both were fully aware of.

Jean Claude also hadn't mentioned the upcoming governor's election, but Marc knew he had to be disappointed; any hopes his cousin had entertained for becoming governor were gone forever.

After the last window was boarded up, they went into the library and Marc uncapped a bottle of bourbon. He poured two drinks and handed one to his cousin. "Dad said you're leaving as soon as the storm is over."

Jean Claude took the drink, then walked to a chair and sat down. "Yes. I think that's best for everyone concerned. I just wanted to stick around in case...in case your father and Dora need help after the storm."

Marc sat down opposite his cousin. "Where will you go?"

Jean Claude shrugged. "I've decided to travel around for a while, and later, who knows?" After an uncomfortable pause, Jean Claude finally said, "The wind is picking up. I hope your dad and Dora get back soon."

The only sounds in the room were the ticking of a clock, and the soft roar of the wind outside and rain beating against the window.

HURRICANE BERTHA fooled them all. And after three days of pounding the coastlines of Louisiana, Mississippi and Alabama, she turned her fury on Florida.

Marc returned to Pass Christian as soon as Bertha's threat ended. As he walked around Samantha's grandmother's yard, he thought back to his meeting several days earlier with Tommy Bailey. The boy had been as closemouthed as the attorney and the receptionist. Marc had talked until he was hoarse trying to convince the boy his intentions were honorable, and even then, Tommy wouldn't say where Samantha had gone; he'd told Marc Sam had made him promise. The only information Marc had been able to worm out of him was her grandmother's address. Then, when he'd started to leave, Tommy had suddenly changed his mind. "Come back in a month," he'd said. "Sam promised she'd be home by Labor Day."

Marc bent over and picked up a tree branch. He'd tried to convince himself he'd come mostly to make sure her grandmother's house had survived Bertha, but deep down he knew that was only part of the reason. Just being at the place where Samantha had lived—and hopefully, to which she soon would return—made him feel closer to her. He picked up another branch and placed it on the growing pile near the front bordering the highway.

The old house had survived with only a couple of broken windows, and Marc suspected it would survive for generations to come. All afternoon, he worked to clear the debris Hurricane Bertha had left. As he labored, a germ of an idea began to take hold. By the time he'd finished, his plan was perfectly formulated. He phoned Tommy and told him he'd arranged to have the windows repaired. He gave Tommy his father's phone number, asking Tommy to notify him once the job had been completed.

Marc figured he had about three more weeks until Samantha showed up, three weeks to accomplish an almost impossible task, but somehow he'd do it. He had to. He only hoped his efforts wouldn't be in vain.

SAMANTHA STEPPED OUT of the rental car and sighed. It was good to be home, she thought as she closed her eyes and took a deep breath. The salty smell of the gulf was ambrosia to her starved senses. Her trip to Europe had served its purpose for the most part—she'd escaped the news media. But she hadn't been able to escape her homesickness or her memories of Marc. Each time she'd seen a dark-haired bearded man, she'd thought of him. It seemed that everywhere she looked and everywhere she went, people came in pairs, and each time she'd seen a couple, she'd felt her life was incomplete. Her last week spent in Paris had been pure torture, and all she'd thought about was going home. Over and over, she remembered all the ways Marc had shown he cared, but she'd been too hung up on her past to accept the truth, to accept what Marc had tried to tell her.

Samantha slammed the car door and looked around. Everything seemed the same. The house had held up like a trooper under Bertha's fury. She'd been in England when she'd heard about the storm and had almost left for home then. But a phone call to Tommy had eased her mind.

Just to reassure herself, she walked around the exterior of the old house. But the only changes she could find were two new windows on the front. Tommy must have had them replaced, she thought as she ran her fingers over the brand label still attached to the clear glass.

Samantha glanced at the gulf, then turned away. It was time to get on with her life. "Buck up, girl," Gram would have said. "The only thing pride is good for is to swallow." Samantha stiffened, then walked purposely toward the rental car to retrieve her luggage.

THE FOLLOWING DAY Samantha spent most of the morning unpacking and washing clothes. Several times she considered going to the beach, but each time, the thought of the holiday crowd kept her away.

She'd just switched off the oven and removed a frozen dinner when the phone rang. She picked up the receiver.

"Samantha, it's Tommy." He sounded winded and panicky. "There's been an accident and I need help."

Samantha stiffened. "What's happened?"

"It's Charlie. God, my mom's going to kill me."

"Slow down, Tommy. What about Charlie?"

"He took one of the catamarans out by himself over an hour ago. I can see the cat with my binoculars, but Charlie's not on it, and with my bum arm, I can't go after him alone."

"Did you call the Coast Guard?"

"Yeah, first thing. But I keep getting a damned busy signal. Samantha, I'm worried and there's no one else around who knows how to sail."

"Surely there's someone on the beach who could go after him."

"Sam, please. There's no one else. Charlie's a good swimmer but he can't keep afloat indefinitely."

"Aren't you exaggerating a bit?"

"Great! Now I'm exaggerating. Just remember I asked for your help."

Samantha took a deep breath. Once before she hadn't listened to Tommy about the *Jenny*, and her stubbornness had got her nothing but heartache. Why me? she thought. Where the hell was everyone? With a sinking feeling, Samantha knew she couldn't sit by and do nothing while a boy's life was at stake. "Hang on, Tommy. I'll be there in a jiffy."

She shoved her feet into her tennis shoes and was sprinting across the sand a few minutes later. Sweat poured down her body and her breath came in painful gasps. Tommy had already pulled another catamaran into the water, and with only one good arm, was having a hard time holding it against the driving surf and the stiff breeze.

"Get on," she shouted. Awkwardly, Tommy climbed up on the tarp and Samantha shoved the cat farther into the water. "Which way?" she asked as she hopped aboard and took control.

"Out toward that yacht." He pointed toward a large boat anchored offshore. "I'm hoping he was able to swim to it."

When she saw the beautiful boat Tommy pointed to, Samantha swallowed hard. It reminded her of the *Jenny*. The size, the smooth lines, everything about it was heartstoppingly familiar. Ridiculous, she told herself. The *Jenny* only existed as a bittersweet memory. Setting her jaw and squinting up into the noon sun at the catamaran's brightly colored sail, Samantha pulled on the tiller. The sail filled with wind and she pointed the cat directly toward the yacht.

"I don't see Charlie's boat," she said and glanced at Tommy.

He shrugged. "By now, it could be all the way to Cuba."

Samantha shivered. Poor Charlie, she thought. Like Tommy, she prayed he'd been able to swim to the yacht.

When she maneuvered the cat alongside the larger boat, there was no one in sight. For a moment an eerie feeling of déjà vu washed over her. Pushing the feeling aside, she concentrated on securing the cat to the yacht's lifeline, then pulled herself over the side.

"Wait here," she instructed Tommy as she struggled to her feet. Cupping her hands over her mouth, she called out, "Hello, anyone aboard? Charlie?"

A muffled answer came from below. Cautiously, Samantha walked toward the companionway. "Charlie, are you there?" She stepped through the opening and climbed down the ladder. For a moment all she saw were spots as her eyes adjusted from the blinding sunlight to the dimness of the cabin.

After blinking several times, Charlie's grinning face came into focus. "Glad you could make it," he said. "Thanks to the captain of this rig, I'm alive and doing well."

Samantha glanced around but the room was empty. "Where is the captain?" she asked.

Charlie inclined his head toward the back stateroom. Samantha's gaze followed his gesture; a tall figure stood in the doorway. Her heart skipped a beat.

"Marc," she whispered. "What—"

Charlie interrupted. "Guess you guys don't need me anymore. See ya later, Sam," he said and sauntered past her.

"Thanks, Charlie," Marc called out. "And thank Tommy for me, too."

Samantha whirled around in time to see Charlie's smiling face looking down at them from the deck. "Sure thing, Mr. Dureaux." Then he disappeared.

Placing her hands on her hips, she spun around to face Marc. "What's going on here?" But even as she asked, she knew.

"Sam, let me explain. Give me a chance—"

Tears stung her eyes as she backed toward the ladder. "I'm...not...sure," she stammered. "Please...give me a minute." To think that he'd gone to all this trouble for her was overwhelming. She'd intended to find Marc, to tell him what was in her heart, but now, face-to-face, the words wouldn't come.

"Please let me explain," he entreated.

Samantha finally nodded.

Marc gestured with his hand. "Let's go up on deck. It's cooler there."

Again she nodded, then turned and climbed up the companionway steps. By the time she reached the deck, Tommy and Charlie were laughing and waving as the little catamaran drifted by; they made two full sweeps around the yacht before heading for shore.

The second time they circled, it suddenly began to dawn on her why everything about the yacht looked familiar. She frowned, trying to remember the little bit she'd seen below. "The *Jenny*," she whispered, as fresh tears filled her eyes.

Marc had prepared himself for a fight. What he hadn't prepared himself for was the sight of Samantha sitting in the cockpit crying. He felt his heart sink. Maybe he'd gone about this all wrong. Hadn't she suffered enough because of him? Had he been so blinded by his own selfish desires that he'd caused her more pain?

"Sam?" When she lifted her head, he felt another stab of guilt. Her eyes were red and filled with emotion. "God, honey. I'm sorry. I didn't mean to upset you by turning up like this."

Samantha lifted her chin. Without a word she stood, turned toward the open gulf, and leaned forward, bracing her hands along the edge of the cockpit. "Why, Marc?" she whispered. "Why did you go to all this trouble?" She turned to face him.

"I tried to tell you before, but you refused to listen."

Samantha crossed her arms beneath her breasts and continued to stare at him.

Marc rubbed the back of his neck and looked away. The silence stretched between them.

"Well? Go on. I'm listening now. Tell me again."

Marc took a deep breath and faced her. "My marriage was over a long time before I met you." He paused. "It was over long before I fell in love with you. Yes... I do love you, Sam. True, I felt guilt and remorse over Angelique, but not for the reasons you thought. I'll admit at first I did have mixed emotions, and I'll admit you were right in one respect. I do sometimes tend to let my basic sense of responsibility overrule my good judgment. Over the past few weeks I've thought a lot about what you said. Regardless of what you think, I would never have taken Angelique back. She was someone to be pitied, not someone I wanted to share the rest of my life with."

Her expression remained the same and Marc had a sinking feeling his declaration of love had come too late. She was listening, but had she heard him? He turned away. "I'll get the dinghy and take you back."

Samantha grabbed his arm as he passed her. "Kiss me."

Marc stopped to stare, first at her hand, then at her face. "What did you say?"

Samantha tugged on his arm and smiled. "I said kiss me."

Marc's face registered his shock. "I don't understand," he said. "I—"

Samantha slowly stepped forward and placed a finger against his lips. Marc felt his body instantly respond to her touch.

For a moment she smoothed her hands against his beard, then gently tugged. "I've missed you," she whispered.

A lump formed in his throat and he wasn't sure if he could utter a word.

"And I want you to kiss me . . . now."

Marc groaned when he saw the blatant invitation on her face. How many nights over the past month had he dreamed of this moment? At best, all he'd dared to hope for was a chance to explain, to tell her what was in his heart. Slowly he cupped his hands around the back of her head. Gently, tentatively, he touched his lips to hers. Her response was instantaneously sweet—all-knowing, all-giving, holding nothing in reserve. For long moments Marc savored the taste of her and breathed deeply as if he could inhale the essence of her very soul. Reluctantly he pulled away, and she sighed.

"Could we try that again?" she asked softly. "I was just getting the hang of it."

Marc chuckled. "Sweetheart, any more of that and I can't be held responsible for the consequences."

She held his gaze with a grave, solemn look. "Promise?"

Marc sobered. "Honey, I'll promise a hell of a lot more than that if you give me the chance. I love you."

"Marc, I love you too," she whispered.

Marc pulled away and held her at arm's length. "Say it again," he demanded. "And say it louder. I want to make sure I'm not dreaming."

Samantha began to laugh and unspeakable joy washed over him at the sound.

"I said I love you," she shouted.

"Are you sure?"

"Absolutely," she answered. "In fact, bright and early Tuesday morning, I was going to make a trip to New Orleans to find you—"

Marc's fingers covered her lips to still her words. His voice was low and filled with need. "No, not now. Tell me later. Much, much later."

His hands moved restlessly up and down her body. "Sam, Sam," he whispered against her mouth. "I need you. I have for a long time."

"Kiss me again." Boldly she reached for his hand. "Touch me." Her voice invited, pleaded, demanded.

For a moment he couldn't move, couldn't breathe. With his hand imprisoned between hers, pressing against her breast...oh, God, she was so soft, so full beneath his fingers. He drew in a ragged breath. Deep down, all along, he'd known this was how it would be.

As he pushed aside the neckline of her shirt, he bent his head. His lips grazed the upper swell of her breast. His soft beard brushed against her sensitive skin, soothing yet inflaming. Samantha closed her eyes against the sharp yearning that twisted and pulled against the center of her desire.

"I love you, Sam." He whispered the words against the pulse of her neck as deftly, one by one, he released the buttons of her shirt. One taste wasn't enough, didn't satisfy. He slipped the shirt over her shoulders, removed her bra and lowered his head. He flicked his tongue over her nipple, back and forth, until it hardened. She tasted salty and sweet and smelled of musky womanhood. Her soft whimper of approval made him bolder. He opened his mouth around the tip of her breast and sucked slowly, deeply, his tongue flicking back and forth. Her hands caressed and pulled against the back of his head urging him to give equal time to her other breast. He complied gladly.

Samantha arched toward him. "Yes, oh, yes." She groaned out each word and buried her face in his hair. Long-forgotten yearnings pulsed with each pull of his mouth until she wanted to scream out for fulfillment.

Recognizing the signs of a deeper need, Marc released her and hugged her close for a moment before swinging her off her feet and into his arms; she linked her hands behind his neck and buried her lips beneath the lobe of his ear. He'd never realized a woman could be so responsive, so sensitive to his every touch. It was an earth-shattering, sobering experience. He wanted to prolong it, make it last forever. He wanted to give and give until there was nothing left to give.

Within seconds he placed her gently on his bed and tugged off her shorts and panties. His eyes devoured her as she leaned back invitingly against the pillows, her hair a pale halo against the dark blue of the pillowcase. In the dim light, her skin seemed to glow. Her breasts heaved with every breath she drew, reaching up, begging to be caressed. Her waist was slim, her hips rounded. Farther down, her long legs, slightly bent at the knees, were demurely pressed together.

Leisurely, savoring the way her eyes followed his every move, Marc unzipped his shorts and slid them below his hips until they fell to the floor. Taking his time, he lowered himself to the bed beside her. Ever so gently, he tantalized and teased her with his fingers, running them over her breasts and down her stomach and farther. She was warm and moist and ready.

Then he tasted her sweet mouth again and she moaned out her need and arched upward toward him. Her hands clawed at him, pulling, begging. He couldn't deny either of them any longer. He moved quickly over her and with one sure surge, buried himself deep within her. For agonizing seconds he held back. Then her legs wrapped around him, drawing him deeper. Her hands moved down his back, pressing against his buttocks. She pushed upward with her hips, leaving him no choice; he lost control. His hungry mouth claimed hers as he withdrew and thrust deeply. A moan of mutual satisfaction vibrated between them. He thrust again and again, building and building more momentum like the flames of a raging fire devouring everything in its path until nothing was left but warm, glowing embers.

Samantha sighed and Marc raised up on his elbows. She slid her arms from his buttocks to his waist and clasped her fingers together, pressing him closer. His skin was slick and warm. "No...don't go yet."

He smiled. Her lips were slightly swollen and still moist from his kisses. With the tip of his finger, he traced the outer edges.

He watched as she slowly opened her eyes. They were shining with adoration, and he felt humble and undeserving. No one had ever looked at him with as much tenderness, as much love.

She lifted her head and gently kissed him, then lay back against the pillow. "I love you, Marc. I didn't realize what love meant until I met you. What happened to me before was nothing compared to what I feel for you."

Marc nuzzled his nose against hers. "You do tend to be stubborn at times, and after we're married I—"

Samantha stiffened beneath him. "Married?"

Marc's eyes began to twinkle with teasing lights. "If you ever want to get off this boat, you'll say yes."

Samantha giggled. "I like this boat. Why would I want to get off—"

"Sam," he cautioned. "Be serious for a moment."

"Yes," she answered quickly. "Yes, I'll marry you."

"Are you sure?"

"Absolutely."

He wrapped his arms around her and closed his eyes. "You'd better be, because, sweetheart, I told my father to hold off firing Dora until I . . ."

"Fire Dora! Why on earth would he do that?"

Marc laughed. "My dad would have made a great diplomat. He finally figured out the only way he would ever get Dora to marry him would be to fire her. Then he could tell her she was no longer the housekeeper. Either she had to marry him or he'd hire someone else to keep house for him. And you know how she'd feel about that."

Samantha smiled, savoring the sound of Marc's voice and the way his body was intimately joined to her own. Her heart felt full to bursting. Nestled in his arms, she knew that at last she'd come home. Outside, the sun spiraled across the heavens to complete its daily journey, and the warm gulf breezes whispered in the sails of the *Jenny III*. Below the deck, other whispers blended in, whispers of passion, of caring, and whispers of eternal love.

Harlequin Superromance®

Coming in August from
Harlequin Superromance
A new novel from the author of
BRIDGE TO YESTERDAY

IN GOOD TIME
By Muriel Jensen

A mad but cunning killer is stalking Paula Cornell.
Reluctantly, Paula must place her faith—and her life—
in the hands of bodyguard Dane Chandler, a man ten
years her junior.

In their secluded mountain hideout, Dane and Paula
fall in love. But unless Paula can overcome a tragedy
in her past, she will never be able to be the wife and
partner Dane needs her to be.

IN GOOD TIME
A story of hope and renewal
Superromance #512

IGT92

WELCOME TO

The quintessential small town where everyone knows everybody else!

Finally, books that capture the pleasure of tuning in to your favorite TV show!

GREAT READING...GREAT SAVINGS...AND A FABULOUS FREE GIFT!

Each book set in Tyler is a self-contained love story; together, the twelve novels stitch the fabric of the community. The covers honor the old American tradition of quilting; each cover depicts a patch of the large Tyler quilt.

With Tyler you can receive a fabulous gift ABSOLUTELY FREE by collecting proofs-of-purchase found in each Tyler book. And use our special Tyler coupons to save on your next TYLER book purchase.

Join your friends at Tyler for the sixth book, SUNSHINE by Pat Warren, available in August.

When Janice Eber becomes a widow, does her husband's friend David provide more than just friendship?

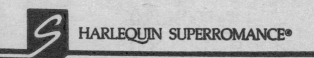

Harlequin Superromance®

COMING NEXT MONTH

#510 CHEYENNE SUMMER • Jenny Loring
Seven-year-old Cheyenne had her new mother all picked
out. Elaine Fielding would be just perfect. It took
Cheyenne a while longer to decide that Matt Cheney
should be her father, but Elaine liked him. One thing
Cheyenne knew for certain: the man her real mother had
married *wasn't* her father. Now he was chasing Cheyenne,
and she didn't know why. Elaine and Matt would protect
her, but she wanted more. She wanted them to be a
family... her family.

#511 JUNIPER • Margot Dalton
Even supposing Buck Buchanan could figure out the
mysteries of Pablum and how to discipline a four-year-old,
how was he going to hide these two kids he'd suddenly
acquired from Claire Tremaine? She was the only woman
he'd ever truly set his heart on, and she didn't *look* to be
the mothering type....

#512 IN GOOD TIME • Muriel Jensen
Pursued by a maniacal killer, Paula Cornell was forced to
go into hiding, with ex-military man Dane Chandler as her
bodyguard. Paula hated the enforced dependency on a
younger man, especially one who, she soon found out, was
as willful as she was. Still, in their secluded mountain
hideout, it didn't take long before other feelings began
to grow....

#513 TOURIST ATTRACTION • Connie Bennett
Beautiful, ambitious Lauren Widmark was so busy
planning vacations for the rich and famous, she had no
time to relax herself. And hotel tycoon Ross McKendrick
had no time to enjoy the luxury resort he'd built in the
Ozarks. Then their paths crossed professionally, and
suddenly, the all-work-and-no-play decree seemed a whole
lot less attractive.

She was a prisoner on his boat

Samantha Bradford was beginning to regret
climbing aboard the *Jenny II* to see if she
could help its captain. Sick as he had been,
Marc Dureaux had set sail, and now Sam was
trapped with a stranger on the open waters of
the Gulf of Mexico.

Marc had his own problems. He'd witnessed an
assassination, and the perpetrators were after
him. No way could he risk returning to land. He
and Sam would just have to make the best of it.
And the best seemed to happen whenever he
kissed her.

Then things took a turn for
the worse....

ISBN 0-373-70507-7

70507

0 65373 00339 3